NICHOLAS TEEGUARDEN

The Copper Scroll

Masa Chronicles

Contents

1 The Spark   1

2 A New World   8

3 A Familiar Path, an Unseen Shadow   14

4 A Clue in the Chaos   21

5 Cracks in the Wall   29

6 Darkness Chased by the Light   36

7 The Crook's Call   42

8 The Museum Breakthrough   49

9 The Museum's Whisper   56

10 Dust on the Horizon   62

11 Shadows at Dusk   71

12 The House of the Cross   78

13 The Order's Shadow   85

14 The Fisherman's Thread   92

15 The Mantle   100

16 The Mantle's Echo   108

17 The Traitor's Shadow   115

18 Flight into the Night   122

19 Echoes of Betrayal   128

20 The Dove's Shadow   136

21 Sanctuary Under Siege   143

22 Caves of Qumran   151

23 The Net's Shadow   157

24 The Shepherd's Echo   165

25 The Road North   173

26 The Fire at the Waters   180

27 The Narrow Way   187
28 April 10, 2025   203
29 Trap of Truth   210
30 April 11, 2025   217
31 August 2025   224
About the Author   229

1

The Spark

Joshua "Masa" Bennett hummed the Villines Trio's familiar refrain, "I'm going all the way, I made up my mind..." as he drove toward the University of Arkansas. The song, a staple from his Lincoln church, bookended his commute, its quiet grace a lifeline since his Army days tromping biblical lands. No atheists in foxholes, they say, and Masa carried that faith into civilian life, fueling his master's in archaeology. Today felt routine, just another class, but a spark flickered beneath it, a path to mysteries buried for centuries, secrets that could shake faith's foundations.

The lecture hall buzzed with late-afternoon chaos. High ceilings arched overhead, intricate moldings catching golden light through tall, narrow windows. Dust motes danced in the beams, stirred by restless students shifting in tiered rows of scarred desks with etched initials, coffee rings, and doodles of bored minds. Chalk dust bit the air, mingling with the musty scent of old books and the hum of flickering fluorescents. At the front, Professor Thaddeus Luke commanded the room, his wiry frame dwarfed by a blackboard scrawled with frantic chalk lines and gray hair flaring like a storm cloud as his voice boomed with passion.

Joshua sat near the back, his lean frame hunched over a desk that creaked under his weight. His leather backpack, a frayed relic from his grandfather's desert-wandering days, slumped against his leg like a loyal dog. Dark hair fell into his eyes as he scribbled furiously in a notebook already thick with ink:

sketches of jagged cave mouths, snatches of Hebrew script, arrows darting between wild theories. Around him, classmates slumped in their seats, some doodling aimlessly, others sneaking glances at their phones beneath the desks. A girl two rows ahead twisted a strand of blonde hair around her finger, whispering to her neighbor with a smirk. Joshua barely noticed. His world was the blackboard, the professor's words, the tantalizing riddle unfolding before him.

Professor Luke's chalk scratched against the board as he recited from the Copper Scroll, his tone reverent yet edged with excitement. "Item four: 'In the cave of the pillar that is in the valley of Achor, which is near the house of the washer, dig three cubits: there are twenty-two talents of silver.'" He paused, turning to face the room, his eyes glinting behind wire-rimmed glasses. "Discovered in cave three at Qumran in 1952, this scroll stands apart from the Dead Sea manuscripts. Sixty-four locations, each a cryptic promise of treasure, not scripture, not prophecy, but a map. A cipher waiting to be cracked."

Joshua's hand shot up, cutting through the low murmur of restless students. "Professor," he began, his voice trembling not with nerves but with a barely contained urgency, "could the 'pillar' be a natural feature, like a stalagmite, rather than something manmade? And the valley of Achor, near Jericho, could the 'house of the washer' refer to a spring, maybe a dyeing site, instead of a literal building?"

A ripple of groans and muffled laughter swept through the room. "Here we go," muttered a broad-shouldered guy in a hoodie ahead of Joshua, slumping lower as if to distance himself from the outburst. "Indiana Jones strikes again."

The jab landed, but Joshua didn't flinch. His gaze stayed locked on Luke, waiting.

The professor halted midstride, dusting chalk from his tweed jacket as a faint smile tugged at his lips. "A bold leap, Joshua. You've been digging deeper than the syllabus, haven't you?" A few snickers broke out, but he waved them off with a dismissive hand. "The Copper Scroll's a maddening tease. Scholars and treasure hunters have chased its shadows for decades, only to come up

2

empty. Your theory's as good as any, though it'd need evidence to stand."

The words "cave of the pillar" hooked into Joshua's mind, pulling him back to a memory as vivid as the lecture hall was real. He was eight again, kneeling in the soft, loamy dirt of his grandparents' backyard in suburban Illinois. The sun beat down, warm and heavy, baking the earth until it released a rich, damp scent that filled his lungs. His chipped plastic shovel, a bright red thing he'd begged for at a garage sale, scraped against the ground as he dug, his small hands gritty with soil.

Beside him, his grandfather crouched, his khaki pants stained at the knees, his voice a warm gravel that seemed to carry stories from centuries past. "Right there, Masa," he'd said, chuckling as he pointed to a spot near the gnarled roots of an old oak tree. The nickname had stuck years before, born on a museum trip when Joshua, barely five, had stared wide-eyed at a Roman mosaic and stammered, "Masa," instead of the word he'd meant. His family seized it, a tender badge of his endless curiosity, and it followed him like a shadow.

That day, his shovel struck something hard. He pried it free, a rusted bottle cap, its edges jagged, and a shard of blue glass that caught the sunlight like a sapphire. To anyone else, they were trash, but to Joshua, they were treasures, relics of a world buried and waiting.

His grandfather handed him an old map of the Middle East, its edges yellowed and curling, and traced a finger across the paper. "This is Jericho," he'd said, his voice low and conspiratorial. "Prophets hid scrolls there, Masa, secrets in the sand. Egypt's tombs, Babylon's ruins, they're all waiting for someone to find them."

Joshua had clutched the map to his chest, its creases rough against his skin, and felt a spark flare inside him, a hunger he couldn't name.

The sharp snap of Professor Luke's chalk against the board yanked Joshua back to the present, the backyard fading into the lecture hall's hum. That childhood moment had lit a fuse in him, and the Copper Scroll was the flame racing along it. It wasn't just a text, it was a summons, a call he'd been answering since he first held that map.

The final exam came two weeks later, and Joshua tore through it with a fierce, quiet focus. The room was stifling, the air thick with the scratch of pencils and the rustle of turning pages. His pen danced across the booklet, spilling answers about the Dead Sea Scrolls' historical context, their scribal peculiarities, their glimpses into Second Temple Judaism. He described the Essenes' rigid purity laws, the War Scroll's apocalyptic fervor, the Community Rule's stark discipline details he'd memorized as easily as breathing. But when he reached the essay question, "Discuss the significance of the Dead Sea Scrolls in understanding Second Temple Judaism," his thoughts swerved to the Copper Scroll.

He pictured its cryptic lines, the promise of silver and gold hidden in desert caves. What if it wasn't just treasure? What if the Essenes had encoded a warning, a prophecy of Rome's invasion, a plea to preserve their legacy? His pen hovered, ink beading at the tip. He could weave it in, stake a claim no one else dared. But doubt crept up that Professor Luke might dock him for straying off topic. Joshua exhaled, opting for caution, and penned a meticulous analysis of the scrolls' sectarian insights. Yet in the margins, he couldn't resist a quiet rebellion: *Copper Scroll Essene code? Cave 4 link?* A dare to get Luke's attention.

He finished early, his booklet thudding shut as others labored on, their pencils gnawed to stubs, their brows creased with strain. Joshua stretched, his shoulders popping, and let his mind drift to Qumran, its cliffs baking under a relentless sun, the air heavy with dust, the faint glint of ancient metal catching his flashlight. The image sent a shiver of anticipation down his spine, prickling his skin like static.

When the proctor called time, Joshua lingered near the front, his backpack slung over one shoulder. He caught Luke's eye as the professor gathered the exams into a teetering stack. "Got a minute, Professor?"

Luke adjusted his glasses, peering over the pile. "Make it quick, Joshua. These won't grade themselves, though I'd pay good money if they did."

Joshua grinned, falling into step as they left the room. "It's about the Copper Scroll."

Luke snorted, a dry, knowing sound. "Of course it is."

The professor's office was a cluttered shrine to a life spent chasing history.

Books teetered on every surface, spines cracked, pages dog-eared, while maps of the Levant plastered the walls, their edges curling from years of thumbtacks and tape. A faint whiff of pipe tobacco wove through the musty air, softening the sharpness of old paper.

Joshua dropped his backpack beside a chair and pulled a crumpled page from its depths, smoothing it on Luke's desk with careful hands. "Dr. Henry Smith's journal," he said, tapping the faded ink. "He wrote, 'A map in cave four hints at hidden messages from the Roman invasion.' Cave four, not three, could it tie to the Copper Scroll?"

Luke leaned back, his chair creaking under him, fingers tented beneath his chin. "Smith was a dreamer, brilliant but half-mad. Chased ghosts across the desert and came back with scraps. Still, his ideas stick with you." He studied Joshua, his gaze sharp. "What's your angle?"

Joshua took a breath, the words tumbling out in a rush. "I want to study it in Jordan, the museum in Amman, the caves near Qumran. I can't get to Palestine, but Jordan's close enough. There's something there, Professor, I can feel it."

Luke chuckled, a deep, rumbling sound that filled the room. "You've got fire, Joshua. Reminds me of myself in Egypt, Saqqara, hunting Imhotep's tomb. Spent weeks in the sand, came up with a shard that mapped a trade route. Small, but real." He paused, his expression softening. "Archaeology's a grind, not a movie: dust, dead ends, disappointment. Are you ready for that?"

"I am," Joshua said, his voice steady, his eyes unyielding. "This could be my thesis, my start."

Luke tapped the desk, then nodded slowly. "I know a scrolls expert in Jordan, Dr. Khalil, sharp as a tack. I'll call him, see if he'll take you on. But the desert's no joke. Watch your step."

Joshua's face split into a grin he couldn't suppress, his fist clenching in quiet triumph. "Thank you, Professor. I won't let you down."

As he turned to leave, Luke called after him. "And don't get shot, Joshua. You're too good to lose over some old metal."

* * *

Home for the holidays, Joshua faced his family across a dining table groaning with food. The air was thick with the scent of roasted turkey, sage stuffing, and his mother's signature cranberry relish, its tartness cutting through the warmth. Ellen Bennett, her auburn hair pulled into a loose bun, passed him a bowl of mashed potatoes, her brow creased with worry. "Jordan, Josh? It's so far, and the news, those protests, the unrest..."

"It's a university program, Mom," he said, spooning gravy onto his plate. "Supervised, safe. I'll be with professors, not wandering alone."

His father, Mark, peered over his coffee mug, his glasses fogging slightly from the steam. "And the cost, Masa? International tuition's no joke. This better not be some wild goose chase."

The nickname landed like a gentle touch, a bridge to the boy who'd dug up bottle caps in the backyard. Joshua smiled, meeting his father's gaze. "It's my future, Dad. If I find silver, that's just a bonus."

Emily, his younger sister, leaned forward, her dark curls bouncing as she smirked. "What, like spies chasing you through caves? You'll need a fedora and a whip."

"Emily!" Ellen snapped, though a grin tugged at her lips.

Joshua laughed, the sound easing the tension. "Just scrolls and sand, Em. No secret agents."

The meal stretched on, plates clinking, voices overlapping in a familiar rhythm. His mother fretted over a news report she'd seen, unrest near Amman, a clash in the streets, while his father grumbled about flight prices and the impracticality of chasing "old junk." But beneath their worries, Joshua felt their support, a quiet pride wrapped in skepticism. When dessert came, pumpkin pie with a dollop of cream, he caught his mother watching him, her eyes soft.

Later, the gifts piled up under the tree. His parents handed him a pair of sturdy hiking boots, "For your cave trekking," Mark said gruffly, while Emily tossed him a sleek tablet, "to prove you're alive out there." Joshua hugged them each in turn, the weight of their faith settling over him like a blanket.

That night, in his childhood bedroom, he lay awake, the suitcase by his door packed and ready. The walls still held echoes of his past, a faded map of the Middle East tacked above his desk, its corners curling; a photo on the nightstand of him and his grandfather, grinning beside that old oak. He reached for a small wooden box on the shelf and lifted the lid. Inside lay his grandfather's compass, its brass dulled but its needle steady, and a worn trowel, its handle smoothed by years of use. He packed them carefully, their weight grounding him.

His mind raced to Jordan, the valley of Achor, the Copper Scroll's secrets whispering through the sand. This was his leap into the unknown, a thread stretching from that backyard dig to a destiny he couldn't yet see. He closed his eyes, the compass cool against his palm, and let the anticipation pull him toward sleep.

He had no idea how deep, or how dangerous, that unknown would prove to be.

2

A New World

The moment Joshua stepped off the plane, the heat slammed into him like a physical force. It wasn't the humidity of an Arkansas summer, but a thick, humid blanket laced with the scents of cardamom, diesel, and a dozen spices he couldn't name. The Queen Alia International Airport hummed with life. Voices in Arabic swirled around him, a melodic chaos he couldn't decipher, punctuated by the clatter of suitcases and the shouts of taxi drivers vying for fares. He clutched his passport tighter, suddenly aware of how foreign he looked in his faded "Calling the Hogs" hoodie and scuffed sneakers. Overhead signs in elegant, looping script pointed to exits he couldn't read, and for a fleeting second, panic gripped him. *You're fine*, he told himself, swallowing hard. *Just keep moving.*

His grandfather's leather backpack felt heavier than it had in Arkansas, stuffed with maps, notebooks, and a well-thumbed copy of *The Dead Sea Scrolls: A New Translation*. He adjusted the straps and pushed through the crowd, dodging a family reuniting in a flurry of hugs and tears then nearly tripping over a suitcase abandoned by a mother wrangling three kids. "Sorry," he mumbled, though no one seemed to notice. The air was thick with sweat and perfume, and a man in a white thobe brushed past him, leaving a trail of oud that lingered like smoke.

Outside, the chaos doubled. Taxi drivers swarmed him, their broken English cutting through the din.

"You need ride? Good price!" one called, waving him toward a battered yellow cab.

Joshua nodded, fumbling with his phone to show the address Dr. Khalil had emailed him.

The driver squinted at the screen then flashed a gap-toothed grin. "Near university! I take you, my friend."

The ride was a sensory assault, honking horns: hairpin turns, and the driver's cheerful chatter about Amman's weather, traffic, and the best shawarma spots. Joshua gripped the door handle, his knuckles white, as the taxi darted through streets lined with stalls selling knockoff sunglasses, piles of dates, and steaming pots of mint tea. The city pulsed with a raw energy Arkansas had never matched, vibrant, unpolished, a kaleidoscope of motion and color. His stomach churned, a mix of jet lag and the overwhelming newness of it all.

They pulled up to his apartment building, a modest sand-colored structure squeezed between a bakery and a mechanic's shop, and Joshua exhaled in relief.

The landlord, a stout woman in a floral hijab, greeted him with a key and a plate of sticky baklava. "Welcome, welcome!" she boomed, her English warm but heavily accented. "You rest now. Tomorrow, you see Amman."

He stumbled into his tiny studio, the bed creaking under him as he collapsed. The room was bare, a mattress, a desk, a kitchenette with a single burner, but it was his. Through the open window, the call to prayer drifted in, its haunting notes weaving through the night air. He lay there, jet-lagged and wired, listening to the city breathe, until exhaustion finally dragged him under.

The next morning, Joshua ventured out to explore. The University of Jordan was a short walk from his apartment, but in Amman, "short" meant navigating a maze of street vendors, honking motorcycles, and hawkers who pegged him as a foreigner instantly.

"American! You want scarf? Cheap!" one shouted, thrusting a bundle of fabric at him.

Joshua smiled, shook his head, and hurried on, the sun already baking the pavement.

The university sprawled across a hillside, a patchwork of modern glass buildings and older, boxy structures that reminded him of faded postcards from the Soviet era. Students milled in shaded courtyards, some in jeans and sneakers, others in hijabs and flowing abayas, their laughter a universal sound that eased his nerves. He wandered at first, awed by the library's towering arches, then got lost twice before asking a passing student for directions. His halting Arabic, "Min fadlik, wain al, qism al, athari?" earned a kind smile and a point toward a squat beige building.

But it was the Jordan Museum that stopped him cold. Sleek and modern, it stood out against the dusty streets, its air-conditioned interior a sanctuary of quiet. The lighting was soft, casting a glow on glass cases filled with ancient coins, pottery shards, and, at the center of it all, the Dead Sea Scrolls exhibit. Joshua's pulse quickened as he approached, seeing the physical scrolls and translations scrawled in the negative space on the walls. The etched lines seemed alive, whispering secrets from centuries past. He leaned closer, his breath fogging the glass. *"In the cave of the pillar that is in the valley of Achor,"* he murmured, tracing the words with his finger.

"Beautiful, yes?" a voice said behind him. He turned to see a security guard, his uniform crisp, his smile wide. "You like history?"

Joshua nodded, testing the Arabic he'd practiced. "Shukran," he said, hoping it sounded right.

The guard's grin widened. "You learn! That's good. Shukran means thank you."

"Shukran," Joshua repeated, earning a hearty nod.

"You come back, I teach more," the guard said, clapping him on the shoulder before strolling off.

As Joshua lingered, he noticed a woman in a headscarf cleaning the cases, her movements slow and reverent. She glanced at him, her eyes sharp, assessing, then turned back to her work without a word.

He left as dusk fell, the sky streaked with pink and gold. The city softened in the fading light, dust hanging in the air like a golden haze. Motorcycles zipped past, dodging pedestrians with impossible grace, their engines a high-pitched whine. Joshua stood on the sidewalk, breathing it in, a mix of awe and isolation swelling in his chest. This was his new reality: beautiful, chaotic, and entirely his own.

His second day brought a lesson in humility. Buoyed by his museum visit, Joshua stopped at a falafel stand near his apartment, drawn by the sizzle of frying chickpea balls and the vendor's enthusiastic pitch.

"Best in Amman!" the man declared, handing him a pita stuffed with falafel, pickled turnips, and a generous drizzle of tahini.

The first bite was paradise, crisp, spicy, a flavor explosion unlike anything he'd tasted back home. He devoured it, licking his fingers with a grin, feeling briefly invincible. But by midnight, that triumph had curdled into misery. His stomach twisted into knots, and he spent the night curled on the bathroom floor, groaning and vowing to stick to packaged snacks. *So much for blending in*, he thought, ruing his overconfidence.

By the time his first class arrived, Joshua was a tangle of nerves and resolve. The classroom was stark, rows of mismatched desks facing a chalkboard, the air heavy with dust and the faint scent of old paper. Dr. Khalil stood at the front, stocky and stern, his blazer sporting elbow patches that screamed archaeology professor. It was comforting, in a way, a thread of familiarity in this unfamiliar world.

But it was the teaching assistant who threw him off balance. Noa, her nametag read, moved with a quiet intensity, her dark hair pulled into a loose bun, tendrils framing a face that was sharp yet soft. Her gaze swept the room, daring anyone to test her, and when she handed Joshua the syllabus, her fingers brushed his. He fumbled his pen, sending it clattering to the floor, and she smirked, an eyebrow arching in silent judgment. His usual bravado evaporated, leaving him flushed and scrambling to recover.

Dr. Khalil's voice cut through the moment, a gravelly baritone that demanded attention. "Welcome to Advanced Near Eastern Archaeology," he said, his accent a blend of Arabic and Oxford polish. "This semester, we'll dissect the Levant's material culture, from the Bronze Age to the Roman period. Expect rigor. Expect discomfort."

Joshua sat straighter, notebook open, pen poised. This was why he'd come, to learn, to push beyond the surface. But when Dr. Khalil mentioned the Dead Sea Scrolls, Joshua's hand shot up before he could stop it. "Dr. Khalil, about the Copper Scroll, do you think some of its locations, like the 'cave of the pillar,' could still hold undiscovered artifacts? With modern tech, I mean."

Noa snorted, her eyes rolling skyward. Dr. Khalil fixed Joshua with a stare that could shatter granite. "Mr. Bennett, yes? Our eager American guest. The Copper Scroll has been pored over for decades. If treasures remained, they'd have been found. Focus on facts, not fairy tales."

The room tittered, and Joshua's face burned. He sank lower in his seat, his confidence in tatters. Noa's glance flicked toward him, unreadable, maybe pity, maybe scorn, and it stung either way.

* * *

Back in his apartment that night, Joshua spread his notes across the bed, the Copper Scroll's lines dancing in his mind. He'd made a fool of himself today, no doubt, but Dr. Khalil's dismissal only steeled him. *They'd have been found by now.* Maybe. Or maybe no one had looked hard enough, or in the right place.

He picked up a sketch he'd made at the museum, tracing the etched words with his finger. But as he flipped it over, something stopped him cold: writing on the back, in a hand not his own. Scrawled in faint pencil were the words *The pillar awaits.*

His heart lurched. He hadn't written that. Someone had slipped this into his bag, the guard? The cleaning woman? A classmate? He stared at the note, pulse racing. It was a clue, a taunt, a thread to pull. Whatever it meant, it confirmed one thing: he wasn't alone in chasing the Copper Scroll's mysteries.

Joshua leaned back against the wall, the sounds of Amman filtering through his window, the distant honk of horns, the murmur of voices, the call to prayer threading it all together. He was a stranger here, out of his depth in a city that didn't care about his ambitions or his stumbles. But he'd crossed an ocean for this, and he wouldn't back down now.

The pillar awaited. And so did he.

3

A Familiar Path, an Unseen Shadow

After a few days in Amman, Joshua could feel the streets between his apartment, the university, and the museum grounds starting to imprint themselves on his mind. The chaos of the city, vendors shouting, horns blaring, the occasional motorcycle weaving through the crowd: it no longer overwhelmed him. He'd learned the shortcuts, cutting through the alley where the spice merchant waved hello, avoiding the stretch where the air reeked of overripe fruit. His leather backpack, slung over one shoulder, had become an extension of himself, stuffed with notebooks, loose letters, and an index he'd begun compiling from the university library's labyrinth of texts. Each step felt less foreign, more like a rhythm he could follow.

Back at his apartment, the walls told a different story. They were no longer bare; they'd morphed into a chaotic tapestry of Copper Scroll notes and translations scribbled in black ink, maps dotted with question marks, and photocopied pages pinned up in no particular order. It looked like the room of a madman, or maybe a genius depending on who you asked. Joshua didn't mind. It was his sanctuary, a place where the ancient puzzle of the scroll felt within reach.

His daily walk to the university took him past a row of falafel stands, their sizzling oil and cumin, heavy aromas tugging at his senses. One stand he avoided after that disastrous first encounter. His stomach hadn't forgiven the greasy aftermath. But another, run by a man named Omar Al-Hussein, had become a ritual stop. Omar was a wiry figure with a quick smile and hands that moved like a maestro's, shaping falafel with practiced ease.

From day one, he'd greeted Joshua in English, "Good morning, my friend!" before slipping in a word or two of Arabic as he worked. "Marhaba," Omar would say, sliding a warm pita across the counter. "Hello. You try this today." Then, as Joshua ate, Omar would point to something, a spoon, the sky, and offer its Arabic name: mil'aqa, sama. It was a small kindness, but it stuck. Omar had a way of putting him at ease, swatting away the kids who swarmed Joshua with trinkets, "American! Good price!" and pointing him toward the best coffee spot or a shortcut to the museum.

In return, Joshua had been open, maybe too open. "I'm doing a study on the Copper Scroll," he'd said early on, leaning against the stand. "Trying to figure out if it's real or just a hoax."

Omar nodded, his eyes sharp but friendly. "Interesting work," he'd replied and left it at that. The streets around them buzzed, people yelling over the din of traffic, horns punctuating the air like exclamation marks, but Omar's stand felt like a pocket of calm.

That changed on day three.

It started like any other morning. Joshua approached the stand, the familiar scent of frying chickpeas pulling him in. "Marhaba, Omar," he said, proud of the word rolling off his tongue.

"Marhaba, Joshua!" Omar grinned, already assembling his order. "You learn fast. Soon you speak better than me." He handed over the pita, stuffed with falafel and a drizzle of tahini, but as Joshua reached for it, Omar's expression shifted. He leaned closer, his voice dropping beneath the street's clamor. "You need to be careful about telling too many people about this scroll."

Joshua paused midbite, the falafel suddenly heavy in his hand. "What do you mean?"

Omar's gaze flicked to the side, subtle but deliberate, landing on a man standing at the corner of the street. The man was lean, his keffiyeh pulled low, a newspaper clutched in his hands but unread. "My cousin fought those ISIS dogs around the caves," Omar said, his tone low and urgent. "They have eyes and ears all over the city here, in the markets, near the university. They'd gut a man at the hint of gold if they thought some guy was unearthing ancient treasure."

The words hit Joshua like a punch. He followed Omar's nod, studying the man at the corner. Was he watching? The newspaper hadn't moved, the man's posture too still against the flow of the crowd. Joshua's stomach twisted, the falafel turning to ash in his mouth. He'd been careless, chatting about the scroll like it was just another academic puzzle, first with Omar then in class with Dr. Khalil and a few others. He hadn't thought it mattered. It was history, not a treasure map. Or was it?

Omar didn't elaborate, didn't need to. The warning hung between them, sharp and unspoken: *You're not as safe as you think.* Joshua forced a nod, muttering a quick shukran before stepping away, his backpack heavier on his shoulder than it had been moments before.

The rest of the day, Joshua couldn't shake the unease. The streets he'd started to know now felt different, their noise more menacing. Every glance from a passerby lingered too long; every shadow seemed to shift. At the university library, he buried himself in his notes, but his focus splintered. He kept glancing at the door, half expecting the man from the corner to walk in. His index grew, another reference to a cave near Jericho, a theory about the scroll's copper being a deliberate choice, but his mind was elsewhere.

By the time he returned to his apartment, the sun dipping low over Amman's hills, the weight of Omar's words had settled deep. He locked the door behind him, double-checking the bolt, and stood in the center of his note-covered room. The Copper Scroll wasn't just a thesis anymore, it was a risk. And for the first time, Joshua wondered if he'd underestimated what he'd walked into.

He set his backpack down and stared at the wall, at the scrawled line he'd pinned up that morning: *In the cave of the pillar...* A clue, a mystery, maybe a trap. Whatever it was, he couldn't unsee it now. And he couldn't shake the feeling that someone else was looking, too.

Joshua's night was a restless spiral of fear and fascination. After spending

hours watching ISIS videos, videos that left him feeling watched and regret-
ting his choices, he couldn't shake the dread that had replaced the excitement
of his upcoming trip. The videos, filled with destruction and chaos, weren't
directly tied to his research, but they amplified his unease. When he finally
turned away from the screen, sleep eluded him. Instead, he turned to the
walls of his room, covered in notes, charts, and theories about the Dead Sea
Scrolls. His mind fixated on one question that seemed unanswerable yet
impossible to ignore: *Who was responsible for all the scrolls?*

The Dead Sea Scrolls, discovered between 1947 and 1956 in caves near
Qumran, are a collection of ancient Jewish texts that have puzzled scholars for
decades. These manuscripts, some of the oldest known copies of biblical texts,
alongside sectarian writings and legal documents, were hidden away over
2,000 years ago. But by whom? Joshua's sleepless night was spent wrestling
with this mystery, comparing his notes on the scrolls to the artifacts found
in the caves, searching for clues. The leading theories about who buried the
scrolls were each a piece of the puzzle that kept Joshua awake.

Joshua paced before his wall, markers in hand:

- **Essenes**: *Close to caves, wrote the rules. But too simple?*
- **Temple**: *Big library, big motive. Logistics tricky.*
- **Refugees**: *Chaos fits the times. Who were they?*
- **Hybrid**: *Best of all worlds? Or just a copout?*

His charts compared scroll contents, biblical texts, war prophecies, purity
laws, to cave findings, seeking patterns. The biggest question, *Who was
responsible for all the scrolls?*, loomed over it all, unanswered and unrelenting.
Each group had the typical means and opportunity, motive may be the key to
unlocking some of the mystery. Or it was just another rabbit hole to go down.

The next couple of days, Joshua was tense, looking over his shoulder, being
short with the usual suspects in his daily routine. Even the library didn't offer
much in the way of distraction, and he was unable to stop thinking about his
parents' worries. The images in his head from the ISIS videos. The weekend
came, the first chance for Joshua to have a couple of days without going to

classes.

Heading to the museum, still somewhat stuck in the funk, Omar pulled him aside, "You're okay, I see you worried. I have my ear to the ground and you're okay."

The words were short and easy, but they lifted a weight off his shoulders, and he enjoyed his falafel on the way to the museum.

Joshua sat on a low bench in the Jordan Museum's Dead Sea Scrolls exhibit, the faint hum of the air conditioning cutting through the stillness. The room was bathed in soft, dim light, the ancient scroll fragments resting in glass cases like whispers from a lost age. His leather backpack slumped beside him, its contents spilling out, notebooks filled with frantic scrawls, loose pages of photocopied texts, and his ever-expanding web of theories. Omar's warning about ISIS and the dangers of his research still echoed in his mind, a persistent shadow he couldn't fully dispel. But Omar's reassurance had lifted some of that burden, and now, here in the museum, Joshua was determined to focus. He had come too far to let fear stop him.

He flipped through his notes, his tired eyes scanning the chaotic lines for a spark of insight. The Copper Scroll's cryptic phrases looped in his thoughts: *In the cave of the pillar that is in the valley of Achor...* He'd pored over it countless times, cross-referencing it with maps of Qumran's caves, each marked with annotations and question marks. Theories swirled in his head, the Essenes hiding their sacred texts, Temple priests safeguarding treasures, refugees burying their hopes, but none clicked into place. Today, he needed something solid, a thread to pull that would unravel the mystery.

As he leaned closer to a glass case, his gaze snagged on a small scroll fragment. It was barely the size of his hand, its edges crumbling and its ink faded to a ghostly brown. But there, etched faintly in the center, was a symbol, a looping mark that resembled a shepherd's crook. His breath caught. He'd seen that shape before, buried in the margins of his notes from a library session weeks ago. It tied to a phrase he'd jotted down: "the shepherd's path," mentioned in an obscure text about ancient trade routes near Jericho.

Joshua's pulse quickened as he rummaged through his backpack, pulling out a crumpled page. There it was, in his own hurried handwriting: *The shepherd's path leads to the valley, where the pillar stands guard.* His mind raced. The valley of Achor was near Jericho, and the Copper Scroll's "pillar" could be a landmark, a rock formation, a stalagmite, something tangible. He grabbed his pen and scribbled furiously, the scratching sound filling the quiet room. If the shepherd's path was a route known to the scroll's authors, this symbol might be a clue to its location.

Excitement surged through him, loosening the knot of tension that had gripped his chest for days. It wasn't definitive proof, at least not yet, but it was a lead, a whisper from the past that felt personal, like the scrolls were speaking to him alone. He glanced back at the fragment, the shepherd's symbol glowing faintly in the exhibit's light. Perhaps the Essenes had veiled their secrets in metaphors, or maybe refugees had marked their hiding spots with signs only they could decipher. Whatever it meant, Joshua was closer now than he'd ever been.

He stood to leave, slinging his backpack over his shoulder, when a flicker of movement stopped him cold. A figure lingered near the exhibit's entrance, half shrouded in shadow. The man was tall, his face hidden beneath the brim of a hat, and he stood with an unnatural stillness, his gaze fixed on the room. Joshua's heart thudded, the hairs on his neck prickling. For a moment, their eyes locked, and then the figure turned and slipped out, his footsteps silent on the polished floor.

Joshua exhaled sharply, his paranoia flaring. *You're imagining things*, he told himself, gripping the strap of his bag. Amman was full of people, tourists, locals, and museum staff. Not everyone was a threat. Still, as he walked toward the exit, he couldn't resist a glance over his shoulder. The room was empty, the scrolls silent in their cases. He stepped outside, the city's heat and noise washing over him, but the unease lingered like a faint echo.

Back in his cramped apartment, Joshua added his discovery to the wall. He pinned the sketch of the shepherd's symbol beside his notes on the pillar, drawing a red line to connect them. Stepping back, he took in the chaos, his theories, maps, and questions sprawling across the plaster like a living thing. It was a map of his mind, a testament to the sleepless nights and relentless curiosity that had brought him here. Exhaustion tugged at him, but beneath

19

it burned a quiet resolve.

He crossed to his desk and picked up a framed photo, its edges worn from years of handling. It showed him and his grandfather, grinning in a sunlit backyard beside a shallow hole in the dirt. In the picture, Joshua held up a rusted bottle cap like a prize, his grandfather's arm slung around his shoulders. That day, years ago, his grandfather had pressed an old map into his hands and said, "History's waiting, Masa. You'll find it someday." The memory anchored him, a reminder of why he'd come to Amman, why he'd risked so much.

Joshua set the photo down, his eyes lingering on his grandfather's smile. The scrolls weren't just a puzzle, they were a bridge to the past, a way to understand the people who'd shaped it. His grandfather had sparked that hunger in him, and now, standing on the edge of a discovery, Joshua felt it more than ever. The risks, like Omar's warning and the figure in the museum, were real, but they paled against the pull of the truth. He wasn't stopping now.

He turned back to the wall, tracing the red line with his finger. The shepherd's path was out there, hidden near Jericho, waiting for him to find it. And he would, no matter what shadows followed.

4

A Clue in the Chaos

Joshua's apartment looked like the aftermath of an archaeological explosion. Papers littered every surface, his desk, the floor, even the sagging couch where he'd fallen asleep too many nights to count. Notes were pinned to the walls in a chaotic collage, connected by strings of red yarn that made the place resemble a conspiracy theorist's lair. A half-eaten falafel wrap sat abandoned on a plate, its greasy wrapper crinkling in the still air, while the faint bitterness of cold coffee lingered from a mug perched precariously on a stack of books. His leather backpack slumped in the corner, spilling its guts: photocopies of the Copper Scroll, a spiral notebook stuffed with sticky notes, and a battered translation he'd practically memorized. It was a mess, sure, but today, it felt alive.

He sat cross-legged on the hardwood floor, barefoot and hunched over a photocopied article he'd dug up from the university library, a German scholar's paper titled *Die Hirtenpfade und die Kupferrolle: Eine Neue Perspektive.* The title alone had nearly put him to sleep when he'd first found it, but now, after the museum trip, it was gold. The shepherd's symbol he'd seen etched into that display case, its looping crook and faint, deliberate lines, had lodged itself in his brain, and he was convinced it meant something. The scroll wasn't just a treasure map; it was a puzzle, and this paper might hold the next piece.

Joshua squinted at the text, his German rusty but serviceable. His finger traced a line he'd highlighted in neon yellow: *Der Hirtenpfad, lange Zeit als wörtlicher Weg betrachtet, könnte stattdessen eine Reise des Glaubens symbol- isieren, bewacht von der Säule der Wahrheit.* He frowned, chewing the end of his pen. A journey of faith? Guarded by a pillar? That didn't jive with the Copper Scroll's blunt, itemized style, sixty-four locations, weights in talents, directions like "forty cubits north." But the scholar, a Dr. Heinrich Voss, wasn't some crackpot; his work was recent, peer-reviewed, and annoyingly dense with footnotes. Joshua flipped to his index notebook, a tattered thing bursting with loose pages, and scanned an entry he'd scrawled weeks ago: *Shepherd's path near Jericho, poss. trade route, check refs.* He'd ignored it then, too focused on the scroll's treasure lists, but now it nagged at him.

He grabbed his sketch of the symbol from the museum, a rough pencil drawing on graph paper, and held it up to the dim light filtering through his blinds. The crook curved like a question mark, its base splitting into two faint lines. If the shepherd's trail was real, a physical path, and the pillar was a landmark, maybe he could map it. His heart thudded, a familiar thrill creeping up his spine. This was why he'd come here, why he'd left the comfort of home for this dusty, relentless chase. He wasn't just some kid playing Indiana Jones; he was onto something.

His phone buzzed on the floor beside him, jolting him back to reality. A text from Emily, his sister: *Still alive, Masa? Or buried under scrolls?*

He grinned at the nickname, short for Masa, and typed back, *Barely. No treasure yet. Thinking of pitching Treasure Hunter Fail to Netflix. Ratings gold.*

Her reply pinged almost instantly: *I'd watch. Just don't get eaten by a camel.*

He laughed, a short bark that echoed in the quiet room. Emily had a way of pulling him back from the edge, reminding him there was a world beyond his obsession. The weekend had been brutal, hours of dead ends, no big revelations, but the museum trip had reignited him. He wasn't giving up. Not now.

Monday morning hit like a slap, the sun already scorching the streets as Joshua trudged across campus. The university's squat sand-colored buildings loomed ahead, their shadows stretching long and thin across the courtyard. He slipped into the classroom just as the clock ticked past nine, feeling the weight of a dozen pairs of eyes as he claimed his usual spot in the middle row, strategic, anonymous, but close enough to engage.

The room hummed with the low buzz of preclass chatter: a guy in the back griping about a paper, two girls up front flipping through flashcards. Joshua kept his head down, flipping open his notebook to the page he'd filled last night, the shepherd theory scrawled in frantic loops.

Dr. Khalil burst in like a force of nature, his stocky frame filling the doorway. "Good morning, everyone," he said, his voice a gravelly boom that silenced the room. He dropped his satchel on the desk with a thud that rattled the chalkboard. "No treasure this weekend, I take it?" His eyes twinkled with mischief, landing squarely on Joshua.

The class snickered, and Joshua felt heat crawl up his neck. He forced a grin, leaning back in his chair with a casualness he didn't feel. "Words are easier than guns and swords," he muttered, barely loud enough to carry. It was his grandfather's old saying, a mantra he clung to when the doubts crept in. Knowledge was power, he just had to wield it right. Maybe it was dumb, maybe it was a bid for Noa's attention—she sat two rows up, her dark hair cascading over her shoulders as she sorted papers—but it steadied him.

Dr. Khalil didn't miss a beat. "Down to business, then. Today, we're tackling the Dead Sea Scrolls' journey to the caves. Who hid them? Why? What does it tell us about their world?"

Joshua's hand twitched, itching to shoot up. He'd spent the weekend neck-deep in those questions, his apartment wall a testament to his madness.

But before he could speak, Dr. Khalil's gaze pinned him again, a smirk tugging at the professor's lips. "Ah, Mr. Bennett. I'm sure you've got something to say."

The room went quiet, all eyes swiveling to Joshua. He swallowed, his mouth suddenly dry. "I, everyone calls me Masa." He threw the name out trying to buy time. "I, uh, did some research after the museum trip. I think—"

"Fantastic," Noa interrupted, her voice cutting through like a blade. She didn't look up from her papers, but the sarcasm was thick enough to choke on. "But I think we'd all rather hear Dr. Khalil first there, Masa."

The jab landed hard, a sharp twist in his gut. *Ouch.* But there was a spark too, she knew his name, at least. He shrugged, playing it off. "Fair enough," he said, loud enough for her to catch. "I'll save my brilliance for later."

A ripple of laughter spread through the room, and Noa's head tilted just enough for him to glimpse her profile. Was that a smirk? He couldn't tell, but it was enough to keep him in the game.

Dr. Khalil cleared his throat, a gravelly warning shot. "Right. Let's start with the Essenes. As you know, they were a Jewish sect, likely based near Qumran..."

Joshua half listened, his mind racing. He'd already charted the theories, Essenes hiding from Roman persecution, Temple priests stashing sacred texts, refugees fleeing chaos. Dr. Khalil's lecture was sharp, methodical, but it skimmed the surface Joshua craved to crack. His thoughts drifted back to the German paper. *The shepherd's path guards its flock.* What if the flock wasn't sheep but something else, knowledge, treasure, even people? His pen tapped a restless beat against his notebook.

Then it hit him like a jolt: what if the shepherd's trail wasn't a path but a person? A guide who knew the caves, who led others to safety, or to secrets. His breath hitched, the idea unfurling like a map in his mind. The Copper Scroll was literal, yes, but maybe it needed a key, a human one. He scribbled the thought in the margin: *"Shepherd = guide? Code name?"* It was a stretch, but it felt alive.

Dr. Khalil's voice broke through. "And that's why the refugee theory has legs. Questions?"

Joshua's hand shot up before he could second-guess it. "Dr. Kalil, what if the shepherd's trail isn't a route but a person? Someone who led people to the caves?"

The room stilled, the air thick with curiosity. Dr. Khalil blinked, his expression a mix of surprise and skepticism. "Interesting, Mr. Bennett. But the scroll's text is precise, locations, measurements. A person doesn't fit."

Joshua opened his mouth to push back, but Noa jumped in. "Unless," she said, her tone thoughtful, "the shepherd was a code name. Like a guardian of the scrolls."

Dr. Khalil's eyebrow arched, his gaze darting between them. "Okay, let's work this out. Answer some questions about who the shepherd might be, how does he fit, and what do we do since he is probably not with us anymore."

Joshua's pulse raced. Noa had backed him, sort of. It was the first time she'd engaged, not just swatted him down. He caught her eye, and for a split second, she held it, a challenge glinting in her dark gaze.

The bell rang, shattering the tension. Chairs scraped, bags zipped, and the room erupted into chaos. Joshua packed up slowly, his mind buzzing.

As he slung his backpack over his shoulder, Noa brushed past, her voice low. "Nice try, treasure hunter. But you'll need more than guesses."

He grinned, the sting of her earlier cut forgotten. "Watch me," he shot back, half to her retreating back, half to himself.

The courtyard was a blur of students and heat as Joshua stepped outside, the sun glaring off the pavement. His thoughts churned, shepherds, symbols, Noa's dare. The German paper was a start, but he needed more. Dr. Khalil had once mentioned restricted archives, scroll fragments too fragile for public view, locked away in the university's basement or the museum's vaults. If he could get in, maybe he'd find a letter, a record, something naming the shepherd.

Joshua's pace quickened as he approached the university library, his resolve hardening with every step. The shepherd theory nagging at his mind was a long shot, wild enough to earn a scoff from any academic worth their salt, but long shots were his bread and butter. He'd chased flimsier threads with nothing but gut instinct to guide him, and this time, he had a symbol, a phrase, something tangible. It wasn't much, but it was enough to keep him moving.

He didn't notice the figure trailing him, a shadow slipping through the crowd of students, eyes fixed on his back like a predator tracking prey.

The library doors swallowed him into a world of cool air and hushed silence, the scent of old paper and polished wood wrapping around him. Joshua made a beeline for the front desk, where the usual librarian sat, her gaze already narrowing as he approached. She peered over the rim of her glasses, sizing him up from behind a barricade of stacked books.

"Excuse me," Joshua said, keeping his tone even despite the urgency bubbling inside. "How would one get permission to see the documents in the safe?"

The librarian's pensive stare didn't waver. "The safe?" she echoed, her voice dry as the pages around her. "You mean the restricted archives?"

"Yeah, that's it," he replied, aiming for nonchalance but missing by a mile. His hands fidgeted at his sides, betraying his impatience.

She leaned back, arms crossing like a gate slamming shut. "You'd need a professor to sign off on a valid research reason. Then a document specialist will schedule an appointment to go with you. It's not a walk-in service."

Joshua's jaw tightened, frustration clawing at him. "Thank you," he managed, forcing the words through a thin smile. He turned away before she could see the irritation flaring in his eyes. *Another wall. Perfect.* Persuading a professor to endorse a weak theory concerning shepherds and scrolls? He could already hear the laughter.

His sneakers squeaked against the polished floor as he headed for the stairs, leaving the librarian's scrutiny behind. The second level was his sanctuary, a dim, dusty corner where forgotten books slumped on sagging shelves, left by seekers who'd come before him and abandoned their quests. The air up here was thick with the smell of aging pages and mildew, the light feeble as it filtered through grimy windows that wrapped around the building. Desk lamps flickered on the tables, their glow weak and yellowed, barely pushing back the shadows.

Joshua sank into his usual spot, a creaky chair wedged between two towering bookcases. The table was a chaos of his own design, books sprawled open, pages marked with scraps of paper, and his leatherbound index notebook lying at the center like a battle-worn relic. When he'd first started coming here, he'd tried to decipher the library's indexing system, only to realize there wasn't one. No one had bothered to catalog these neglected volumes, so he'd taken it upon himself. He'd begun scribbling names, many unfamiliar, plucked from faded spines, and keywords into his notebook, building a makeshift map through the mess. He left it on the desk between visits, a lifeline he could pick up where he'd left off.

He still held out hope that one of these old voices, buried in ink and dust, would speak to him. That it would fill in a blank he didn't even know was missing, the piece in the middle of the puzzle that would make the whole picture snap into focus.

His fingers brushed the cover of a book he'd been poring over last time: *Die Hirtenpfade der Antike*. The German was rough going, but he'd wrestled enough meaning from it to catch a thread. Shepherds weren't just herders, they were guides, their paths hiding something deeper. He flipped to a marked page, eyes hunting for a line that had lodged in his brain: *The shepherd's path guards its flock.* If the flock wasn't sheep, could it be knowledge? Secrets? People, even? The idea tugged at him, slippery but persistent.

A faint squeak broke his focus, the floorboards groaning somewhere in the stacks behind him. Joshua stiffened, his pen freezing over the page. The library wasn't empty; other students drifted through the aisles, their steps softened by the carpet. But this felt closer, sharper. A chill prickled up his spine, the hairs on his neck standing on end.

He twisted in his chair, peering into the shadows between the shelves. Nothing, just the dim glow of the windows and the distant rustle of pages. He exhaled, shaking his head. *Get a grip.* Too many late nights and cryptic warnings were making him jumpy. But as he turned back to his notes, the unease clung to him, a whisper he couldn't shake.

In the shadows, a pair of eyes watched. The figure stood motionless, half concealed behind a row of crumbling books, cataloging Joshua's every move. The way he hunched over his journal, the frantic scratch of his pen, the muttered thoughts spilling from his lips, all of it was noted. The open notebook on the desk was a treasure trove, its pages dense with names and keywords, though too far to read. It didn't matter. The boy's intensity, his obsession, told the watcher everything: Joshua was digging into something dangerous.

The figure shifted, a careless step brushing a book on the shelf's edge. It toppled to the floor with a soft thud, the floorboards creaking under the weight. Joshua's head snapped up, his eyes darting toward the sound.

The watcher melted back into the darkness, breath held tight. For a tense moment, the library hung in silence, the air heavy.

Joshua stood, his chair scraping loudly as he took a cautious step toward the stacks. "Hello?" he called, his voice low and uncertain.

No answer came. The figure waited, statue-still, until Joshua muttered something to himself and retreated to his desk, his focus shattered. Only then did the watcher slip away, footsteps silent on the carpet, leaving no trace but the chill in the air.

Joshua slumped back into his chair, rubbing his eyes. The words on the page blurred, the library's quiet turning oppressive. He couldn't shake the feeling that someone had been there, watching him from the shadows. It was absurd, he was alone in a corner no one cared about, but the sensation gnawed at him.

He snapped his notebook shut, shoving it into his backpack along with the German book. He needed air, a break from the dust and the weight of the past. As he stood, a scrap of paper slipped from between the pages, fluttering to the floor.

Frowning, he bent to retrieve it. The paper was rough, its ink faded but clear: *The shepherd's path is not walked alone.* His breath hitched. This wasn't his handwriting, wasn't part of his notes. Someone had planted it in his book, in his space. A warning? A clue? His pulse quickened as he gripped the scrap tighter.

He wasn't alone in this hunt. And whoever was watching was closer than he'd feared.

5

Cracks in the Wall

Within weeks, Joshua sensed a shift, Noa's defenses were cracking. It wasn't friendship yet, but she'd stopped treating him like just a punching bag. The classroom had become their arena, each lecture a chance to trade theories and barbs, and today was no different. Joshua slid into his usual seat, the old wooden chair creaking as he dropped his backpack and flipped open his notebook. The room smelled of aged books and chalk dust, morning sunlight cutting through the windows in hazy beams. Dr. Khalil stood at the front, shuffling papers with a scowl that suggested he'd rather be buried in a dig site than babysitting undergrads.

Joshua's gaze drifted to Noa, two rows ahead. She leaned back in her chair, her dark hair spilling in loose waves over her shoulders, catching the light like polished obsidian. Her hazel eyes, sharp and restless, shifting like sunlight on sand, were trained on her notes, but he knew she was listening, waiting for him to strike. She wore a faded denim jacket over a plain white tee, sleeves rolled to her elbows, and a silver pendant hung at her throat, a small, intricately carved relic that seemed older than the room itself. Joshua squinted at it, wondering if it was a family heirloom or a thrift store trinket. Either way, it screamed her obsession with ancient history.

"All right, let's dive in," Dr. Khalil said, his voice a gravelly sigh. "We're picking up with the Dead Sea Scrolls' historical context. Who wants to recap?"

Joshua's hand shot up, but Noa was faster. "The scrolls were likely hidden during the First Jewish-Roman War, around 66 to 73 CE," she said, her tone crisp and confident. "Probably by the Essenes, given their proximity to Qumran."

Dr. Khalil gave a curt nod, but Joshua couldn't resist. "Or maybe not," he interjected, leaning forward. "I've been digging into some German scholars from the 1930s, Heinrich Voss and his crew. They mapped physical locations in the desert, spots that could tie to the Copper Scroll's clues. It's not all about the Essenes."

Noa's head whipped toward him, her eyebrow arching like a drawn bow. "The Germans in the '30s were chasing trade routes, not scrolls, Masa. You're off by a decade." Her voice carried a teasing lilt, but there was a bite beneath it, a challenge flashing in her smirk.

The class snickered, and Joshua felt the familiar sting of her jab. "Maybe," he fired back, "but their maps could still point to something. Not everything's about the grail, Indy."

Her smirk deepened, hazel eyes locking onto his with a mix of amusement and defiance. "You're not the real Indiana Jones, Masa. Stick to the syllabus."

Dr. Khalil cleared his throat, his patience visibly unraveling. "If you two are done with your little performance, perhaps we can return to the lecture?"

Joshua sank back, his pulse kicking up a notch. Noa's barb had hit its mark, but the way she'd held his stare, half-annoyed, half-intrigued, lit a spark in him. She was paying attention, and not just to mock him. His eyes flicked to her pendant again, the carved symbol glinting like a whispered secret. Maybe she wasn't just a skeptic; maybe she had her own stakes in this game.

As Dr. Khalil droned on about sectarian politics, Joshua's mind wandered. Noa's precision, her quick wit, it wasn't just academic posturing. He'd caught a snippet once, an offhand remark she'd made weeks ago about her grandfather trekking Qumran's caves, spinning tales of lost troves. To her, this wasn't textbook trivia; it was personal. That pendant, could it be his, a memento from those dusty expeditions? The idea stuck, a thread he couldn't untangle yet.

The lecture slogged on, but Joshua barely registered it. His pen tapped a restless rhythm against his notebook, his thoughts circling Noa. She was a

30

wall of sharp edges and guarded glances, but those cracks were showing. He just needed the right angle, the right theory to pull her in.

When the bell finally rang, students flooded the hall, but Joshua lingered, watching Noa pack up.

She slung her bag over her shoulder and glanced his way, her expression unreadable. "Nice try, treasure hunter," she said, her voice low, almost conspiratorial. "But you'll need more than old maps."

He grinned, hoisting his backpack. "Watch me," he shot back, again half to her, half as a promise to himself.

She rolled her eyes, but there was a flicker in her gaze, a spark that hadn't been there before. Joshua stepped into the courtyard, the sun glaring off the pavement, his resolve hardening. Noa was a puzzle wrapped in a challenge, and he was nowhere near done.

* * *

A few days later, Joshua spotted Noa in the library, hunched over a table strewn with books and photocopies of scroll fragments. He approached cautiously, like a hunter stalking prey, and dropped into the chair across from her.

She didn't look up, but the slight stiffening of her shoulders told him she'd clocked him. "Voss again?" she asked without preamble, her pen scratching notes in tight, precise script.

"Nah," Joshua said, leaning back. "I'm onto something new, topographical overlays from the '50s. Matches some of the Copper Scroll's coordinates."

Her pen paused, and she lifted her eyes to his. Up close, he noticed faint freckles dusting her nose, a detail he'd missed in the classroom's dim light. "You're still chasing that treasure myth?" she said, but her tone lacked its usual bite.

"Maybe it's not a myth," he countered. "What if it's a lead your grandfather missed?"

Her jaw tightened, and for a split second, her guard slipped. "You don't know anything about him," she said, voice low and clipped.

"I know he was out there," Joshua pressed, nodding at her pendant. "That's his, isn't it?"

Noa's hand brushed the silver relic, her fingers lingering as if weighing whether to answer. "It's just a necklace," she said finally, but her eyes betrayed her, distant, like she was seeing Qumran's caves instead of the library.

Joshua leaned forward, lowering his voice. "Come on, Noa. You're not here for the grades. You're after something bigger."

She studied him, her hazel eyes narrowing, then shoved a photocopy across the table. "Fine. Look at this, line seventeen of the Copper Scroll. 'In the cave of the pillar.' Voss's maps don't match it, but your overlays might."

He blinked, caught off guard by her shift. "You're helping me now?"

"Don't get used to it," she said, smirking faintly. "I just want to see you crash and burn with better evidence."

Joshua laughed, the sound echoing in the quiet library, earning a glare from a nearby student. "Deal," he said, pulling the photocopy closer. "But when I'm right, you're buying the coffee."

Noa snorted, but she didn't argue. As she bent back over her notes, Joshua caught the glint of her pendant again, and a thrill ran through him. The walls were cracking wider, and he was slipping through, one theory, one jab at a time.

* * *

Joshua's laugh still echoed in his ears as he left the library, the memory of Noa's snort and her uncharacteristic lack of argument replaying in his mind. The photocopy he'd clutched felt like a small trophy, proof of a victory in their ongoing dance of banter and bets. The late afternoon sun hung low over the university campus, painting the stone pathways in hues of gold and amber. He adjusted his backpack, the weight of books and notes a familiar comfort, and made his way toward the classroom building. The air carried the faint tang of dust and the sweetness of blooming jasmine, scents that had woven themselves into his daily life in Amman.

The library had been his sanctuary these past weeks, a place where he could burrow into the past and chase the threads of history. His usual haunt, a cluttered corner of shelves and worn tables, had become a battlefield of sorts. He'd cataloged most of the books in his section, earning a rare, approving glance from the librarian, a woman whose stern face softened only for those who respected her domain. Joshua had devised his own system for the books: *useless*, *more useless*, and *utterly useless*. The pre-1940 journals fell squarely into the last category, their pages filled with outdated musings and theories that crumbled under scrutiny. He'd set them aside with a sigh, their brittle edges a testament to time's indifference.

But not everything was a dead end. A handful of maps had caught his eye, their faded lines whispering secrets he couldn't yet decipher. He'd spent hours tracing them, combining them into a consolidated overlay that stretched across his desk like a patchwork quilt. It wasn't a breakthrough, not yet, but it was a start, a skeleton he could flesh out with more data. The journals that focused on the who behind the scrolls were more promising. They didn't offer concrete answers, but they sketched a vivid picture of the factions, religious zealots, political schemers, and curious scholars who'd sought physical artifacts over the centuries. A couple even mentioned communication scrolls, tantalizing hints of messages penned around the time of Jesus's ministry. These writings came from diverse hands, Essenes huddled in desert caves, Temple priests guarding their sacred stores, refugees fleeing chaos, each leaving a mark on the historical tapestry.

The museum visits had been a lifeline, too. Joshua had taken to sketching the scrolls displayed behind glass, his pencil capturing curves and symbols that cameras couldn't quite grasp. He'd made imprints when permitted, pressing paper against ancient surfaces to feel the weight of time. Back at the library, he'd paired these with the journals, correlating dates and details until a fuzzy image began to emerge. It wasn't evidence, not the kind that would hold up in Dr. Khalil's class, but it was enough to keep him pushing forward, one painstaking step at a time.

As he walked, Joshua's thoughts drifted to the eyes that had shadowed him since his arrival. They were still out there, though he noticed them less these days. Maybe it was a false sense of security, a trick of his mind settling into this new life. Even Oman, ever watchful, had stopped pointing out the figures that lingered at the edges of his vision. They'd laughed about it over falafel one evening, how the watchers didn't need to trail him to the food stands anymore. His routine was predictable enough that the street kids knew to wait for him, their small hands outstretched for coins or scraps. Joshua had picked up enough Arabic to catch fragments of their chatter now, words like shukran and sala slipping into his vocabulary. The city was starting to feel less alien, its pulse syncing with his own.

But today, his mind wasn't on the shadows or the scrolls. It was on Noa. Her snort in the library, the way she'd bent over her notes without a comeback, it was a shift, subtle but real. He'd caught the glint of her pendant again as she worked, a small silver piece that seemed to carry a story she hadn't shared. He wondered if it tied her to the past she hinted at, the grandfather who'd roamed Qumran's caves and filled her head with tales of lost treasures. She guarded it like a secret, her fingers brushing it absently, and Joshua felt a pull to know more, not just about the pendant but about her.

He reached the classroom building, the old wooden door creaking as he pushed it open. The room buzzed with low chatter, students sprawled across mismatched desks. Joshua's eyes scanned the rows, and his breath caught when he saw Noa. She was sitting closer than usual—just one row ahead, her denim jacket draped over her chair like a casual flag. She didn't look up as he slid into his seat, but the tilt of her head suggested she knew he was there. His pulse quickened, a mix of nerves and something brighter threading through him

Dr. Khalil swept in moments later, his broad shoulders filling the doorway. "Quiet down," he said, his voice a gravelly command as he dropped his satchel on the desk. "We're diving into the scrolls' cultural ripple effects today. Who's got the rundown?"

Joshua's fingers twitched toward his notebook, but he stayed silent, letting another student stumble through a recap. His mind was elsewhere, on Noa's nearness, on the library's small victories. He doodled absently, tracing the shepherd's symbol he'd found on a scroll, a question mark curling beside it. The pieces were there, scattered across his notes and sketches, but they hadn't clicked yet. Still, he was closer than he'd been weeks ago, and that fueled a quiet fire in him.

The lecture blurred past, Dr. Khalil's words a distant hum. When the bell rang, students surged toward the exit, but Joshua lingered, packing his things with deliberate slowness. Noa did the same, her movements unhurried as she zipped her bag. Their eyes met across the emptying room, and the air tightened for a heartbeat.

"Next coffee's on you," she said, her tone light but her gaze steady.

Joshua grinned, hoisting his backpack. "Only if I'm wrong."

She smirked, brushing past him as she headed for the door. Her shoulder grazed his, a fleeting touch that sent a spark through him. He watched her go, her dark hair catching the hallway light, and felt the walls between them crack just a little wider.

Stepping into the courtyard, the sun dipping below Amman's hills, Joshua took a deep breath. He wasn't the same fumbling newcomer who'd arrived jet-lagged and lost. He belonged here now, tied to the city's rhythm, its people. The eyes that had once loomed large felt distant, their menace dulled by his growing roots. Maybe they'd moved on. Maybe he'd outpaced them.

But as he walked into the twilight, he didn't see the figure step from the shadows, eyes fixed on his retreating form, a silent promise that the game wasn't over yet.

6

Darkness Chased by the Light

J oshua's pulse quickened as he crossed the university courtyard, the late afternoon sun stretching shadows across the cobblestones. In his hand, he clutched the permission slip, a fragile piece of paper that felt heavier than it should. Access to the restricted section of the library had just been granted, a privilege he'd hardly dared to hope for. His thesis, tied to his status as an international student, hinged on this moment, and now it was real. Dr. Khalil had come through with the approval faster than anyone expected, a sign that Joshua's work was starting to turn heads.

He glanced at his watch. Noa would be here soon, fresh from her last class. She hadn't seen the restricted section either, and her excitement matched his own. They'd been buzzing since Dr. Khalil had burst into the seminar room two days ago, waving the permission slip like a victory flag. Normally, approvals took weeks, bogged down by bureaucracy, but this time, it was different. Joshua's research on the Copper Scroll, an enigma from the Dead Sea Scrolls, had caught Dr. Khalil's attention, and the professor's influence had cut through the red tape.

The library loomed ahead, its stone walls exuding an air of quiet authority. Joshua's mind raced with possibilities. What would he find in those forbidden shelves? Rare manuscripts? Lost fragments? The answers to questions he'd been chasing for months? His excitement was electric, but a flicker of doubt gnawed at him. *Am I ready for this?* The thought lingered, unbidden, before he pushed it aside.

He reached the library steps, his sneakers scuffing the worn stone, when a jolt of panic stopped him cold. His notebook, he'd left it in the classroom. His sketches, his notes, his entire framework for the thesis were in there. How could he have been so careless? Heart pounding, he spun around and bolted back across the courtyard. The classroom was empty, the door ajar, and there it was, his notebook, sitting innocently on the desk, pages fluttering in the breeze from an open window. He snatched it up, relief flooding through him as he tucked it into his backpack and raced back to the library.

Noa was already there, leaning against the wall near the entrance, her dark hair glinting in the fading light. "Thought you'd bailed," she said, her tone teasing but her eyes bright with anticipation.

Joshua held up the permission slip, a grin breaking across his face. "Not a chance. You ready?"

She nodded, falling into step beside him as they pushed through the library doors. The front desk librarian peered at them over her glasses, her expression skeptical until Joshua slid the permission slip across the counter. She accepted the note, a small hum of disapproval she seemed to have developed over Joshua's visits. The librarian pushed a button, within a few moments another academically dressed man stepped to the desk. Without saying a word, he started walking, the two decided at the same time to follow him. A short time later the man's key unlocked, what could reverantly be referred to as, the secret passage.

The door creaked open, revealing a room steeped in shadow and reverence. Rows of ancient books lined the walls, their leather spines cracked with age. Glass cases held fragile manuscripts, yellowed and delicate, while the air carried the faint, musty scent of history. Joshua's breath caught in his throat.

Noa, usually quick with a quip, stood silent beside him, her wide eyes reflecting the same awe he felt. "Where do we even start?" she whispered, her voice barely breaking the stillness.

Joshua scanned the rows of glass encased drawers. "Cave 4's scrolls, they are tied more to the Copper Scroll's origins. Only having today and tomorrow, we should start as close as we can to the source." He pulled a drawer, its soft scrape revealing scroll fragments pieced together like a puzzle. Faded Hebrew writing struggling to be highlighted under the protective glass. Each reveal meant an exposure causing light damage, making this a privilege not lightly granted, amplifying the weight of this quest.

They dove in, the thrill of discovery charging the search with anticipation, soon the sheer volume would be overwhelming. Scanning every word proved too slow, causing frustration of reality to join the fear of missing vital clues. "We're drowning in parchment," he muttered, sliding another drawer shut.

Noa's multi-tool tapped her notebook, her eyes sharp. "We change tactics, read the first lines, and skip the unrelated. Focus, Masa." Her nudge, steadied him. They adapted, skimming fragments, the hum of the library more insistent as the day came to an end.

Dusk fell, the day's progress was slim, and exhaustion was creeping in. Noa smirked, pocketing her notes, "let's grab some coffee." They left the library and stepped into Amman's twilight, the city's call to prayer weaving through the spice laced air. Noa elbowed Joshua, her gave flicking to a man across the street. He was out of place, with sharp eyes, and chilling glare. Joshua tensed, recalling the falafel vendor's warning. "That one's ISIS, watching you."

He nodded hurrying them to the coffee shop, his pulse still racing as they walked inside. The sounds of the street exchanged for the clatter of cups. As they sat, Joshua confided what the falafel merchant had told him. "I'm being watched, coming and going."

Noa slid her annotated notebook across, her tone firm. "We're not backing down. Drowning in parchment's bad enough—focus, Josh, game on." Her index detailed Cave 4 finds, a lifeline. Joshua flipped pages, pausing at a line: Shepherd's path leads... "This," he said, voice rising, "I've seen it before, but I can't remember where exactly. Is the line incomplete?"

Noa shushed him, smirking. "Cave 4, column 2, drawer 4—my indexing's smarter than you." Her finger tapped the page, grounding his excitement.

A figure glided toward them, cassock rustling—a priest, incongruous in the shop's bustle. He sat at the next table, voice calm. "Good evening. No need to hide our talk—folks wouldn't believe we're not discussing your work." He nodded streetward, hinting at the watcher. "You've been busy." The priest smiled, cross glinting. "Father Nance. I've heard of your access, impressive for students." He eyed their notebooks. "Be careful. We're watching, can't guarantee your safety, well hers, maybe, not yours." He whistled, teasing, then stood. "We're keen on what you find."

Joshua exhaled, "Good Lord."

Noa winked, "I think that's his line."

He let out a shaky laugh, but the priest's parting words, *We will keep an eye on you*, echoed in his mind, sharp and unsettling. Who was "we"? And why did a priest, of all people, care about his thesis on the Copper Scroll? Joshua's fingers tightened around his coffee cup, the warmth seeping into his palms as he tried to steady himself.

He glanced at Noa, who had already flipped open her notebook again, her brow creased in focus. The coffee shop buzzed around them, conversations blending with the clatter of cups, but Joshua's thoughts were elsewhere. His eyes flicked to the window, scanning the street beyond. The suspicious man from earlier was nowhere in sight, but the prickling sensation of being watched lingered. The falafel maker's warning from weeks ago surfaced in his memory: *You're being watched, coming and going.* Now, with Father Nance's cryptic visit, it felt less like paranoia and more like a fact.

"Josh," Noa said, her voice snapping him back to the moment. She tapped her pen against the notebook. "We've only got tomorrow left in the restricted section." Noa leaned in, her shoulder brushing his as she peered at the page. "You mentioned a journal. Any idea which one?"

Joshua closed his eyes, pictured the library's restricted section, the dusty shelves, the scent of aged leather. "It was from the 1950s, an archaeologist's field notes. I logged it under cave four theories in my index, but it didn't stand out until now."

Her eyes sparked with excitement. "That's a start. If we can track down that journal tomorrow, it might fill in the blanks, or at least point us somewhere."

"Yeah," he said, a flicker of hope cutting through his frustration. It wasn't a solution, but it was progress, a thread to chase in the labyrinth of scrolls they'd been sifting through. With Noa's knack for detail, it felt within reach. "We'll hit that first thing in the morning."

She smirked, a teasing glint in her hazel eyes. "Good thing I'm smarter with the indexing, huh?"

Joshua chuckled, the tension in his chest easing. "Don't get cocky."

They sipped their coffee in a comfortable silence, the shop's ambient hum wrapping around them like a buffer against the day's chaos. Joshua's gaze drifted to Noa's pendant, a small, carved piece she wore like a second skin. He'd noticed her touching it absently during their library search, a quiet habit that hinted at a story she hadn't shared. Was it tied to her grandfather's tales of Qumran? He almost asked, but her voice broke the thought.

"You know," she said, softer now, twirling her spoon in her cup, "my grandfather always said the scrolls weren't just about treasure or history. They were about people, who they were, what they believed." Her eyes grew distant, lost in memory. "Maybe that's what we're missing here. The human piece."

Joshua tilted his head, intrigued. "You think the Copper Scroll's more than a treasure map?"

She shrugged, a half smile tugging at her lips. "Maybe. Or maybe I'm just exhausted."

He didn't press her, but the idea lodged itself in his mind. The Copper Scroll's list of gold and silver had always felt mechanical, weights and locations, cold and precise. What if it was a story hidden in plain sight? A new angle to explore, one he hadn't considered before.

They finished their drinks, the weight of the day settling into a shared fatigue. As they stood to leave, Joshua zipped his backpack and froze. A folded scrap of paper jutted from the side pocket, its edges yellowed like the scrolls they'd spent hours studying. He hadn't put it there.

Noa noticed his pause. "What's that?"

He unfolded it carefully, revealing a scrawled message in faded ink: *The shepherd's path is not for the faint-hearted.*

His breath hitched. The handwriting wasn't his, or Noa's. Someone had slipped it into his bag, maybe in the library, maybe the classroom when he'd left his notebook behind. A chill ran through him. Father Nance? The man outside? Or someone they hadn't even noticed?

Noa read over his shoulder, frowning. "That's... creepy. A warning?"

"Or a clue," Joshua said, though his voice betrayed his uncertainty. He tucked the note into his pocket, his mind spinning. Whoever left it knew exactly what they were searching for, and they were closer than he'd realized.

They stepped into the evening air, the city's hum enveloping them.

Noa nudged his arm, her touch light but steadying. "Hey," she said, her tone gentle. "We'll figure it out. One step at a time."

He met her gaze, the streetlights catching the gold flecks in her eyes. For a moment, the mystery, the watchers, the notes, and the endless questions receded. It was just them, standing on the brink of something vast and unknown, together. "Yeah," he said, a small smile breaking through. "One step at a time."

As they walked into the night, Joshua couldn't shake the sense of eyes on his back. But with Noa beside him, it didn't feel like a threat. It felt like a challenge. And he was ready to face it.

7

The Crook's Call

The library doors creaked open, and Joshua and Noa hurried inside, the morning chill still clinging to their jackets. The librarian, her smirk firmly in place, shot Joshua a look that could curdle milk.

Noa elbowed him as they climbed the stairs to the restricted section. "Wow, did you spurn her love or something?"

Joshua tilted his head away, biting back a retort. "Let's just focus on the scrolls," he muttered, though the corner of his mouth twitched.

Once inside the restricted section, they settled into a familiar rhythm.

"I'll check the spots where we found the shepherd's path mentioned yesterday," Noa said, heading toward the drawers they'd already flagged. "You keep going on that new one."

Joshua dropped his bag on the table, pulling out his notebook. The pages were a mess of scribbles, translations, theories, and quotes from a 1950s scholar whose work had become his lifeline. He slid a manuscript under the glass toward him, his eyes darting between the ancient text and his notes. The shepherd's path stared back at him, its recurrence across scrolls from different caves a tantalizing thread. The scholar had written: *A recurring theme in some scrolls, even from different caves... may ultimately hint at who was responsible for their creation.*

He turned to Noa, excitement creeping into his voice. "This guy read these lines over and over. He was convinced the shepherd's path could point us to the scrolls' authors."

Noa nodded, peering at her own fragment. "We've got two mentions from cave four so far, on separate scrolls. But it's still nothing concrete."

"Yeah," Joshua agreed, "and we can't afford tunnel vision."

"Exactly," she said, her tone firm but encouraging. "Still, it's the first time you've linked any scrolls together. Seeing it with your own eyes, that's huge."

Joshua grinned, the thrill of the hunt sparking through him. "It's amazing."

They worked in silence for a while, the only sounds the soft scrape of drawers and the rustle of their notes. Joshua's focus narrowed to the scroll in front of him, his fingers tracing the glass as he read. Then, something caught his eye, a tiny symbol etched in the margin beside the shepherd's path phrase. A staff with a crook, like a shepherd's tool. His breath hitched. He'd seen it before on a scroll fragment at the museum.

"Noa," he said, his voice low and urgent. "Come look at this."

She crossed the room in three quick steps, leaning over his shoulder. "What'd you find?"

"This symbol." He pointed to the shepherd's crook. "It's next to the shepherd's path mention. I saw the same mark on a piece from Qumran at the museum."

Noa's eyes widened. "Check the others."

He pulled out the two cave four scrolls they'd flagged yesterday, and there it was, faint but unmistakable, the same crook beside each shepherd's path reference. "It's on all of them," he said, his pulse racing. "This can't be random."

"It's like a signature," Noa murmured, her fingers hovering over the glass. "Maybe it marks scrolls tied to the shepherd's path, or the people who wrote them."

Joshua nodded, his mind spinning. "If we can figure out who used this symbol, we might know who's behind the scrolls. Maybe even the Copper Scroll itself."

They exchanged a look, the weight of the discovery settling between them.

This was more than a recurring phrase, it was a lead, a crack in the mystery they'd been chasing.

But before they could dig deeper, the librarian's voice cut through the silence. "Time's up. You're done for today."

Joshua groaned, glancing at Noa. "We just got started."

She packed her notes, her movements brisk. "We've got enough to chew on. Let's regroup outside."

As they stepped into the thick evening air, Joshua couldn't shake the librarian's glare, or the prickling sensation at the back of his neck. He scanned the street, half, expecting to see the shadowy man from the night before. No one stood out, but the unease lingered.

Noa nudged him toward the coffee shop down the block. "You're jumpy. What's up?"

"Just a feeling," he said, shoving his hands in his pockets. "Like we're not the only ones interested in those scrolls."

She frowned but didn't press. Inside the shop, they claimed a booth, the warmth and chatter a stark contrast to the library's stillness. Noa leaned forward, her voice low. "That symbol, it's a game-changer. We need to cross-reference it with everything we've got."

Joshua nodded, flipping open his notebook. "If it's a marker, it could tie the shepherd's path to a specific group. A sect, a secret society, something the 1950s guy missed."

"Or something he didn't have access to," Noa added. "We've got better tech now. Photos, databases..."

"Right," Joshua said, his excitement building. "We'll dig into the museum records tomorrow. See if that crook shows up anywhere else."

Noa sipped her coffee, her gaze steady. "One step at a time, Josh. We're getting close."

He met her eyes, the tension easing just a fraction. "Yeah. One step at a time." But as he glanced out the window, a figure lingered across the street, too still, too watchful. Joshua's grip tightened on his mug. The shepherd's path was leading them somewhere, but it was starting to feel like they weren't the only ones following it.

Noa's eyes flicked to the window, her spoon clinking softly against her mug as she stirred her coffee.

"Of course, this could be a thread that leads to nothing," Joshua said, his voice steady, grounding himself in the realism he'd learned from years of chasing historical leads. The shepherd's path symbol, a tiny shepherd's crook etched beside the recurring phrase, had ignited a spark of hope, but he knew better than to let it blaze unchecked. History was a maze of dead ends, and he'd stumbled into plenty before.

Noa nodded, her expression calm but thoughtful. "So, one more day in the restricted section. We should come up with a plan of attack for tomorrow." She tapped her notebook, where her neat handwriting cataloged their findings—the two Cave 4 scrolls, the symbol's appearances, and a growing list of questions. Despite the uncertainty, there was a quiet satisfaction in her tone, a sign she was pleased with their progress, even if it was just a foothold in a much larger climb.

Joshua leaned back, swirling the last of his coffee. "We'll start with the Cave 4 fragments again. Check for more symbols, maybe compare the handwriting. If the Shepherd's Path is a code or a marker, there could be other clues we've missed."

"Smart," Noa said, jotting a quick note. Then her gaze shifted, her voice dropping to a near whisper. "Aside from that, what do you think of your, or our, shadows?"

Joshua's grip tightened on his mug, the warmth doing little to chase away the chill that crept up his spine. He glanced out the window, where the streetlights cast long, shifting shadows across the pavement. The figure he'd spotted earlier was gone, but the prickling at the back of his neck lingered, a nagging echo of the falafel maker's warning and Father Nance's cryptic words. "Nothing much so far," he admitted, keeping his tone even. "I prefer the priest, at least he informed me. That other one, the one who stays in the shadows... it's a little worrying."

Noa's brow furrowed, her usual steadiness giving way to a flicker of concern. "You think they're connected?"

"Maybe," Joshua said, his mind racing through the possibilities. "Or maybe they're after different things. Either way, it's clear someone's watching what we're doing."

She leaned forward, her voice firm despite its quietness. "We'll be careful, Josh. But we're not backing down."

He met her gaze, her hazel eyes sharp with resolve, a mirror to the determination steadying his own nerves. "No," he agreed, his voice solidifying. "We're not."

For a moment, they sat in silence, the coffee shop's hum wrapping around them like a fragile cocoon. Joshua's thoughts drifted to his grandfather, to the old man's gravelly voice: *History's a puzzle with missing pieces, Masa. You just keep looking.* That persistence had driven him here, to this table, with Noa beside him and a symbol that might finally fit a piece into place.

Noa broke the quiet, stirring her coffee absently. "Think we'll ever figure this out?"

Joshua shrugged, a half smile tugging at his lips. "Maybe. Or maybe we'll just end up with more questions."

She laughed softly, the sound light and grounding in the midst of their tangled chase. "Sounds about right."

They finished their drinks, the day's fatigue settling into their bones, but tempered by a shared purpose. As they stood to leave, Joshua zipped his backpack, his fingers brushing the folded note still tucked in his pocket: *The shepherd's path is not for the faint-hearted.* A warning? A clue? He wasn't sure. But with Noa at his side, it felt less like a threat and more like a dare. Joshua paused at the coffee shop's door, Amman's streetlights casting shadows through the glass, the note in his pocket—"The shepherd's path is not for the faint-hearted"—ringing like Matthew 3:3's cry, urging him toward the Copper Scroll's secrets. Noa's hand brushed his arm, her multi-tool tucked away, her voice low, "Museum records tomorrow, Masa—ready?" Two paths loomed: the scroll's perilous truth, marked by the shepherd's crook, and the unspoken pull of her steady gaze. Could he answer both calls without faltering, with watchers lurking beyond the glow?

They stepped into the night, the city's pulse thrumming around them. The air buzzed with the hum of distant traffic, the chatter of late-night vendors, and the faint strum of a street musician's oud. Joshua couldn't shake the sensation of eyes on his back, a prickling that had followed him for days. He resisted the urge to turn, his focus split between the shadows and the woman beside him.

Tomorrow, they'd return to the restricted section of the museum with a plan: dig deeper into the shepherd's path, cross-reference the shepherd's crook with archival records, and follow the thread wherever it led. The mystery was unraveling, one fragile piece at a time, and they were in it together, shadows and all.

For the last few nights, Joshua had walked Noa to her apartment. Tonight, as she slipped through the door with a quick smile, his heart thudded hard enough to drown out the city's noise. He lingered at the threshold, watching her disappear inside, a warmth spreading through him that he couldn't ignore. He wasn't a stranger to relationships. He'd had girlfriends before, but this felt different, deeper than a fleeting crush. A working connection had blossomed into something more, and it left him unsteady.

The walk home should have been simple, but Amman's streets were a labyrinth. The first night he'd escorted her, he'd gotten lost, the alleys twisting around him like a riddle he couldn't solve. Tonight, he navigated by instinct, the flickering streetlights and maze-like turns mirroring the tangle in his mind. By the time he reached his apartment, his pulse hadn't settled.

Inside, the wall greeted him, a chaotic tapestry of notes, maps, and scribbled theories about the shepherd's path. He sank into his chair, staring at the mess. Two forces pulled at him: the thrill of the discovery and the growing pull of Noa. Both were the most exciting things to happen in his life, twin flames that could illuminate everything or burn it all down if he lost focus. The shepherd's crook, that ancient symbol they'd uncovered, promised answers to a historical puzzle he'd chased for years. But Noa, her sharp mind, her quiet strength, had become a puzzle of her own, one he hadn't expected to care about solving.

He leaned forward, elbows on his knees, and ran a hand through his hair. Was he letting emotion cloud his judgment? His grandfather's voice surfaced, steady and firm: *History's a puzzle, Masa. Don't lose the pieces.* The words had guided him through late nights and dead ends, but they didn't account for this, for her. He reached for a scrap of paper and sketched the crook, its sharp curve grounding him. The mystery had to come first. It was why he was here, why he'd poured years into this work. Losing sight of it now would unravel everything.

But as he tucked a cryptic note, one they'd found tucked in an old manuscript, into his pocket, Noa's face flickered in his mind. Her laugh from earlier that day, the way her eyes caught the glow of the streetlights. He couldn't shake it. Outside, the shadows shifted, a faint creak of a floorboard beyond his window, a flicker of movement in the dark. The feeling of being watched hadn't faded, and his distraction tonight made him vulnerable. Someone else was chasing this thread, and they were close.

Joshua exhaled, pinning the sketch of the crook to the wall. He couldn't afford to falter, not with the shepherd's path within reach, and not with Noa counting on him. One puzzle at a time, he told himself. For now, the mystery would anchor him. But his heart, still racing, whispered that Noa wasn't a puzzle he could set aside so easily.

8

The Museum Breakthrough

The morning sun barely crested Amman's skyline as Joshua and Noa met outside the university library, their breath misting in the crisp air. Noa's dark hair swung in a loose ponytail, her worn backpack slung over one shoulder. She flashed Joshua a grin, her brown eyes glinting with mischief. "Morning, Masa. Ready to unravel the scroll's secrets?"

Joshua returned the smile, the nickname warming him like a familiar tune. "Always. Let's see if Dr. Kalil's in a sharing mood today."

They climbed to their second-floor nook, a cluttered table wedged between towering bookshelves heavy with the scent of aged paper. The library hummed faintly, its silence broken by the rustle of pages and a chair's occasional creak. As they spread out their notes—Joshua's notebook brimming with sketches and Noa's marked with precise annotations—Dr. Kalil appeared, his stocky frame casting a shadow across the worn floor. His eyes twinkled with curiosity as he pulled up a chair.

"Morning, you two," he said, his voice laced with amusement. "Heard you've been chasing shadows. What's new with the Copper Scroll?"

Joshua flipped open his notebook, revealing a chaotic spread of scribbled theories and a sketch of a shepherd's crook. "We're zeroing in on the 'Shepherd's Path.' This symbol—a crook—keeps appearing in Cave 4 scrolls, tied to those phrases."

Dr. Kalil leaned in, his thick fingers tracing the sketch's curves. "Intriguing.

You think it points to the scroll's authors?"

Noa nodded, tucking a stray hair behind her ear. "Maybe. If we identify who used it, we could link it to the Copper Scroll's creators."

Kalil stroked his chin, his expression cautious but engaged. "A good lead, but the Copper Scroll's an outlier. Its purpose might not match the other scrolls."

"That's why we need to see it up close," Joshua said, his voice electric with urgency. "The Jordan Museum has it. I think the real thing could spark something."

Kalil's eyebrow arched, a faint smile tugging his lips. "The museum, huh? Ambitious."

"I've been there before," Joshua pressed, leaning forward. "The staff know me. They might let us get closer."

Kalil chuckled, leaning back. "If anyone can charm their way in, it's you, Joshua. Go for it, but don't expect the scroll to whisper its secrets."

As Kalil shuffled off, Noa turned to Joshua, her eyes gleaming with resolve. "He's skeptical, but I'm with you. Let's hit the museum after lunch."

The Jordan Museum loomed like a modern fortress amid Amman's ancient sprawl, its glass facade shimmering under the midday sun. Joshua and Noa crossed the bustling plaza, heat radiating from the pavement. Inside, the air was cool and reverent, exhibits glowing under soft lights, the hum of air conditioning barely audible.

At the front desk, Ahmed, the security guard, broke into a wide grin. "Joshua! Back again?" His handshake was firm, his eyes warm. "What's the draw today?"

"The Copper Scroll," Joshua said, keeping his tone light but hopeful. "Any chance for a closer look?"

Ahmed glanced around, then leaned in with a conspiratorial wink. "For you, my friend, I'll make it happen. Follow me."

He led them through a maze of exhibits—past weathered clay jars and mosaics faded by time—to a secured room. Behind thick glass, the Copper Scroll gleamed, its greenish patina catching the light like aged bronze. Etched symbols and cryptic lines sprawled across its surface, a treasure map frozen in time.

Noa's breath hitched as she stepped closer. "It's unreal," she whispered. "Centuries old, still hiding something."

Joshua nodded, his eyes scanning the scroll. "There—'Behind twin pillars that split the waters, guarding the island, it lies buried upon the mantle.'"

Noa squinted at the faint etchings. "Twin pillars... maybe rock spires near a spring?"

"Exactly," Joshua said, his mind racing. "Ein Feshkha has springs that could 'split the waters.' Caves there have ledges—a 'mantle.'"

Noa tilted her head, skeptical. "Ein Feshkha's been scoured. Wouldn't someone have found it?"

"Maybe we're misreading it," Joshua countered, tapping the glass. "The 'island' could be a raised platform in a cave, surrounded by water channels."

Their ideas sparked, bouncing between them with growing intensity. Joshua's gaze drifted to a topographic map of Qumran nearby, and a memory snapped into focus. "Wait," he said, stepping toward it. "My grandfather's old map marked two rock formations near the Jordan River—the Twin Pillars."

Noa joined him, her interest sharpening. "That fits."

Joshua's pulse quickened as he traced the map. "There's a plateau nearby, almost like an island, with caves beneath. That's our 'mantle.'"

Noa's eyes lit up. "The scroll's pointing us there."

"We need to cross-check this in the library archives," Joshua said, grabbing her arm in a surge of adrenaline. "There could be maps or records to confirm it."

They hurried out, footsteps echoing on polished floors. As they passed through the main hall, a figure lingered in the shadows—an older man with sharp features and a weathered coat. He watched them go, his gray eyes narrowing, his German accent thick as he muttered, "Too close." He reached for a radio clipped to his belt, his movements deliberate.

Joshua and Noa burst from the museum, the afternoon heat hitting like a wave as they jogged toward the library, backpacks bouncing. The thrill of discovery drowned out their exhaustion, Amman's noise fading into a blur.

Behind them, the dark figure stepped into the sunlight, his gaze locked on their retreating forms. He lifted the radio, his voice low and urgent. "They're heading to the library. Watch them."

The library's second floor was a frenzy as Joshua and Noa stormed their table, spilling maps and journals across its surface. Joshua pulled a frayed, yellowed map from his bag—his grandfather's, its ink faded but legible. "Here," he said, pointing. "The Twin Pillars, marked clear as day."

Noa leaned in, tracing the lines. "And there's the plateau, near the river."

"If we find excavation records for that area, we can pinpoint the cave," Joshua said, his voice taut with focus.

Noa grabbed a stack of journals, flipping through with practiced speed. "Let's check the Jordan River surveys."

Time blurred as they dug in, the quiet corner a war room of research. The sun sank, painting the windows gold, but they pressed on, fueled by the promise of answers. Noa's shout broke the silence. "Found it!" She held up a 1960s expedition report, a sticky note flapping. "They surveyed caves near the Twin Pillars—nothing major, but they mention a ledge in one cave, looked man-made."

Joshua's eyes widened. "That's the 'mantle.' If they didn't dig deep, the treasure's still there."

Noa grinned, the excitement contagious. "We've got a lead, Masa."

The library's closing announcement crackled, jolting them. They packed up, stepping into Amman's cool evening, the city's lights flickering to life. Exhilaration mixed with unease in Joshua's chest—Elias's shadow loomed, a reminder of unseen eyes.

Noa nudged him as they walked toward her apartment. "Field trip to the Twin Pillars next?"

Joshua laughed, tension easing. "Maybe. Let's run it by Kalil tomorrow."

At her door, Noa paused, her expression sobering. "Be careful, Josh. We're stirring something big."

He met her gaze, nodding. "I know. Together, though?"

"Always," she said, her smile soft. "Goodnight, Masa."

"Goodnight, Noa."

Joshua navigated Amman's winding streets home, the city closing in. The Copper Scroll's secrets felt within reach, but so did the danger. Sleep eluded him that night, his mind racing with the weight of discovery and the echoes of his grandfather's backyard digs.

The next morning, Joshua approached Dr. Kalil's office, voices spilling from within—serious, but not heated. "He's getting close?" A voice, familiar yet jarring.

Joshua knocked, the voices hushing. "Heard you down the hall," he said, stepping in with a grin, moving books to claim a chair. "Keep talking about me."

Dr. Kalil's eyes sparkled with amusement. "These gentlemen were discussing your work. You know Father Nance, but meet Rabbi Cohen."

Rabbi Cohen, a reclusive scholar from Jerusalem, was a legend in Dead Sea Scrolls circles, his theories on their ties to sacred history both revered and debated. Father Nance, a Vatican-connected priest, remained an enigma, his presence tied to museum work but his motives unclear.

"We're up to speed on your progress," Cohen said, his monotone voice dry as dust. "The restricted section, your access to the scroll—impressive."

Joshua leaned back, cautious. "Noa and I have been grinding, but it's for my thesis. No solid evidence of physical treasure yet."

"Masa," Father Nance said, his tone eerie but calm, "we're not here to hijack your work. We've studied the scroll for years and haven't made your connections. We have information you might need."

Joshua relaxed, catching Kalil's satisfied grin. "Good to hear. I take it you're not with the other guys?"

"No," Cohen replied sharply. "Some groups fund terrorism with artifacts, selling them on the black market, not destroying them."

"Be careful," Nance added, producing a notebook. "This outlines what we think each scroll line leads to—potential artifacts."

Joshua's pulse quickened as he took the notebook. "My big question is who hid the scrolls. I think it was the Essenes, collecting not just religious texts but synagogue letters." He pulled his index from his bag, flipping to a marked page. "I've logged letters mentioning 'the shepherd.' I think it's

Jesus."

A collective breath rippled through the room—skepticism or surprise, hard to tell. Joshua pressed on. "The symbols and dates align with first-century timelines. I found a letter in the general archives, not restricted, from a Pharisee urging supporters for Jesus's trial before Pilate. It's marked with a dove emblem."

Cohen's eyebrow arched. "A bold claim."

"It's real," Joshua insisted, pointing to his index. "The letter's script and materials are first-century. It mentions a jar of synagogue correspondence."

Kalil's grin widened. "That's monumental, Joshua. You and Noa need to be certain before your thesis." He glanced at the guests. "Any concerns beyond safety?"

Cohen and Nance exchanged a glance, unreadable but charged. To Joshua's surprise, neither objected. Cohen's fingers tapped his chair, his gaze distant.

"Noa's on her way," Joshua said, breaking the silence. "You're welcome to stay and dig into this."

The room settled into a heavy quiet, each person lost in thought, Joshua's theory a spark waiting to ignite.

Noa strode in, her backpack thudding as she froze, eyeing the group. "Interrupting?"

"Just in time," Joshua said, waving her in. "We're on the shepherd theory—Jesus and the scrolls."

Noa's brow arched as she pulled up a chair, glancing at Cohen and Nance. "Jesus, huh? Big audience for that one."

Nance inclined his head. "We're here to help, not hinder. Your work intrigues us."

Cohen leaned forward, his voice sharp. "The dove emblem ties to messianic figures in Jewish tradition. Your theory has legs."

Noa shot Joshua a look, surprised. "You think he's right?"

"It merits investigation," Cohen said. "The Essenes were obsessed with messianic hope. Letters about 'the shepherd' could suggest early Christian ties."

Nance nodded. "The Vatican's long sought such links in the scrolls. If true, this could reshape history."

Kalil cleared his throat. "Let's not get ahead of ourselves. Joshua, show us that letter."

Joshua flipped to his index, his voice steady. "It's in the general archives—a Pharisee's letter about Jesus's trial, marked with a dove. I've seen it."

Noa's eyes widened. "That's huge. If it's real."

"It is," Joshua said, meeting her gaze. "And it ties the Essenes to the scrolls' purpose."

Cohen's fingers stilled, his gaze intense. "We need to see it."

Nance nodded. "If authentic, it could explain the Copper Scroll's treasure."

Noa frowned. "Why hide Jesus's letters with sacred texts? And what's the treasure link?"

Joshua leaned back. "What if the treasure is knowledge—documents that rewrite history?"

Kalil chuckled, intrigued. "A stretch, but compelling."

Cohen's voice dropped, deliberate. "A legend speaks of forbidden texts, hidden to shield them from destruction."

Nance's eyes narrowed. "The Vatican knows similar tales—lost gospels, smuggled to the desert."

Joshua's breath caught. "So the Copper Scroll's a map to those texts?"

"Perhaps," Cohen cautioned. "But it's dangerous. Some would kill to keep them buried—or exploit them."

Noa's grip tightened on her notebook. "Like those black-market groups?"

"Exactly," Nance said grimly. "Proceed with care."

The stakes settled like dust, heavy and real. Joshua's thoughts flickered to Elias—the shadowed figure, the radio's crackle. Danger was close.

Kalil broke the tension. "Focus, you two. Verify that letter tomorrow."

"We will," Joshua said, resolve hardening.

Noa stood, slinging her bag. "Rest first. Long day."

As they left, Joshua lingered, Amman's lights twinkling beyond the window. With Noa, Cohen, and Nance behind him, the Shepherd's Path felt closer—but so did the shadows trailing it. There was no turning back.

9

The Museum's Whisper

T
he morning sun barely crested Amman's skyline as Joshua and Noa slipped into the museum, the air still cool from the night. Joshua had walked Noa home after Dr. Khalil's office, their chatter as light as that first evening: falafel stands and stray cats, not scrolls or shepherds. Now, though, the museum hummed with a different energy, charged like static before a storm. They carried their notes from the restricted section like scribbled gold, Noa called them, and spread them across a worn wooden table in the archive room, the scent of dust and old paper thick around them.

Noa hunched over a magnifying glass, tracing the faint curve of a shepherd's crook etched into a parchment fragment. "If this is Essene," she murmured, "it's not shouting Jesus at me yet." Her voice was tight, guarded. She'd seen scholars crash chasing religious ghosts, ignoring history's grit for miracles.

Joshua nodded, flipping through his notebook. "I'm not saying it's a neon sign. Just... look for the who and why. If it's them, why hide it?" He kept his tone even, sensing her edge. Noa got like this when the stakes climbed: quiet, sharp, a bear better left unpoked. "Don't poke the bear," he muttered, a half smile tugging at his lips.

Her head whipped around, dark eyes flashing. "Did you say something?" Her voice sliced through the stillness, louder than the hum of the overhead lights.

He raised his hands in mock surrender. "Just thinking aloud, Noa. You're the boss here."

She snorted, softening a fraction, and turned back to the fragment. "Good. Keep it that way."

The door creaked open, and a woman stepped in, tall, with a confident stride and a backpack slung over one shoulder. "Morning," she said, her accent a soft blend of local and something foreign. "I'm Amina. Heard you're digging into Second Temple stuff. Mind if I join?" She flashed a smile, setting her bag down near theirs. A pendant glinted at her neck, a cross with flared ends, Templar if Joshua's memory served.

Noa glanced up, wary but polite. "We're not advertising. How'd you hear?"

Amina shrugged, pulling out a sketchpad. "Word travels in tight circles. I've studied Jerusalem's archives, thought I might help." She tapped a pencil against the table, her gaze flicking to Joshua's notebook. "Those emblems of the dove, crook, and any others tied to this?"

Joshua's brow furrowed, but he slid the notebook closer. "Maybe. This one's from a letter, a Pharisee calling for supporters at Pilate's court. First century, dove in the margin."

Amina leaned in, her pendant catching the light. "Interesting note: the Sadducees, not Pharisees, led the push against Jesus in Jerusalem. Templars guarded relics from that era, some say they hid more than they found." Her tone was casual, but her eyes lingered too long on the page.

Noa's fingers stilled on the magnifying glass. "Templars? That's a leap from Essenes."

"Not if the Essenes passed something on," Amina replied, sketching the dove with quick, precise strokes. "Jerusalem's a crossroads. Secrets don't stay with one group."

The room grew quiet, her words settling like dust. Joshua felt a prickle at his neck, someone watching, or just the museum's old bones creaking? He shook it off. "All right, Amina. You're in. Let's find more."

Noa shot him a look, half warning, half curiosity, but nodded. "Fine. Facts, not legends."

They worked into the morning, the table piling with fragments and notes.

Amina pointed out a shepherd's crook on a clay seal, Noa cross-checked dates, and Joshua traced a dove to a scroll edge. Nothing screamed Jesus, but the pieces fit too well to ignore.

Then Noa unrolled a long sheet she'd been building, a working scroll of their own connections, theories, and justifications scrawled in her tight script. "Look at this," she said, voice low but firm. "John the Baptist, an Essene, Jesus's baptizer. One scroll annotates it, found with others we think are apostolic. Letters, maybe from John or his circle, post-trial."

Joshua leaned over, pulse quickening. "Apostolic? You mean..."

"Yeah," Noa cut in. "They're about preserving John's ministry. The Essenes knew the caves' preservative power hostile with Pharisees and Sadducees; they'd want their guy canonized. After Jesus's execution, it's John and Jesus the twin pillars." She tapped the sheet. "Shepherds for John, doves for Jesus."

Amina's pencil paused. "Twin pillars? That's in the Copper Scroll, 'behind twin pillars that split the waters.' You're saying it's them?"

"Maybe," Joshua said, enthralled by Noa's logic, though Amina's input tugged at him too. "The Essenes could've hidden these to protect their link, John to Jesus."

Noa frowned, sensing his drift toward Amina. "What spot at the Dead Sea hasn't been touched, Amina? Wouldn't it be smarter to chase what we've already mapped, Masa?" Her use of his nickname was sharp, a bid to pull him back. She pointed to her scroll, indexed locations like Ein Feshkha, red team notes underneath: *Twin pillars could be older, David, Elijah, Samuel. Teacher, student, not John, Jesus.*

Amina smiled faintly, tucking her sketchpad away. "Fair point. But I know a cave near Qumran, unmapped, whispered about in Templar lore. Could be your pillars."

Joshua caught Noa's eye, torn between her rigor and Amina's allure. The tension between them, still not romantic, crackled, now with Amina wedging in.

Noa's grip tightened on her scroll. "We stick to our plan," she said, voice steel. "Ein Feshkha first."

Amina glanced at a scribbled note then stood. "Excuse me a moment." She slipped out, her footsteps fading down the hall.

Joshua stared after her, a dumb grin creeping onto his face, half captivated, half oblivious.

Noa's jaw tightened. She wasn't about to let this new girl run unchecked. Muttering, "Be right back," she followed her, rounding the archive door just as Amina's voice drifted through low and clipped. "Yes, they still have their site circled. Yes, sir..."

Noa froze, heart thudding. That was all she needed to hear. She darted back, hissing, "Josh!" But before she could spill it, Amina strode in, all smiles.

"Okay, sorry about that," Amina said, unfazed. "Now, let's look at the map and go over potential locations. I'll show you my spots, and you judge if they're worthwhile." She spread a weathered map across the table, pointing to a mark near Qumran.

Joshua leaned in, nodding like a puppy at her every word.

Noa bit her tongue, her eyes narrowing. She played along, unrolling her scroll beside the map. "Ultimately, we won't know till we're on the ground," she said, elbowing Joshua hard. "My vote's Ein Feshkha first."

He mumbled, rubbing his side, then nodded. "Yeah, Ein Feshkha."

Amina shrugged, rolling up her map. "Suit yourselves. I'll tag along, I know the area well."

Noa folded her scroll, her mind racing. Amina's call wasn't innocent. Templars, or someone worse, were watching. Joshua's crush-blindness was a problem, but she'd handle it.

Joshua hefted his bag, oblivious. "Tomorrow, then. Dead Sea."

"Right." Noa looked at Joshua. "Are you walking me home, or have I been replaced in that too?" She said it with a surprising amount of venom, giving her the thought to check her feelings on the situation. Noa nodded curtly, her gaze flicking to the window.

A shadow flickered past, brief, gone in a blink. Her breath caught as Amina strode out, missing the tense exchange. They packed in silence, the museum's walls feeling tighter.

As they stepped into the hall, Noa grabbed Joshua's arm. "Outside. Now."

The walk back was familiar, Amman's streets alive with dusk, vendors hawking wares, but Noa's urgency cut through.

"Amina's not clean," she said, voice low. "I heard her say, 'They still have their site circled.' She's reporting to someone."

Joshua blinked, the puppy-dog haze fading. "Templars?"

"Maybe. Or worse." Noa pulled the note from her sleeve, handing it over. "This came after she left."

He read it, jaw tightening. "Watched... the shadowy figure?"

"Could be. Point is we're not alone in this." She stuffed her hands in her pockets, glancing sidelong. "You were too busy drooling to notice."

Joshua groaned, a sheepish grin breaking through. "Okay, I was an idiot. She's got that... thing. But I'm with you, Noa. Always."

She smirked, elbowing him lighter this time. "Good, 'cause I'm not losing you to some Templar spy." The teasing flowed, joking about his puppy-dog act. Her bearish glares mostly at Joshua's expense. He took it, laughing, the weight lifting a fraction.

Then he stopped at a flower stand, its jasmine blooms stark against the dusty street. He plucked a few, their scent sharp and sweet, beauty in the barren, like the desert itself. Turning to Noa, he held them out, voice unsteady. "I've felt like this for a while now, probably since you first called me out in class. My kid sister'd be less nervous than I am right now."

Noa's eyes widened, her smirk faltering into something softer. She took the flowers, fingers brushing his, and studied them. Jasmine, a marriage of the wild and the lovely. Joshua, who'd leapt from Christmas in the States to a semester in Jordan, was leaping again. The rest of the walk was silent, not the tense kind from the museum but heavy with unspoken things. His nerves buzzed, but her quiet wasn't rejection, just Noa processing.

At her door, she turned, clutching the jasmine. "Tomorrow's big, Masa. Don't screw it up." A faint smile flickered, then she was gone.

Joshua stood there, heart pounding, the city's hum fading behind him. Whatever watched them, Elias, Templars, or worse, could wait till morning. For now, he'd laid something bare, and Noa hadn't thrown it back. That was enough.

He trudged back to his apartment, head spinning: scrolls, Amina's call, the note, and now this. He couldn't shut it off. Sitting at his desk, he fired up his laptop and typed an email to his sister, Emily, who'd been hounding him to date. *Met someone, well, been with her all along. Noa. Gave her jasmine tonight. I want a sister-in-law too, twerp, but don't jinx it.* He could hear her voice reading it, giggling, "I want a sister, Masa!" She'd said it before then added, "Don't screw it up."

He hit send, half expecting to regret it by morning. Sleep came fast, exhaustion pulling him under, until a crash jolted him awake. Glass? Metal? Outside his window. He stumbled out of bed, knocking over a chair in his haste, heart hammering. By the time he reached the window, the street was empty, just shadows and the faint glow of streetlights. A coincidence, or them?

Breathing hard, he checked his phone, an email from Emily, timestamped minutes ago. *Don't screw it up, Masa,* it read, with a winking emoji. He laughed, nerves fraying, and sank back into bed. Tomorrow was big, Ein Feshkha, Amina, the watchers. He'd laid his heart out tonight, and something else was circling. Sleep wouldn't come easily now.

10

Dust on the Horizon

Joshua barely slept, the crash outside his window pounding in his skull like a drumbeat. He'd tossed until dawn, Emily's email tangling with Noa's faint smile and the jasmine haunting his dreams. The note Noa found, *The shepherd's path is watched*, sat on his desk, edges curling in the dry air. Shadowy man? Templars? The feeling of eyes lingered as first light seeped through Amman's dusty streets.

He showered quickly, grabbed his backpack, notebook, flashlight, and water, and checked the window. Just a stray cat nosing trash. Still, his gut twisted. Yesterday was scrolls and flowers; today was caves and answers or traps. He slung the bag over his shoulder and stepped out, the city stirring slowly around him.

At the museum, Noa leaned against the wall, theory scroll tucked under her arm, wilted jasmine peeking from her jacket pocket, a quiet echo of last night. Her eyes were sharp, scanning the street. "Sleep any?" she asked, voice dry.

"Barely," Joshua said, rubbing his neck. "You?"

"Enough." She straightened as Amina approached, Templar pendant catching the sunrise. "Crash outside my place woke me."

Noa's brow flicked up at Joshua's "Crash?" Her glance at him asking, *The same as you?*, but Amina cut in.

"Probably nothing," she said, too smoothly, hefting her bag. "Ready for Ein Feshkha? Bus leaves in ten."

Joshua nodded, but Noa's silence roared. They boarded a rattling bus, groaning over Jordan's roads, and claimed seats near the back: Joshua by the window, Noa beside him, Amina across the aisle. The desert unrolled south, cliffs and salt flats blurring past.

Joshua traced the twin pillars in his notebook. "John and Jesus," he murmured. "If they're there..."

"Might not be," Noa said, low. "Red team's got David, Elijah..."

"Or a decoy." Amina leaned in. "Templars mapped caves, some were traps. Ein Feshkha's too obvious."

Noa's jaw tightened. "Then why'd you agree?"

Amina's smile thinned. "To see what you find."

Joshua glanced out, heart lurching. A dust plume trailed them, a jeep flickering in the haze. "Guys," he said, voice tight. "Company."

Noa twisted, peering past. "Same as the crash?"

"Maybe." He gripped his bag, the note searing his mind, *watching*. They weren't waiting for Ein Feshkha.

A white truck roared past, just beyond the city, then slowed, forcing the bus to the roadside. Another screeched behind, boxing them in. Shouts erupted, Arabic, maybe Farsi, Joshua couldn't parse them as hooded figures spilled out, crossed swords stark on the truck doors. Not friendly. They yanked passengers off, herding them into the dust. Joshua, Noa, and Amina were singled out, shoved to the scorching pavement.

Heat seared Joshua's knees as they rifled through his bag, tossing notebooks and pens.

A tall figure loomed, snatching his leather satchel. "Where are the maps?" The voice was gravel, accented.

"What maps?" Joshua bluffed, pulse hammering. "We don't know what you're after."

The man froze then backhanded him, splitting his lip. Joshua hit the dirt, tasting blood. The figure turned to another, a shadow too familiar, months of trailing locked in that stride.

"No, I believe it's you finding the treasures," the hooded one said, kneeling to Joshua's eyes. "Answer, or my friend shows you what he's capable of."

A second grabbed Amina's hair, wrenching her head back. She hissed, but the crowd broke, passengers scrambling for the bus's cover. Gunfire cracked, rounds pinging off metal as return fire flashed from nowhere. The interrogators cursed, bolting for their truck and peeling out, dust choking the air.

Joshua scrambled, grabbing his bag as Noa snatched her scroll. They ducked with the others by the bus's front, the firefight stretching seconds into forever. When it stilled, four figures approached, tactical gear gleaming like G.I. Joes.

One pulled his mask down, a face Joshua half knew. "Mossad," he said, voice clipped. "Rabbi Cohen figured you'd need eyes."

Joshua blinked, wiping blood. "You?"

"Been watching you for days," the agent said, nodding to Noa and Amina. "Marked others tailing you too. Last night's guests? We scared them off." His team collected guns, snapped photos, and smashed gear. "Two minutes."

Amina dusted off, cool as ever. "Joining us?"

"No." He tugged his mask back. "Watch your surroundings. Good luck." They vanished into a black SUV, gone as fast as they'd come.

The bus driver waved, shouting another ride was inbound. "Wait if you're continuing!" He boarded with the shaken crowd, engine rumbling as they pulled away. Joshua, Noa, and Amina didn't move, bags clutched, eyes on the horizon where dust still hung.

"What just happened?" Joshua muttered, voice raw, wiping his lip again.

"Don't know what to call it but impressive," Amina said, brushing sand from her hair. She pieced herself together with eerie calm. Shocked, sure, but not rattled like Joshua and Noa. As she repacked, her fingers darted to her phone, a quick text sent with a sidelong glance to mask it.

Noa caught it, eyes narrowing. Templars, ISIS, Mossad, now? The list swelled, each shock jarring her nerves. She nudged Joshua, nodding toward Amina, subtle, urgent.

He missed it, turning to Amina instead. "Letting your folks know you're okay?"

Amina didn't answer, just zipped her bag. "How long till this bus gets here?" she asked, voice flat.

Joshua shrugged, feeling the tension coil. "Few minutes. Twenty, maybe." He sidestepped the brewing clash, rubbing his bruised jaw.

The wait dragged, the desert sun climbing, heat shimmering off the cracked asphalt.

Amina broke the silence. "We should hit my caves. Qumran's less exposed after this."

Noa's stance hardened. "No. Ein Feshkha, our plan, our evidence."

Joshua sighed, caught in the middle. "She's right, Amina. We've got enough to say something's there, physical items, even if it's not the endgame. It backs our thesis." He'd worked this too long to ditch it, every scrap of proof mattered.

Amina shrugged, conceding with a thin smile. "Fine. Ein Feshkha it is."

The replacement bus rolled up, dust-caked and creaking, its driver barking for boarders. Joshua, Noa, and Amina climbed on, settling into the same seats: Joshua by the window, Noa close, Amina across. The engine growled, pulling them south again. Joshua stared out, the horizon clear now, but his pulse didn't settle. A glint flickered in the distance—Metal? Dust?—then vanished. *Watched*, the note whispered. Always watched.

The bus lurched over ruts, its shocks groaning as the desert swallowed them. Joshua pressed his forehead to the glass, the bruise on his jaw throbbing in time with the engine.

Noa shifted beside him, her scroll unrolled across her lap. "You okay?" she murmured, voice low enough Amina wouldn't catch it.

"Lip stings," he said, touching it. "You?"

"Fine." She paused, eyes flicking to Amina, who stared ahead, too still. "She texted someone."

Joshua frowned, glancing over. "When?"

"While you were playing peacemaker." Noa's tone was sharp, but her fingers brushed the jasmine in her pocket, grounding herself. "Templars, maybe. Or worse."

He swallowed, the note's weight sinking deeper. "She didn't flinch back there. Not like us."

"Exactly." Noa rolled her scroll tighter. "We're walking into this blind,

Masa. Keep your eyes open."

The road dipped, salt flats giving way to jagged hills.

Amina turned, catching their hushed exchange. "Problem?" she asked, voice light but edged.

"Nope," Joshua said, too quickly. "Just... processing."

"Smart." She leaned back, pendant glinting. "Ein Feshkha's close, half hour if this heap holds up. What's your play when we get there?"

"Find the pillars," Joshua said, steadier now. "John and Jesus, or whatever's left. Pots, scrolls, something physical. It's there."

Amina nodded, but her eyes lingered too long. "And if it's a bust?"

"Then we've got Qumran," Noa cut in, dry. "Your turn."

The bus rattled on, dust swirling in its wake. Joshua flipped his notebook open, sketching the pillars again, twin shapes, stalagmites maybe, from Noa's notes. The ambush replayed in his head, crossed swords, the shadowy man, "maps" and "treasures." Who knew what? Mossad had their backs, but for how long? He glanced at Noa, her profile set against the sun-bleached window. The jasmine was a wilted lifeline between them, proof they weren't just chasing ghosts.

A sign flickered past: Ein Feshkha, 10 km. The desert grew wilder, cliffs clawing up from the flats, shadows pooling in their creases.

Joshua's stomach knotted. "Almost there," he said, more to himself.

Noa nudged him, pointing out her window. "Look." A faint dust trail snaked parallel, miles off, too far to pin, too close to ignore. "Jeep?"

"Maybe." He squinted, the glint from earlier flashing in his memory. "Or wind."

Amina leaned over, peering past. "Wind doesn't follow roads." Her tone was casual, but her grip on her bag tightened.

The bus slowed, tires crunching gravel as it pulled into a sun-scorched lot. Ein Feshkha, springs and ruins sprawled ahead, the Dead Sea glinting beyond. The driver barked, "End of the line!" Passengers shuffled off, but Joshua, Noa, and Amina lingered, bags in hand.

They stepped into the heat, the air thick with salt and silence. Joshua scanned the cliffs. Caves pocked the rock like eyes, some low, some high.

"Noa's scroll says twin pillars near water," he said, shielding his eyes. "Springs are that way."

"Lead on," Amina said, falling in step.

Noa hung back, watching her then the horizon. The dust trail was gone, but the unease clung.

The trek was short, boots crunching over parched earth, the sun a hammer overhead. A spring trickled ahead, its banks fringed with reeds and cracked stone.

Joshua's pulse surged as they rounded a bend, and a cave mouth yawned, flanked by two stalagmites, jagged and paired like sentinels. "There," he breathed, flashlight out.

Inside, the air cooled, damp with the spring's breath. Shadows danced as Joshua swept the beam: rock walls, a low ceiling, a passage stretching beyond the light. Water lapped at their feet, shallow but insistent. He edged along the side, crawling where the rock pinched tight, Noa and Amina behind him. The tunnel stretched on, a wet, endless throat. Minutes bled into forever.

"Come on," Noa's voice echoed then faded ahead, swallowed by the dark. The slow trickle beside them swelled, a rush of running water humming deeper in.

"Stop," Joshua said, halting so fast Noa bumped his back. He flashed the light over a dark void yawning before them, the sound of a waterfall spilling into it, not a big drop but steady. The beam caught a sandy shore, maybe twenty feet off. "Care for a swim?" He didn't wait, jumping in but hitting rock bottom four feet down, the water knee-deep. "Or wade?"

He slogged toward the shore, Noa and Amina splashing behind. The island was small, ten by ten at its widest, sand gritty underfoot. In its center, a black rock jutted out, Hebrew script scarring its face.

Joshua knelt, tracing the letters, heart pounding. "Noa, read this."

She crouched, squinting. "It's old, Essene, maybe. 'Push where the shadow falls.'" She glanced at the rock's lean. "We need to tip it."

Joshua and Amina joined her, shoving where it tilted. The stone groaned then slid, crashing onto its side with a thud that echoed. A hole gaped beneath, jagged where the rock had split. Joshua dug in, pulling out clay pots—five, six—heavy with age.

"Masa!" Noa exclaimed, voice bright. "You did it! This is amazing." She pried one open. Silver coins spilled out. A few scrolls curled inside others, brittle and brown.

"Treasure," Amina said, crouching beside him, voice dry. "Not yours, though."

Joshua's jaw tightened, pocketing a coin, proof but not the prize. He unrolled a scroll fragment, Aramaic, faded, no stone case in sight. "It's something, hides were here. Thesis holds." Disappointment gnawed at him. The pillars were right, the endgame wrong.

Amina stood, brushing dust off. "Qumran next?"

Before Noa could snap back, a shout pierced the cave, harsh, distant, Arabic again. Joshua froze, beam flicking to the entrance. Shadows shifted beyond the reeds, boots crunching gravel.

Noa grabbed his arm. "Not wind."

"Any chance Mossad's still out there?" Joshua asked, fear leaking through despite his steady tone.

Amina flashed her light deeper in. Water flowed toward the back wall, slowly but surely. "There," she pointed. "It's going somewhere."

"Right," Noa said, nodding. "Water leads out."

They stuffed coins and scrolls into their bags, leaving two empty pots in the hole. The water deepened as they waded toward the wall, ankle- then hip-deep, ducking under a low overhang. The tunnel twisted in and out of water, a mile of cold, slick stone. Joshua's legs ached, the flashlight dimming, but a pinprick of light winked ahead, just around a bend.

They reached a rock wall, daylight seeping through cracks. Joshua pushed, and the slab gave, tumbling them into a ravine. They landed hard, twelve feet from the bottom, wind whistling through the narrow gap. The top loomed close, climbable, maybe. Light cast their shadows long on the far wall, the day's heat seeping back, a stark contrast to the cave's chill.

Echoes of Arabic yells drifted from the tunnel, faint, not closing in, too far to hear outside shouts. Joshua exhaled, shaky, brushing sand from his hands. "They didn't follow. Yet."

Noa scanned the ravine, scroll damp but clutched tightly, her breath fogging in the cooling air. "Or they're waiting."

Amina adjusted her bag, pendant glinting as she steadied herself against the rock. "We're not done running."

A jeep's engine growled, low and distant, outside the ravine, circling somewhere above. Joshua's stomach dropped.

"Wait until nightfall?" Amina suggested, pointing to a narrow ledge along the side. "We crawl over there, climb up when it's dark." The ledge led to a slanted section, rough but scalable with care.

"Right," Noa said, waving a hand across the ravine's expanse. "This place throws sound around, can't tell how far those voices are, or if they're just across the road up there."

"We do know the crawl and wet walk it took to get here," Joshua said, easing down to sit on the sandy floor, back against the cool stone. "They might leave, might stay to see if we pop out, but dark's our best shot to slip away unnoticed."

Noa nodded, sliding down beside him, her damp scroll resting on her knees. "Agreed. Gives us time to dry out, figure out what's next." She glanced at Amina, who crouched a few feet off, scanning the ravine's rim with a calm that prickled Noa's nerves.

Joshua rubbed his bruised jaw, the split lip stinging as he shifted. "Those scrolls, Essene, you think? Not John's, but something."

"Could be," Noa said, unrolling one carefully, the damp parchment crackling. "Dates fit, first century, maybe trade records. Nothing big yet." She tucked it away, eyes flicking to Amina. "What's your take?"

Amina shrugged, her light sweeping the ledge again. "Find's a find. Doesn't change Qumran's odds." Her tone was flat, but her fingers lingered near her bag, too close to her phone, Noa thought.

The wind picked up, whistling sharper through the ravine, tugging at their damp clothes. Joshua pulled his notebook out, sketching the black rock's Hebrew by memory, *Push where the shadow falls.* "It's a start," he muttered. "Proof they hid things, even if it's not the case."

Noa leaned closer, voice low. "Keep her in sight, Masa. That text, she's still playing us."

He nodded, the jeep's growl fading then surging, a restless hunter above. The light dimmed, shadows stretching as the sun dipped. Nightfall wasn't far, hours, maybe less. Watched, always watched, but now they'd wait it out, coiled and ready.

11

Shadows at Dusk

The colors of sunset bled across the sky, crimsons and golds smearing into the desert's deep blue, time ticking closer to nightfall. Joshua had lasted ten minutes slumped against Noa's shoulder, his soft snores rumbling through the ravine's stillness before sleep claimed him. Noa held out longer, thirty minutes more, fighting heavy lids to keep Amina in her sights. The damp scroll rested on her lap, her free hand brushing the wilted jasmine in her pocket, a tether to sanity amid the day's chaos.

Amina outlasted them both, perched near the ledge, eyes tracing its narrow curve upward. She tilted her head, listening. Wind whistled through the ravine, but the yells in Arabic had faded hours ago, the jeep's growl gone silent. Nothing moved toward them now. She nudged Joshua's leg with her boot. "It's almost time."

He jolted awake, blinking at the dimming light. "Right, I'm ready. Noa must've..." He elbowed her, grinning as she stirred.

"That wasn't me snoring," Noa muttered, rubbing her eyes. She shot Amina a look, half glare, half gratitude. "Thanks for keeping watch."

"No problem," Amina said, standing, brushing sand from her knees. "Let's grab our stuff. We can start crawling." She hefted her bag, pendant glinting faintly. "I was thinking we could've left earlier. Joshua's snoring didn't tip them off, we'd have been fine."

"Easier to crawl that ledge with some light," Noa countered, rising stiffly.

She clapped a hand on Amina's shoulder, a knowing squeeze, trust still thin. "Less chance of slipping."

"Got it," Joshua said, scrambling up. "Just let me—" He turned, grabbing his bag, then froze. "Oh, funny guys." The ravine was empty, they'd started without him.

He caught up as they belly-crawled the ledge, sandstone scraping his elbows, the angled climb looming ahead. The air cooled, stars pricking through the twilight as they hauled themselves over the ravine's lip, sand dusting their damp clothes. They froze midbreath. A black SUV idled ten yards off, headlights dark, a figure leaning against its hood.

"Father Nance said you could use a pickup," the man called, voice calm, a faint smirk tugging his lips.

"Oh, come on," Noa groaned, throwing her hands up, sand raining from her sleeves. "How could he possibly know that?"

"I'm starting to think everyone's in on this with him," Joshua said, pointing skyward, half joking, half spooked.

"Nothing so spiritual as that," the man replied, stepping forward, boots crunching gravel. "Though I wouldn't put it past Father Nance." He swung open the SUV's back door. "Rabbi Cohen tipped me where you were headed. Saw the others peel out an hour ago, figured you'd crawl up eventually."

"Who are you?" Joshua asked, bag clutched, his split lip throbbing as he eyed the stranger.

"Oh, right, I'm Paul." The man tipped his head, a Templar cross pendant glinting at his neck, smaller than Amina's but unmistakable. "I'm with a small Templar group. Think you've been made aware of us. If not, well, I'm Paul."

Noa's eyes narrowed, darting to Amina, who didn't flinch, just adjusted her bag with that eerie calm.

Joshua swapped a glance with Noa. Paul's pendant matched Amina's too closely. "Templars, huh?" he said, voice tight. "Friendly ones, I hope?"

"Friendly enough to pull you out of this mess," Paul said, chuckling low. "Get in, night's not done with you yet."

The desert stretched dark around them, the Dead Sea a faint sheen to the east, Jerusalem's hills a shadowed promise west. Noa's hand brushed Joshua's arm, *Let's go*, and they climbed in, Amina sliding in last, her silence loud as Paul fired up the engine. The SUV growled to life, tires biting gravel as they swung northwest.

"Where to?" Joshua asked, leaning forward, the bruise on his jaw pulsing.

"Jerusalem," Paul said, eyes on the road. "Nance wants you at his church, says it's time you saw something. Safer than out here."

Noa frowned. "Safer how? ISIS knows we're moving."

"They've scattered east," Paul said, glancing in the rearview. "For now. Mossad spooked them at Ein Feshkha, Cohen's call. But they're not gone."

"Mossad again?" Joshua muttered, rubbing his neck. "What's Nance got there?"

Paul smirked. "You'll see."

The road climbed, desert flats yielding to rolling hills, the Dead Sea dropping away behind them. Headlights carved through the dark, Route 90 bending toward Jerusalem's glow.

Noa unrolled her damp scroll, squinting at the smudged ink. "Church better have answers. Coins and scrolls aren't cutting it."

Amina stayed quiet, her pendant catching the dashboard light.

Joshua watched her, too still, too calm. "You good with this?" he asked, testing.

"Church, Templars, whatever," she said, shrugging. "Just keep moving."

Forty minutes later, the SUV rolled into Jerusalem's eastern edge, the Mount of Olives looming black against the city's halo. Paul turned onto a narrow road, parking outside a small, teardrop-shaped church, Dominus Flevit, its stone walls aglow under floodlights.

Father Nance stood at the door, cassock fluttering, his gaunt face unreadable. "Thought you'd need sanctuary," he said as they climbed out, voice soft but firm. "Inside, quick."

Joshua hesitated, the air thick with incense and old stone as they stepped in. Pews lined the dim nave, a wooden cross looming above the altar. Nance led them to a side chapel, a cracked stone slab etched with a shepherd's crook catching Joshua's eye. "What's this?" he breathed.

"Clue," Nance said, tapping it. "Templars kept it, Cohen vouched for you to see it."

Amina's fingers twitched, and Noa's narrowed gaze flicking to her. Outside, a jeep's engine purred, close then gone.

Paul stiffened. "Mossad's here," he muttered. "Or them."

Four shapes emerged from the jeep. One held the door, another stepped out, shadows blurring in the dark. Hard to see from inside.

Nance strode to the entrance, voice steady. "Welcome, everyone, come in. The group arrived minutes ago."

Mossad agents marched down the aisle, tactical vests glinting, with Rabbi Cohen trailing behind, his gray coat swaying. Father Nance fell in step with him, whispering low.

Joshua nudged Noa, pointing past them. "Another set of lights."

Headlights swept the courtyard, a second car pulling alongside the Mossad jeep. "That must be our last guest," Nance said, reaching the altar. He waved a hand toward a side door. "Let's move to the conference room. Joshua, bring that relic."

They filed into a cramped room, a large wooden table ringed with chairs.

"Take those seats," Nance said.

Rabbi Cohen settled across from him, Nance in the middle, Dr. Khalil sliding in beside, his tweed jacket rumpled from the drive. Mossad agents and Paul took the rest, Amina hovering near the edge, pendant glinting.

"Okay, I think everyone knows everyone," Nance began, nodding to Dr. Khalil. "Thank you for joining us, not an easy trip."

"Sure," Dr. Khalil said, eyeing the trio. "Be nice to know why I'm here."

"For us too," Noa cut in, voice sharp.

Joshua rested a hand on hers, steadying her edge. "What Noa means, gentlemen, is what are we doing here?"

Nance hesitated, opening a worn book, leather cracked, pages yellowed. "It's hard to explain. We've never known what the Copper Scroll truly leads to. But when ISIS started sniffing around you, we had to act, in case…"

Rabbi Cohen cut in, voice grave. "We feared if you found something, ISIS would intervene, capture you, auction it off at best. Kill you and destroy it at

74

worst."

Dr. Khalil leaned toward Nance, picking up the thread. "The other day in my office, we mapped where I thought you were, your focus. Amina's a Templar, studying the scroll for years. She was sent for two reasons: she's invested, and we'd back her if needed."

"All this for us?" Joshua asked, incredulity creeping in.

"Yes," Cohen said, gesturing to the agents. "Mossad got a directive, watch you, respond if needed."

An agent nodded, face hard. "We've been on you since Amman. Ein Feshkha was close."

"Well, thank you," Joshua said, concern etching his brow. "But this is a lot. Should we even keep going?"

"Yes," Amina said, stepping forward, voice firm. "We can't let ISIS stop us. If they snag something, they'll auction it to fund their fight, or destroy it if it challenges Islam."

Noa's jaw tightened, her hand still under Joshua's. "And you're sure about this, after everything?"

Amina met her stare, unflinching. "I've chased this longer than you. It's worth it."

The room fell quiet, the relic's shepherd crook casting a faint shadow on the table. Outside, tires crunched gravel, another jeep, closer now. Paul's hand slid to his side, and the Mossad agents shifted.

Nance closed his book, voice low. "Decide fast, they're not waiting."

"Of course I'm in," Noa said, first after Amina's stand, her tone fierce despite the strain.

"Well, yes, okay," Joshua said, exhaling. "Would you all like to see what we've found so far?"

The three across the table, Nance, Cohen, and Khalil, exchanged glances, a silent ripple of surprise. Before anyone could answer, Amina pulled a clay jar from her bag, Noa unrolled the damp scrolls, and Joshua spilled the silver coins onto the wood with a clatter.

He flipped open his notebook, pointing to the Hebrew he'd copied from the black rock. "'Push where the shadow falls,'" he read. "So we didn't find what we were after, but we got this. Left a couple more jars behind, couldn't carry them."

The room stilled, the coins glinting under the dim bulb.

Dr. Khalil moved first, lifting the jar, his fingers tracing its weathered curve. "This is amazing. You've proved the Copper Scroll's intent, physical caches, just not your specific target yet."

Father Nance leaned in, studying the coins, their edges worn smooth by time. "And you left more behind?"

"No, padre," Joshua said, shaking his head. "We brought all the contents except two empty pots. No room in our bags. This jar's in the best shape, no markings different from the others."

Rabbi Cohen chuckled softly, a rare crack in his gravitas. "So I take it you'll be keeping this haul, or might you leave some for us to study?"

Noa tucked the scrolls closer, her grip firm. "We'll hold the scrolls, might have info we need. The rest, jar, coins, we're happy to leave here, for now."

Khalil nodded, setting the jar down gently. "Smart. These could tell us plenty, but those scrolls... they're your thread."

Amina crossed her arms, pendant catching the light. "Ein Feshkha's a start. Qumran's next, closer to the source."

Paul shifted, glancing at the door as the gravel crunch grew louder, tires rolling slowly, deliberately. "They're circling," he muttered.

The Mossad agents rose, hands near holsters, eyes on Nance.

Nance stood, book under his arm, voice steady but urgent. "You've got our backing, ours and theirs." He nodded to the agents. "But move soon. They're not here for tea."

Joshua scooped the coins, leaving them with the jar, his pulse hammering. Noa rolled the scrolls tight, jasmine brushing her fingers, a quiet vow. Amina met their eyes, a rare flicker of fire in hers. Outside, a shadow crossed the window, boots on stone, a muffled shout in Arabic. The door rattled.

Paul stood, voice sharp. "Come on, I'll get you to the Templar house for the night. Dr. Khalil, you joining us?"

"Yes," Khalil said, rising, his tweed jacket crinkling as he grabbed his bag. The group moved fast, flanked by Mossad agents, spilling out to the courtyard. Joshua clutched his notebook and Noa the scrolls, while Amina's pendant swung as they piled into Paul's SUV, Khalil abandoning his car for the Mossad jeep ahead. Engines roared, but two trucks screeched in, blocking the exits. No technicals here in Jerusalem's tight streets, but gunmen leaped out, rifles up, shouts in Arabic slicing the night.

The Mossad jeep's back doors flew open, two agents erupting, submachine guns flashing silent sparks, suppressors muffling the chaos. Joshua ducked, glimpsing one side: bullets stitched the trucks, glass shattered, bodies dropped. The other side was a blur, too fast to track. Burnt powder stung his nose, tires smoked, and the crackle of burning metal filled the air as the agents dragged corpses clear, tossing them to the street.

The Mossad jeep rammed through the wreckage, grille smashing a truck aside. Paul's SUV didn't pause, tires squealing as it raced after the other, the two agents leaping onto the step rails, guns still hot. Less than a minute and it was over, debris and blood in their wake, the church's glow fading.

Blocks away, police sirens wailed, blue lights flashing past. Joshua caught an officer's glance—two figures clinging to a speeding SUV, weapons glinting—but they sped on, unhindered, as if it were routine.

Noa gripped his arm, scrolls tight against her chest. "That was too close."

Amina, beside Khalil, stared ahead, voice low. "They'll keep coming."

Paul's knuckles whitened on the wheel, the Templar house minutes away, sanctuary or snare, Joshua couldn't tell. His split lip throbbed, and the shepherd's crook etching burned in his mind.

12

The House of the Cross

The SUV rolled to a stop outside the Templar house, its weathered stone facade blending into the night near Jerusalem's Sacred Heart. The Mossad jeep idled just long enough for the two agents, still clinging to the rails, submachine guns slung low, to vanish inside, Rabbi Cohen's gray coat a fleeting shadow as they sped off. Joshua watched them go, unease prickling his neck. Were they out in the open now, allies in plain sight, or enemies still lurking in the wings, ready to strike from nowhere?

He slid out of the truck, Noa's grip tight on his arm as they stepped onto the cobbled street. Paul and Amina led the way, Dr. Khalil trailing close, his tweed jacket dusted with Jerusalem's grit. The old rock building loomed ahead, indistinguishable from the city's ancient sprawl.

"How does one know which is which?" Joshua muttered, peering at the seamless stone.

"That's your question!?" Noa snapped, her voice a jagged mix of fear and frustration. She clung harder, scrolls pressed against her chest. "We just survived a *Call of Duty* firefight, tailed a jeep with armed Mossad agents, and now we're following two Templars everyone thought were extinct. And *that's* what you ask?"

Joshua grinned despite himself, her fire grounding him. "Fair point."

The large wooden doors groaned open before them, a creak straight out of a knightly saga: heavy, historic, echoing through the dark. No torches flickered inside, instead, low, level LEDs cast a soft glow across the foyer, blending old stone with new light in a classic, reverent vibe. The circular room was small, maybe twenty feet wide, but its ceiling soared thirty feet up, arches worn by time, moss clinging to the cracks. Myrrh and frankincense hung thick in the air, a scent that whispered of altars and secrets.

Templar vestiges lined the walls, tunics from ages past, faded and stained with wear, each beneath a small brass plaque. Joshua squinted at one: *Frater Anselm, 1147.*

"You won't recognize the names," Paul said, catching his gaze. "They mark a Templar story from the Book of Deeds, our ledger of the faithful."

Noa's grip didn't loosen, her eyes darting from the relics to Amina, who stood silent, pendant glinting like a quiet claim.

Joshua tilted his head. "Combat order or church outpost? History's fuzzy on that."

Paul smirked, starting up a narrow stone stairway. "Both. Neither. Depends who's asking." Doors flanked each landing, but he climbed to the fourth before stopping, the group trailing, Joshua with Noa's hold now feeling less like nerves and more like something he'd roll with, Khalil's footsteps soft behind Amina's steady stride.

The door swung open to a hallway lined with rooms like a hotel, the warm scent of Joshua wood trim cutting through the stone's chill. At the end, a large chamber glowed, fire crackling in a hearth on one side, leather chairs and a private club vibe sprawling opposite a massive wooden conference table. The table's surface bore a Templar cross carved down its center, the sword's blade pointing toward the flames, its handle at the head. Chairs sat askew, worn from use.

"Have a seat," Paul said, gesturing. "Just not these three." He tapped the head chairs, where the sword's grip lay. He vanished through a back corner door, leaving them in the firelit hush.

Joshua sank into a chair, Noa beside him, her grip easing, though her scrolls stayed close. Amina sat across from them, her calm unshaken, while Khalil settled near the fire, rubbing his hands against the chill.

"Okay," Joshua said, voice low, "is anyone else feeling in over their heads?"

Noa snorted, a shaky laugh breaking through. "You think? Templars, Mossad, ISIS, this isn't digging pots anymore, Masa."

"Understatement," Khalil muttered, his tweed crinkling as he leaned forward. "That ambush... I've read about chaos, not lived it."

Amina's eyes flicked to the corner door, her pendant catching the firelight. "It's not over. They'll regroup. ISIS doesn't quit."

Joshua rubbed his bruised jaw, the shepherd's crook relic flashing in his mind. "So what's this place? Safehouse or headquarters?"

"Both," Amina said, voice steady. "Templars don't advertise, but we endure, here, Qumran, beyond."

Noa's brow arched. "We?"

Amina didn't blink. "I've been clear, I'm in this as deep as you."

The fire popped, embers dancing up the chimney.

Joshua flipped his notebook open, tracing the Hebrew from Ein Feshkha, *Push where the shadow falls*. "Scrolls might say more," he said, glancing at Noa. "Qumran's next, right?"

"Unless they find us first," she replied, her hand brushing his arm, less cling, more anchor.

Footsteps echoed from the back door. Paul reemerged, a leather-bound tome under his arm, his pendant swaying. "Rest here tonight," he said, setting the book on the table. "Tomorrow, we plan, Qumran's close, but so are they."

Khalil frowned. "Who's 'they' now? ISIS or—"

"Both," Paul cut in, eyes hard. "And maybe more. Sleep light."

A distant rumble rolled through the night, two heavy vehicles, tires grinding stone just beyond the street wall. A moment later, the entry doors thudded shut below, a heavy echo rippling up.

"I don't know how much more suspense I can handle right now," Noa said, her voice strained, frayed from the last hours' toll.

Footsteps pounded down the hall, slow, deliberate, like a century's wait condensed. Two men in fine suits swept in, claiming two of the head chairs with quiet authority. Silence settled, the fire's crackle the only sound breaking it.

Paul returned from the back door, followed by an older man, white beard spilling over a dark robe, eyes sharp beneath a weathered brow. Paul took the empty seat beside Joshua and across from Amina. "Okay, introductions," Paul said, nodding around the room.

Names and ranks spilled out, too quick to catch. The bearded man spoke last, voice deep and steady.

"Am I supposed to remember all that?" Joshua whispered to Noa, leaning close.

"No, just know who we are. Names don't matter here," the man at the table's head replied, catching Joshua's murmur with a faint smile. "I'm Grand Master Elias de Vaux, but call me what you like. Eli's fine."

"Yes, and we," one of the suited men added, gesturing to his companion, "are the deputies, Gideon and Thomas. 'Hey, you' works. We get this is a lot."

Paul stood again. "The team left the coins and vessels with Father Nance at the church. Noa's been clutching those scrolls since I met her."

Noa blinked, a sheepish grin breaking through. "Guess I have. Thank you for saving us, so far at least. I'm remembering manners again, I hadn't said that." She stood, easing the scrolls onto the table, unfurling them carefully. There was room to roll them out along both sides, firelight dancing over brittle edges.

The scrolls bore two thousand years of weight, brown and curled at the margins, ink fading near the ends but holding strong deeper in. The longer one stretched six feet, the other just shy, Hebrew script spilling across the parchment like a whispered code. The group slowed, hands trembling to keep the fragile sheets intact.

"Yes, I expected them to be delicate," Eli said, his voice low. He murmured something to Thomas, who nodded and slipped out the back door. "He's fetching supplies, gloves, weights, to hold these together. We won't ruin them."

Dr. Khalil stood, staring at the scrolls, awe softening his academic edge. "I've seen the Qumran finds, safe behind glass, locked in vaults. To think these sat in a cave since the mid-first century, unfurled now for our eyes to be the first..."

"Yes, it's easy to get lost in the moment and forget the weight," Paul said, running a gentle hand over a small, uninked patch, his touch reverent.

"Thomas will bring those supplies," Eli said, pacing the scrolls' length, taking them in. "Gideon, fetch some sheets. We'll cover the table, reveal sections as we go. Moisture's a risk out here."

"Perfect," Noa said, her strain easing into a tired smile.

"Yes, it wouldn't be practical to haul these everywhere," Amina added, her gaze lost in the script, pendant glinting as she leaned closer.

"This is fascinating," Joshua said, squinting at the start of the longer scroll. "Quick translation, looks like a name, 'Dear Dan' style." He grabbed a candle from the table, tilting its light across the ink.

Eli peered over his shoulder, beard brushing the air. "While we take this in, I invite whoever wishes to stay here as our guests while you work."

"That'd be great," Noa said, exasperation giving way to relief. "After all this action the last few hours, I don't feel safe in my Amman apartment."

"Ditto," Joshua mumbled, too focused on the script to look up.

"Paul, set up rooms in the upper hallway out there," Eli said, pointing to the corridor they'd entered through. "You're welcome as long as you like. Study the scrolls, take field trips. You'll get keys; use this as your headquarters."

Noa nudged Joshua. "Oh, huh?" He snapped back, blinking. "That's more than fantastic. Amman's not safe, but one thing I need is stuff off my walls there."

"Okay," Paul said, poised like he was taking a list. "Anything you need, we'll fetch."

Dr. Khalil rejoined, shaking off his scroll-induced trance. "I'll head back, no danger for me. I can tell the community about this find, might push ISIS off your trail." He looked at Joshua and Noa. "I'm behind you staying here. I'll clear it with faculty, keep your progress safe."

"This sounds like a great plan," Eli said, a satisfied note in his voice. "No one's breaking in here. They know what we're capable of in a scrap."

"Sometime, I'd love the history of this group," Joshua said, lifting his head for the first time. "Last anyone knew, Friday the thirteenth happened."

Eli chuckled, a rumble deep in his chest. "Long story, one we've outlived."

"I get it," Noa said. "Thanks, Paul, I've got a notebook beside my couch, could prove handy. Doc, if you head back, be safe; they know you're tied to us."

"Here are the supplies," Thomas said, returning with a box of gloves and weights. "Gideon's right behind with the sheets."

"Okay," Eli said, gesturing to Amina. "You're aware of your freedom here. We ask Amina to join you. Not just for safety, but she's hunted scroll secrets for years. It'd be good if she's with you two."

Noa rested her hand on Joshua's, a tired smile flickering. "Honestly, I don't think we've a choice, but now I know what she was hiding, I'd appreciate her joining us."

Joshua jolted at her touch. "What?"

"Amina, joining us?"

"Oh, I thought she was already part of the team."

"Ha, okay," Eli said, amused. "With that, I'll leave you to it. I'll check in later." He slipped into the darkness beyond the back door.

"Should we go over where we stand?" Amina asked, moving to an uncovered table section, laying out her notebook.

"Joshua, it's late," Noa said, nudging him again to snap him from the scroll. "Let's cover this up, do a status check, give it a rest."

"Teams were dispatched to your apartments," Paul said, turning for the hallway. "They'll be back with your stuff by morning. I suggest rest."

"I'm tired, but it's one of those nights," Joshua said, pointing to the leather chairs. "Maybe if we talk shop, we'll drift off reading."

The log fire's smoky scent filled the room, soft leather chairs forming a horseshoe around the hearth. Dim lamps flanked each seat, classic books stacked on a round table between the chairs, and a bear rug sprawled before the flames, a scene straight out of a castle designer's playbook. Joshua pulled his worn leather bag closer, fishing out his notebooks, opening to the directions that led them to Ein Feshkha. "Okay, we can review these, our original location was right, but we missed what we'd find."

Amina draped sheets over the scrolls, her pendant glinting as she worked. Noa sank into a chair, kicking off her boots, exhaustion settling in. Paul's footsteps faded down the hall, Gideon and Thomas lingering near the door, hands near their hips.

The three talked for a few hours before the weight of the past day pulled at their eyelids. Gideon and Thomas retreated, leaving the room in peace.

13

The Order's Shadow

A mina woke first, the faint scent of jasmine curling through the slit window, a soft intrusion against the stone's chill. Dawn light bled across the Templar house, glinting off covered scrolls on the conference table. She stretched, her pendant swaying, and noted a pile of belongings, notebooks, wall scraps, and odds and ends from Joshua's and Noa's Amman apartments stacked near the door, delivered overnight as Paul had promised. Her boots echoed faintly as she slipped from the room, descending the narrow stairwell two flights from the fourth-floor hallway.

She paused at a heavy oak door, its surface carved with a faint Templar cross, and knocked, sharp and deliberate.

Silence stretched, then the door creaked open, Paul's face in the gap. "Enter, sister," he said, stepping aside. "We're just going over our side of the plan."

Amina crossed into a large chamber, its walls draped with faded tapestries and studded with brass plaques, names, and stern likenesses of past Templar leaders staring down, eyes etched in time. A long table dominated the center, maps and parchments scattered across it, a single candle flickering beside a leather tome, its flame dancing in the draft. "What of the Mossad?" she asked, voice low, joining Paul near the table. "We've never worked with them before."

Paul adjusted his pendant, glancing toward the door. "They're a wildcard, useful but not ours to command. We're briefing the Grand Master now."

The trio entered then. Eli, his white beard catching the candlelight, was flanked by Gideon and Thomas, their suits crisp despite the hour.

"Yes, I was about to explain our involvement with Mossad," Paul said, turning to them. He waited until Eli settled into the high-backed chair at the table's head before sitting, a gesture of deference. "With our numbers, we can't take ISIS head, on. They're watching, too much at stake to let this slip."

Eli's sharp eyes swept the room, settling on Paul and Amina. "Have we learned anything new these past days? We must ensure anything tied to the Savior stays with the Temple. I've sent word to our brothers and sisters in Europe, reinforcements if it comes to it."

Amina frowned, hand brushing her pendant. "Might be early for that, sir. We've only found one site, Ein Feshkha. The new scrolls aren't translated yet. We should wait, see what they say before pulling in the order."

Eli leaned forward, fingers steepled, robe rustling faintly. "Caution's wise, Amina, but time's short. ISIS won't wait for parchment to speak. They'll burn it first. Mossad's kept them at bay, but only just. Paul?"

Paul nodded, spreading a map across the table, Qumran's jagged cliffs marked in red ink, smudged by use. "They're circling closer, scouts near the Dead Sea, chatter on intercepted lines. The scrolls could point to more caches, maybe the big one. If it's tied to John or the Savior, we can't let it fall."

Gideon shifted, suit crinkling as he leaned back. "Mossad's in for now, Cohen's directive. But they're stretched thin, and we're not their priority. We need a move, Qumran, soon."

Thomas crossed his arms, voice gruff. "And if it's another dud like Ein Feshkha? Coins and trade lists won't save us from a bullet."

"It's not a dud if it leads us," Amina countered, tone firm, eyes flashing. "The shepherd's crook, the Hebrew, 'Push where the shadow falls,' it's a thread. We just need time."

Eli's gaze softened, but his jaw stayed set. "Time's a luxury we don't have. ISIS knows you're here, those trucks last night weren't lost tourists. Paul, wake the others. We translate today, plan tonight. Qumran by dawn if the scrolls give us anything."

Amina's face twisted with frustration, voice rising. "If anything, we should push off, ensure a clear site. Move in the dark, use Mossad to our advantage, sneak around ISIS if needed."

Gideon twisted in his seat, voice calm, cooling the room's heat. "I'm with Amina, sir. That scroll sat dormant for over fifty years, it's only because of the two upstairs and her efforts we've found anything."

Thomas shot Gideon a hard look, gruff edge sharpening. "And what if we find a site, get there, and ISIS is waiting?"

"Then we wait," Amina snapped, words bouncing off the stone walls with quiet fury. "I've a theory: give them time, they'll think we've stalled, can't crack another line. Or we pinpoint a site, feint to a decoy while others hit the real one. Let ISIS chase us until they're dizzy."

Paul raised a hand, tone steady, a voice of calm amid the storm. "We don't need to decide this minute. Gentlemen, let's adjourn, leave you with our thoughts and get to work on the next site. Without that, this is all pointless." He shot Amina a glance, half warning, half support, and started for the door, pausing until she rose to follow.

"Right," Eli said, fingers drumming the table's edge, clearly unnerved. "We'll convene this evening for a meal, see where we stand then." His robe swished as he leaned back, the candle's flame trembling in his shadow.

Amina and Paul stepped out, the heavy oak door gliding shut with a resonant thud. They climbed silently to the fourth-floor hallway, boots scuffing the worn stone steps.

"Just keep working," Paul said, breaking the quiet as he slipped through a side door. "We'll sort logistics when it's time."

Amina continued to the large chamber, the fire now a low smolder, its smoky scent mingling with Joshua wood. The scrolls lay draped under sheets on the Templar table, and Joshua's and Noa's chairs were empty, them still asleep upstairs, she assumed. The room had transformed overnight into the trio's planning cell: Noa's notes stacked against one wall, pinned with string and hurried scrawl; Joshua's sprawled across another, maps and Hebrew tracings tacked up; Amina's journals and sketches completed the chaos, piled near the hearth. A computer hummed softly in the corner, a projector beside it, ready to cast their findings on the bare stone wall. In a short window, the Templars had turned this into a scholar's bunker, efficient, focused, a fortress for the scroll work ahead.

She crossed to the window, jasmine thicker now, carried on a morning breeze. A faint hum undercut it, sharper than last night's drone, insistent. Amina leaned into the opening, her pendant catching the dawn light, and froze as a small, black drone swung low, dipping below the roofline. Its lens glinted, a cold eye in the sky. She noted the time, barely past six, and its arc over the street below. Could be coincidence, could be Mossad keeping tabs, but her gut screamed ISIS, spying for movement, tracking the Temple's pulse. They'd seen the trucks, heard the chatter. This wasn't a watch; it was a hunt.

Amina pulled back, breath sharp, and glanced at the scrolls. The sheets rippled faintly, as if stirred by more than the breeze. Footsteps scuffed the hall, soft, uneven, not Paul's steady tread. She turned, hand brushing her pendant, as the door creaked open, a shadow stretching long across the Templar cross.

Noa and Joshua shuffled in, walking in stride, bleary-eyed but deep in chatter about the day ahead. Amina opened her mouth to warn them about the drone, but they breezed past, locked in their own orbit, stopping at the table's sword-tip end.

"Hey, listen," she said, sharper now, snapping their focus. "We're being spied on. I'll update the team, but we need to plan every move outside this Temple carefully."

Joshua shook his head, frustration creasing his brow, disbelief in his tired eyes.

Noa snorted, kicking a chair leg. "Well, just welcome them to the club, whoever they are."

The trio turned to their haul, spreading notes across the planning cell. Amina's stack stunned them: decades of scroll data, journals thick with cryptic leads that dwarfed their own. Joshua moved fastest, pinning his notes to the wall, arrows and highlighted lines, weaving a web of obscure archaeologist quotes from the past few decades. He rigged the projector next, casting a map on the stone: Ein Feshkha circled with an X, linked to a journal entry detailing every find down to the last coin; Qumran circled, tied to Amina's suggestion, cross-referenced with credited sources. The labor was grueling, each ached to chase sites not sift paper, but the drone's hum demanded scrutiny over haste.

Midmorning, Joshua checked his laptop, an email from his sister glowing onscreen: *Updates?* He typed a slow reply, fingers heavy from lack of sleep: *We're safe with the Templars.* A response waited when he refreshed: *I mean between you and Noa. That's her name, right?* The question bounced in his skull, an itch he couldn't scratch, tugging his focus from the hunt. He glanced at Noa, hunched over her notes, then back at the map, Qumran's red circle blurring as the drone's hum pulsed louder through the window.

Noa finished pinning her notes, glancing at Joshua's screen as he adjusted the map projection. "Yes, that's a great way to start," she said, nodding at the circled sites. "Should we list each location on the side, reasons it's there, why we think it fits X or Y?"

"Great idea, Noa," Amina said, looking up from her journals, pen pausing midscratch. "Since we've all got our own sources, we could red-team each site before locking it in, tear the arguments apart."

"Right, I'll update that," Joshua said, fingers hovering over the keys. "Let you get back to your notes." Both girls shot him a glare before he finished, stares pinning him like a bug. "Or... do whatever you want."

Amina smirked, flicking her eyes from Joshua to Noa. "I don't know if you've ever had a girlfriend, but that'll only dig the hole deeper."

Noa laughed, leaning back, arms crossed. "Oh, Masa, there's a lot to learn." She winked at him, grin sharp. "Why Qumran again? We've got the crook, the shadow clue, sure, it's Essene turf, but ISIS is crawling all over it."

"Masa?" Amina asked, still chuckling.

"Masa's his nickname from a kid," Noa said, jumping in before Joshua could. "Introduced himself in class that first day, stuck ever since. I use it when he's being stupid."

Joshua's mind snagged, Amina's quip echoing his sister's email: *Between you and Noa?* He wondered if Noa caught the same vibe, but the location debate yanked him back. "Amina pitched it," he said, tapping Qumran's red circle. "Two miles from Ein Feshkha, Dead Sea Scrolls hub. The Copper

Scroll's from there, lists caches. 'Push where the shadow falls' fits: caves, cliffs, shadows everywhere. 'Shepherd's crook' could be John's wilderness, right there."

Amina nodded, tracing the circle with her finger. "It's close, defensible, caves for cover. John's link to the Essenes, maybe the Savior too. Safest bet."

Joshua frowned, sliding his finger north along the Jordan River. "But Elijah and Elisha parted the Jordan, 2 Kings 2, near Jericho, east bank. Bethabara's there, John's baptism spot, 'Savior' tie through Jesus. Eight, ten miles north of Qumran. 'Crook' could be Elijah's staff, 'shadow' the river's split when it parted."

"Riskier," Amina said, eyes narrowing as she leaned over the map. "Farther from here, open terrain, no caves, less cover. But ISIS might not expect it, could buy us time if we feint."

Noa smirked, tapping both circles with her pen. "Feint one, hit the other? Your dizzy plan in action?"

"Maybe," Amina said, voice dropping, glance flicking to the window where the drone's hum pulsed sharper, a low growl needling the air. "Qumran's safer, Bethabara's bolder. Scrolls decide, we need them cracked."

Joshua rubbed his bruised jaw, his sister's email still itching. He sighed, staring at the map, Qumran's red circle blurring. He'd been itching to hit the scrolls all morning, but they'd been diligent, too diligent. "Maybe one of us could red-team it with the Templars," he said, "and the others start on the scrolls. We're wasting daylight."

Noa raised an eyebrow, approving. "Smart, Masa. I'll take Templars, Eli's meal is tonight, I can push Qumran and Bethabara at them." She stood, stretching, and grabbed her notes.

Amina nodded, peeling back a sheet from the longer scroll, gloves snapping on. "Good, I'll dig in with you, Joshua. Let's find something fast." She slid the projector aside, unrolling the parchment's first foot, its brittle edges curling under the dim light.

Joshua pulled on gloves, pulse ticking up as he leaned over the Hebrew script. The ink held strong midscroll, and there, a jagged line. "By the crook's curve, where the shadow bends, twelve paces north from the parted stone."

He froze, tracing it again. "Amina, look. 'Crook's curve, ' 'shadow bends', and a stone split. That's not vague."

Amina's eyes widened, pendant glinting as she bent closer. "Twelve paces north, specific. 'Parted stone...' Bethabara's river split? Or Qumran's cliffs?"

Noa paused at the door, turning back. "What's it say next?"

Joshua unrolled another inch, squinting. "Smudged, something about 'dove's rest,' rest of it's faded." He glanced up. "Is there any mention of dove's rest in any notes or maps?"

"Not that I recall," Amina said, turning to her notes, fingers flipping pages.

14

The Fisherman's Thread

The sun dipped below Jerusalem's horizon, casting golden rays across the Holy City. Purples and reds streaked the sky, gilding the hills, Mount Zion, and Gethsemane, alive with tourists chasing divine echoes, rabbis and priests threading the throng. A quiet calm draped the streets, but inside the Templar house, the air crackled with unrest.

Joshua and Amina hunched over the long scroll, its Hebrew script taunting them under the lamplight. "By the crook's curve, where the shadow bends, twelve paces north from the parted stone, dove's rest," they'd scrawled on a notepad hours ago, but the words yielded nothing new. Tempers flared as daylight bled away.

Joshua snapped, "This is going nowhere."

Amina shot back, "Keep looking, Masa."

The drone's hum pulsed through the window, a relentless jab at their stalled progress.

Paul stepped into the planning cell, boots scuffing stone. "Evening meal's ready, if you'd care to join." The trio's heads whipped up, eyes blazing, and he recoiled into the hallway. Too late.

"Of course," Noa bit out, papers slapping the table.

"Perfect," Amina muttered, shoving her journal aside.

"Seriously?" Joshua growled, chair scraping back.

Their frustration erupted in a jagged chorus, chasing Paul down the hall.

"Well, third floor, Amina knows the way," he called, retreating fast to the door's end.

"Fine," Noa said, letting her notes drop with a thud. "Lead on, Amina."

The trio stormed out, irritation trailing like smoke as they descended to the dining hall. A long oak table greeted them, laden family-style with roasted meat, potatoes, and dates, their sweet scent cutting through woodsmoke. More Templars than expected filled the seats, Eli at the head flanked by Gideon and Thomas, Paul by the hearth, leaving three chairs opposite Eli vacant.

They sat, plates clinking as Eli opened his mouth. Paul coughed loudly, breaking his focus, and tapped his watch with a subtle headshake.

Eli nodded. "Right. Paul, threat updates?"

Paul scooped potatoes onto his plate. "That drone Amina spotted, we knocked it down, checked it out. No operator. Watched the street after, hoping it was some kid from the apartments." He paused, fork hovering. "No one came."

Gideon leaned in, voice low. "Supports our theory, eyes on the Temple. We briefed Mossad, told them where we're at. They said Rabbi Cohen wants to see the scrolls."

Joshua perked up, the first spark in hours. "That'd be welcome. His Hebrew's sharper, could crack this mess."

Noa and Amina straightened, nodding. "Absolutely," Noa said. "I'd kill to have him in on this."

Eli's eyes softened, a faint smile tugging his beard. "Progress slow, then?" He glanced at Gideon. "Tell Cohen we'd be happy to host him tomorrow. Room with you three if he stays."

Amina set her fork down, clearing her throat. "What about Father Nance? Coins or jars?"

Paul shrugged, spearing meat. "Checked in, mostly to see how he's holding up post-chaos. He's enjoying it, but nothing big. Jars are standard, no scroll clues."

"Too bad," Joshua muttered, staring at his plate. The Rabbi's promise dimmed under Nance's dead end.

Amina pressed on. "We've got a site list, Qumran, Bethabara. Best play's a head fake to one, hit the other. Scrolls hint north, dove's rest, parted stone."

Gabriel opened his mouth, but Thomas gruffly cut in, "We thought the same. Did one better, Gideon and I unblocked the Sacred Heart tunnels today. Sneak the team out, no eyes."

Noa's eyebrow arched, a smirk tugging her lip. "Tunnels? Now we're talking."

The meal wound down, plates clattering as Templars dispersed. The trio retreated to the planning cell, but Joshua veered from the table, grabbing a notebook and dropping into a lounge chair by the hearth.

Noa paused, blinking. "You know what, that's not a bad idea." She snatched her notebook and sank opposite him.

Amina lingered, eyeing them, then gathered the map, her notes, and a site list scribbled with pros and cons. "Not a bad idea," she echoed, settling on the floor between them. She spread the map across the coffee table. "Let's go over the sites, two main ones we've got?"

"Right, Bethabara and Qumran," Joshua said, leaning forward. "I favor Bethabara. The twin pillars splitting the water, Elijah and Elisha at the Jordan crossing, east of Jericho. The mantle passed from one to the other, poetic-like." His take wove the scroll's crook and shadow into prophetic succession, sidestepping the scholar's dry line.

Noa nodded, tapping her pencil. "I agree. The new scroll's stalled, 'By the crook's curve, where the shadow bends, twelve paces north from the parted stone, dove's rest,' no fresh secrets. Instead of banging our heads, refocus on what we had. Amina, you were Qumran from the start, which now?"

Amina exhaled, tracing the map's edges. "Pre-new scrolls, I'd have said Qumran, closest to the Essenes, Copper Scroll's home." She circled Qumran's cave system, crossing out known duds. "These were my picks, caves, cliffs, shadows aplenty. But with dove's rest and Ein Feshkha outside Qumran, the big find's elsewhere."

Joshua pointed to her circles. "So those go yellow, questionable at best?"

"Exactly," Amina said, nodding.

"That bumps anything outside Qumran higher," Joshua said, voice quickening. "Crook's curve as Elijah's staff, parted stone where the Jordan split, Bethabara."

Noa leaned over the table. "Not bad. We don't ditch Qumran, just lower its priority after Ein Feshkha. Bethabara's got legs, dove's rest as John's baptism, tying Elijah to Jesus."

Amina slid her finger to Bethabara, east of Jericho. "This is the modern spot." She edged down half an inch, half a mile on the ground. "Here's where the river ran in Elijah's day, shifted over centuries. That's where the parted stone might sit, where Elisha struck after the mantle passed."

Noa's eyes lit up. "And why no one's found it, wrong riverbank all these years."

Joshua flipped his notebook, rereading the scroll. "'Twelve paces north from the parted stone,' a boulder split by the Jordan, or Elisha's strike. Dove's rest, John baptizing Jesus, the Spirit descending. Bethabara, not Qumran." He glanced at Amina. "Feint Qumran via tunnels, hit Bethabara quietly?"

Amina's pendant glinted as she nodded. "Tunnels give cover, ISIS expects Qumran after the drone. We sneak north, check that old riverbed."

Noa smirked, tapping the map. "Let's get the team up here, get this moving."

Amina started down the hall.

Noa turned. "Masa, I'm pumped. After Ein Feshkha, we'll find something. Your guess?"

"Wow," Joshua grinned, "the possibilities are wild, could shake things up either way."

They buzzed over ramifications, voices low by the hearth.

* * *

Downstairs, Templars quibbled, Eli in his chair, Paul, Gideon, and Thomas on their feet, motives veiled from Joshua and Noa. Templars once stashed biblical treasures in their heyday, but since the order's 14th-century fall, they've lacked church backing to hoard relics. The itch to reclaim relevance simmered, a present drive the trio didn't grasp. Their chatter hushed as footsteps neared.

"Yes, Amina, just hashing the plan," Eli said, eyes sharp as she entered, the others rising.

"Hmm," Amina said, voice cutting, "the plan to secure the treasure for the world or to snag it yourselves, claw back Templar glory?" She'd suspected their desire but hadn't voiced it till now, with the prize in reach.

Paul stepped forward, calm. "Amina, you've known since we tasked you with the Copper Scroll, we want our name on what it hides."

Eli's fingers drummed the armrest, gaze steady. "It's both, preserve and claim. The world sees it, but through us. Tunnels are ready, Qumran feint, Bethabara hit?"

"I don't like it," Amina said, voice sharp. "We would not have found anything if it wasn't for those two upstairs."

Paul raised his hands. "Listen, nothing has been decided, we don't have anything in hand. Let's get the items and decide from there." He turned to the group. "Gideon and Thomas will leave the temple in two vehicles. Take them on a joyride while driving to the site, the rest of us will go to the real location."

"Right," Amina said, turning and walking back to the others.

Paul followed, catching them at the hearth. "Let's get moving, this will be easier at night." He led them down to the tunnel, exiting through the side of the Sacred Heart temple. "Dig team ready," he whispered on the radio. He cracked the door, watching for movement. Two SUVs sped by, Gideon and Thomas on the feint. After a few moments, a truck rolled past, no sign of the drone hovering. The group walked to a nearby garage where an SUV waited. Paul drove out, doing his best to not draw attention.

Joshua sat shotgun, Noa behind, her knee brushing his seat, a jolt he hid. Amina stared out, pendant catching the streetlight. Paul wove through Jerusalem's backstreets, headlights off where he could, avoiding eyes. The drone's absence gnawed at Joshua, his gut twisting.

"Looks like the ruse worked," Paul said, checking the mirrors constantly. "We should be there in thirty to forty-five minutes."

Amina scribbled a note, "Templar double-cross," then palmed it to Noa, keeping it from Paul's glance.

Noa grunted, unable to mask her reaction.

"Everything good back there?" Paul glanced to the back seat.

"Of course," Noa said, clearing her throat, "just ready to get going."

Joshua's ears perked up, they hadn't been together long, but long enough to catch her tones. He turned his head then thought better than to ask.

Paul pulled to a stop next to the current banks of the Jordan. "Okay, where to?"

Joshua began directing him to the site they circled back in the planning room. It was a little off-roading, but the moonlight made it possible to move without headlights. Once they arrived, the team split up.

"I'll go with Amina down this way, you two that way. Check in every thirty minutes," Noa said.

She wanted to find out what Amina really meant, and the thirty-minute limit would keep Amina from ditching her.

"I can't see the boys, so what's up?" Noa asked after a few minutes of walking.

Amina spelled out the issue, her fear of the Templars confiscating any finds. "They might try to detain us to secure it for themselves."

"Perfect," Noa said, a little too loud. "Let me think, we need to make sure they can't hold us."

Behind the two girls, Joshua walked the other way through some brush with Paul. "So, Paul, what are your thoughts?" he asked, using the moonlight to spot any hint of stone sticking out of the ground, a trace of the old banks visible.

"This could get very interesting," Paul said, flashing his light here and there.

Joshua wasn't sure why he asked, maybe a hangover from Noa's tone in the car, or an intuition something wasn't right. His stomach had been in knots since they left the temple.

"Wait," Amina said suddenly. "Check here, I just saw a blank spot on the ground. A break in the ground and a split down the middle." Noa wheeled around, flashed her light where Amina stood. Sure enough, a large stone cleaved in the middle, the top just peeking out over centuries of ground buildup.

Joshua heard it too, and by the time he got to the spot, Noa and Amina were outlining the edges. "Nice find. This could be the spot. Now what do you think, down the middle or dig on the outside?"

Paul was right behind Joshua. "Looks like just enough space between for a shovelhead. I'll get the jeep, it will be easier than dragging four shovels down here."

While Paul was gone, Amina brought Joshua up to speed.

"Great, I knew something was off. What's your idea?"

"Well," Amina said, slowing them down, "we already have support coming tomorrow with the rabbi and Mossad. Let's plan to leave with them."

Noa and Joshua nodded in agreement as the jeep's headlights lit the spot up.

Joshua, Noa, Amina, and Paul dug around the split boulder, ten paces north, along the edges, between the halves. Dirt piled under moonlight, shovels scraping. Paul's flashlight swept the dark, jittery. Gideon and Thomas had sped off in two SUVs toward Qumran, selling the feint, but no word came. Amina's shovel bit between the stone's halves, Joshua pacing north, Noa close, her elbow brushing his once, a spark he buried.

Paul's phone rang, slicing the quiet. "I understand," he said, clipped, hanging up. "Decoy team lost containment. ISIS is back in the wilderness," he told them, voice flat.

The trio swapped a glance, unseen by Paul, loaded with Amina's warning. Headlights flickered on the highway, not at them, but the first in a while.

Noa squinted. "If that's them, could someone tell me how they found us," she quipped, her tone sharp, eyes catching Joshua's.

Minutes later, the headlights bounced straight toward them. "Kill the lights," Paul snapped.

Joshua's shovel thudded, metal hitting wood. Noa and Amina whipped their heads his way. Tap, tap, the sound rang again. Paul watched the lights, but the trio scrambled, dirt flying, uncovering a crate wedged in the hole.

A truck stopped two hundred meters out. A deafening boom hit, ears ringing, sound gone, dirt slamming them. They clawed at reality, hauling the crate free as small splashes of earth pelted around them. The jeep sat meters away, a mile in their daze. Adrenaline surged, glass shattering nearby, the crate clutched between Amina and Noa.

Paul kept his head, battle-hardened but rattled by the attack's ferocity. They piled in, Joshua shotgun, Noa and Amina cradling the find. The jeep swerved, bouncing wildly, a ledge dropping the seat from under them. Desert dirt swirled behind the vehicle, cloaking them as attackers faded in the cloud. Tires screeched onto pavement, sliding toward Jerusalem.

"Did you lose them?" Joshua screamed, ears ringing, voice lost to himself.

Paul drove hard, either not hearing or ignoring, eyes fixed ahead.

15

The Mantle

The jeep's tires screeched on pavement, sliding toward Jerusalem, dust swirling behind. Paul gripped the wheel, silent. Joshua's ears rang from the Bethabara blast. Noa and Amina clutched the crate between them in the back, its wooden edges digging into their legs. Joshua's stomach churned, his "Did you lose them?" scream still echoing in his head, unanswered. Two sets of headlights flared ahead, cutting the night.

"Hold on," Paul barked, swerving, but flashes sparked off the sides, gunfire popping.

The windshield exploded, glass shards slashing Joshua's cheek, stinging hot. Noa yelped behind him, a sound swallowed by a boom under Paul's feet. The jeep lurched, spinning off the road, metal groaning as it rolled onto its side. Joshua's head slammed into the dashboard, world tilting black, the last glimpse of Noa's arm flung wide, crate tumbling.

* * *

He blinked awake, bouncing hard in a truck bed, head throbbing, blood crusting his face. Two hooded men loomed over him, screaming in Arabic, AKs spitting fire off the tailgate. The moon and stars glared down, cold and bright, the truck sliding and jolting down a rough road. Joshua's wrists burned, tied tightly, his body aching like it'd been thrown a mile. The crate sat wedged beside him, dirt-streaked, lid intact, a mute prize from Bethabara. How long had he been out? Minutes? Hours? No sign of Noa, Amina, or Paul, just the engine's roar and the men's shouts.

He shifted, pain spiking his ribs, piecing it together. The ambush hit fast, headlights, bullets, that blast. ISIS, they'd tracked the jeep, Gideon's feint useless. The crate pressed his leg, a taunt. "Under the crook's shadow, the fisherman's truth rests," he'd read. Andrew's hint was now theirs. His gut twisted, Noa's "If that's them, how'd they find us?" sharp in his mind, her elbow brush a ghost on his arm. Where was she?

The truck swerved, slamming him against the crate, one captor glaring down, eyes hard above the hood. Joshua stayed still, breath shallow, ears straining past the ringing. The gunfire faded, gravel crunched, and wind whipped his face. Jordan's desert swallowed them whole.

A jolt later, a mind-numbing slam cracked his head. Darkness took him again. He came to, bound to a chair, wrists chafing from rope, a cold room glowing orange under a bare bulb swinging overhead. A wall loomed ahead, plastered with a map, notes in Arabic, pins marking spots he couldn't read. The crate sat in front of him, no longer a rough box but a small chest, its dirt sprayed off, wood polished dark, mocking him as it was untouched. It was a scene ripped from a terrorist video, stark and chilling. No clue where he was, how long he'd been out, or if Noa and Amina were alive. Just him, the chest, and a bad feeling sinking deep.

A slap across his face snapped his attention sharp. "Tell us how to open this," a voice behind a mask barked in Arabic, pointing at the chest.

Joshua blinked, cheek stinging, blood trickling from his lip. "What have you tried?" he asked, voice steady, genuinely curious.

Another slap answered, harder, rocking his head back. "You will answer my questions, you will direct us to the treasures," the mask demanded, switching to broken English.

The questioning rolled on, slaps punctuating his silence then his willingness to talk. Joshua offered guesses, pry the lid, check for a latch, but each earned a hit, his face swelling, left eye puffing shut. When a camera rolled out, his stomach dropped. YouTube bait. One set it up, tripod steady, while the other shoved a script into his hands, paper creased and smudged. The red light blinked on.

"Read," a voice boomed from behind.

Joshua scanned the page, words blurring through pain, an apology to the Muslim community for Western pillaging, a rant against the "evil Israeli beast." He swallowed, jaw tight, and read haltingly, voice flat, buying time. The chest sat there, a silent witness, its dark wood catching the bulb's glow.

* * *

The rest of the team was waking up. The world of explosions had left, and they were in the back of a dark SUV. Two men up front spoke English with Israeli accents.

"I think they're waking up," Avi said from the driver's seat.

Tal turned from the passenger side with a small flashlight waving across their faces. "Are you okay," he asked. "Can you hear me?"

Amina squinted, trying to block the light, nodding faintly. Noa groaned beside her, head throbbing. Paul slumped, stirring slow. Every bump, noise, or light kicked the pain alive again.

Amina spoke first. "What happened?" she croaked, then winced as Tal answered.

"Definitely concussions," Tal said, eyeing them. "But otherwise they look fine. We found you in the heap you call a jeep. It looked like you hit a bump or two."

"Great, a bad sense of humor," Noa groaned, her voice rough. Joshua's absence was a dull ache she couldn't shake.

"That is not any way to thank your saviors," Tal replied, smirking. "We didn't see the other one with you, Joshua, I think his name was."

Avi nodded agreement, hands steady on the wheel.

"The crate?" Amina growled, sitting up, pain spiking.

"No crate either, it must be with Joshua, wherever he ended up," Tal said. "I'm Tal, this is Avi"—tapping him on the shoulder—"and we are part of the team that saved you, yesterday it feels like. You could have given us a heads up you were leaving."

Paul groaned, hauling himself up, bristling at the savior bit. "We were in a hurry, and we thought we had tricked them by leaving from the temple lot while the others went out the front."

"Well, tricked us," Avi said, voice dry.

"Hey, don't give that information away. Classified," Tal jumped in, half grinning. "Anyway, the other two are trying to track where your friend could have ended up."

Noa's head began to clear. "We have to find him. Where are we?"

"No, we in that," Tal responded. "Don't worry, the other two are pretty good. Meanwhile we are on the way back to Jerusalem, meeting up at the Templar's."

"Great, now we are safe, eh," Noa said, elbowing Paul in the side.

"Hey, why are you elbowing me?" Paul snapped.

Noa elbowed him again. "I'll be hitting once I regain the use of my arms. I know you Templars were planning on betraying us."

"What did you tell her, Amina?" Paul squealed.

"Nothing, but thankfully, you just did," Amina responded. "I didn't tell her that you all were planning on taking all the pieces and controlling access. Trying to regain the relativism of the Templars."

The team continued on toward Jerusalem.

* * *

Gideon and Thomas camped outside a stale concrete building on the edge of the Syrian border. "We found the location," Gideon said into a radio.

Thomas peered through binoculars. "I've counted six," he said.

"We need to move soon, we will lose the darkness," Gideon added.

"Negative," Thomas said into the radio. "Strike in five, four, three," then the boom hit. "I take it back, I count two," he said, laughing with Gideon as they moved up.

An explosion rocked outside the building near the trucks, shaking the room. Joshua flinched, ears ringing anew, the script dropping to the floor. The two captors screamed in Arabic, bolting out the back, away from the blast.

"There's the other two." Gideon pointed behind the building, two figures disappearing into the fading night. "Hit it," he said, stacked on the door.

Thomas triggered a small explosion, cracking it open. They entered, clearing the room with top-tier precision.

Gideon lifted his mask, kneeling by Joshua. "Joshua?" He looked into his eyes. "Joshua, you okay?"

Joshua groaned. "Yes, I think I'm fine."

"Okay, let's get you out of here," Gideon said, cutting the ropes and lifting him from the chair into the darkness outside.

Thomas grabbed the chest as a helicopter dropped in just beyond the burning trucks. Waiting by the chopper, Thomas steadied Joshua, wind whipping their faces. "Okay, the others were picked up by the Mossad guys. We are linking up back at the temple," he said.

Joshua's eyes grew heavy, hard to keep open with the wind and pain. Other than the aircraft's roar, the ride was quiet, vibrations through the platform tugging at his lids until exhaustion won. He drifted, head lolling, the chest a dark blur beside Thomas.

Gideon held him up as they landed, walking into the temple from the top down to the planning room, a mercy over stairs. Sunrise painted Jerusalem in purples and reds again, a blur that felt like five minutes since the crash. Joshua stumbled in first, falling into a chair, sore and bruised, face a map of cuts and swelling.

Outside, two black SUVs pulled up, voices climbing the stairs and spilling down the hall. The room buzzed alive.

Rabbi Cohen strode in, voice sharp. "We need that chest opened, now. See what they died for."

Father Nance followed, hands clasped, murmuring, "A gospel, perhaps, Andrew's voice."

Tal and Avi flanked Amina and Paul, who slumped into chairs while Eli paced, his Templar calm fraying, snapping.

"It's ours to protect, not parade." Amina stood, glaring at Eli. "You'd lock it away, like you planned all along."

Joshua mumbled, voice thick through swollen lips, "They had maps, notes, copies from our apartment, more than keeping up."

Noa knelt beside him, pressing cold packs to his face, her touch steady, eyes tightening at his words. She froze, whispering, "Our wall, Joshua?"

He nodded faintly, pain flaring, the memory of his Amman chaos, scroll translations, Jericho lines, shepherd's crook, mirrored in that orange-lit room.

Rabbi Cohen spun, eyes narrowing. "They stole your work? How?"

Avi stepped forward, voice low. "A leak, someone close, we've got ears in Amman checking now."

Tal nodded, adding, "Explains the ambush. They knew Bethabara, pinned it exactly."

Father Nance clutched his cross, muttering, "A betrayal, then, but whose?"

Eli's pacing stopped, fists clenching. "Not us, we lost men too. Gideon and Thomas barely made it out."

Amina snorted, crossing her arms. "Convenient, your men save the day, chest in your hands, just like you wanted."

Paul shifted, wincing, voice hoarse. "Enough. We're here, it's done. Open it and decide."

The chest sat on the table, dark wood gleaming, drawing every eye.

Rabbi Cohen pressed forward, insistent. "If it's a scroll, it's scripture, belongs to the world."

Eli countered, sharp, "It's Templar legacy. We guard it, not you."

Father Nance interjected, soft but firm. "If Andrew wrote it, it's Christian truth, not yours to hoard."

Amina glared at Paul, voice cutting. "You'd have sold us out for this, admit it."

Paul groaned, rubbing his head. "We'd have shared it, after securing it. Stop twisting things."

Tal leaned in, dry. "Secure it how, with ISIS breathing down our necks?"

Avi nodded, grim. "They had your notes, your maps, someone fed them."

Joshua looked at Noa, nodded slowly. "I'll be okay. I would love to know what's in that chest."

Gideon fetched a pry bar, handing it to Thomas, who popped the lid with a crack.

Noa peered in, voice lifting. "Okay, Joshua, we have two more scrolls, more coins, and a somewhat tattered cloak. Oh, and the cloak seems to have another small scroll inside it."

The others gathered, laying out the items with care: two parchment scrolls, brittle but intact; a handful of silver coins, glinting; a cloak frayed at the edges with a tiny scroll tucked in its folds.

Noa glanced back, eyes bright. "Dr. Khalil is on his way. He will be over the moon with this latest find."

Rabbi Cohen exhaled, reverent. "Three scrolls could be Essene, or something more."

Father Nance smiled faintly. "The cloak, a mystery that maybe the scroll within will solve."

"I think the remainder of the team might need some rest and healing time. Maybe Father Nance and I can work through some translation," Rabbi Cohen suggested, a welcome thought to the battered group.

"Just leave me here. It will hurt too much to move anywhere else," Joshua groaned, sinking deeper into the chair.

"I expect that's a play to get some more, um, caring attention," Tal replied, sparking laughter through the room except from Joshua and Noa. "You sure, my man? I can help you up there."

"Seriously, just let me wallow in pain," Joshua said, more pathetic than before.

"Okay, now I am on to you, Masa," Noa smirked, her eyes glinting. "His nickname he earned as a kid. He only earns it now in mocking."

A sense of brevity filled the room for a few minutes before Paul, Amina, and Noa retired to their rooms. Joshua lay snoozing on a leather couch nearby.

An hour or so later, Dr. Khalil knocked, stepping in with a grin. The others, Tal, Avi, Gideon, Thomas, and Eli, were dismissed, leaving Rabbi Cohen, Father Nance, and Dr. Khalil to talk quietly, Joshua dozing in the corner.

The next several hours unspooled, translating the scrolls, numbering them one through five with the earlier finds. They pinned translations to the rock wall, Rabbi Cohen reading aloud, slowed by faded ink. He guessed at gaps, the older trio marking them as he called out. The first two scrolls from Qumran were lists, judgments by a local priest, notable but tame.

One of the new larger scrolls was a gem, correspondence between synagogues, rare for the cutoff Essenes, hinting at 2 Kings events. The tiny scroll in the cloak dropped a bombshell, naming its owner. Twin pillars tied the split rock at Bethabara to Elijah and Elisha, meaning the cloak was the mantle passed between them.

Rabbi Cohen paused, voice low. "This is Elijah's, handed to Elisha, scripture alive."

Father Nance nodded, awed. "A relic of prophets."

Dr. Khalil scribbled fast, eyes wide. "The Copper Scroll led us here, unbelievable."

16

The Mantle's Echo

T he day bled into dusk, Jerusalem's golden light fading as the scents of dust and jasmine seeped through a crack in the Templar house wall. The planning room buzzed with the team's presence, some perched on chairs, others leaning against the stone, all eyes fixed on the cloak unearthed the night before. It lay draped across the conference table, its coarse weave and frayed edges glowing faintly under the lamplight, a relic too real to fathom. The mystery of it, the sheer weight of its story, could move any soul to tears, and the air thrummed with unspoken reverence.

Rabbi Cohen broke the silence, his voice steady but brimming with excitement. "Much of the cloak's significance flows from Melachim, 1 and 2 Kings in your Christian Bibles. It begins in 1 Kings 19:19, when Elijah casts it over Elisha, marking him as his successor." He couldn't help himself; this was no mere explanation, it was a d'var Torah, a teaching from the Torah's broad embrace, and he dove in like a man unrolling a scroll. "This mantle isn't just fabric; it's a vessel of divine favor."

Father Nance leaned forward, eyes glinting, not about to let the rabbi hold the floor alone. "And tying it to what we've found, consider Elijah raising the widow's son in 1 Kings 17:17, 24, the first pillar of his miracles."

It was almost a faith-off, a friendly duel of sacred knowledge, and the team settled back, rapt. Normally, this might've been a dry lecture, but tonight, with the cloak tangible before them, it felt electric.

Rabbi Cohen grinned, undeterred. "Then there's 1 Kings 18:36, 38, Elijah calls down fire from heaven, consuming a water-soaked altar, proving God's supremacy over Baal. The mantle marks him as God's mouthpiece, though the miracle rides on his prayer." He gestured to the cloak, its threads seeming to hum with the echo of that fire.

Father Nance jumped in, voice rising, "And finally, Elijah strikes the Jordan in 2 Kings 2:8, splitting the waters for him and Elisha to cross, just before his ascent in the whirlwind. A messianic nod, you see, to Jesus's transfiguration, where Elijah appears again." He leaned back, arms crossed, as if daring the rabbi to top that.

Cohen chuckled, a warm rumble. "Well, Elisha takes it up in 2 Kings 2:13, 14, parting the Jordan again, and throughout Melachim Bet, his miracles outnumber and outscale Elijah's, fulfilling his request for a double portion of Elijah's spirit in 2 Kings 2:9. This cloak"—he nodded at it—"is a wearable testament to that succession, a relic of God's power."

Father Nance's grin widened, ready to land his trump card. "Yes, of course. But then there's Malachi 4:5, 6, 'See, I will send the prophet Elijah to you before that great and dreadful day of the Lord comes. He will turn the hearts of the parents to their children, and the hearts of the children to their parents; or else I will come and strike the land with total destruction.' A promise of Elijah's return."

Rabbi Cohen matched the grin, leaning in. "You mean Malachi 3:23, 24, from the Tanakh, same promise, just our numbering. Elijah's spirit endures, a herald of redemption."

The room erupted in laughter, the tension of their scholarly sparring dissolving into shared joy. The cloak sat there, unassuming yet profound, a bridge from Melachim to Malachi, from Elijah to Elisha, and with the scrolls, perhaps to John. The thought of such an item before them, the possibilities of what still lay hidden, tugged at their imaginations like a thread from a tale too wild to believe. Yet here it was, real as the stone beneath their feet.

The buzz simmered down after a few moments, the team's exhilaration tempered by a quiet hunger for what lay next.

Joshua broke the spell, his voice rough from the night's ordeal. "I hate to cut this off, but can we see what the scrolls translate to?"

Dr. Khalil stood, hands raised with a wry smile. "So, to prevent any spiritual wars breaking out here, I'll take the scrolls."

The room buzzed with laughter again, easing the shift.

"The first two from Qumran were local judgments by a high priest, names and rulings here." Dr. Khalil pointed to the translations pinned on the left wall, a row of parchment replicas stretching rightward. "The large one and the small one rolled into the cloak named this find, Elijah's mantle, Elisha's legacy." He flipped on the projector, casting the team's notes onto the stone. "It's the last one we need help with. We've got the words, but they're cryptic, like the Copper Scroll itself."

The screen glowed with a translation: a letter from a Qumran scribe to a synagogue near Bethabara, dated around 6 BCE, mentioning a priest named Zechariah serving at the temple.

Amina's eyes widened, her voice cutting through. "If that's who I think it is, Zechariah, father of John the Baptist, we need to dig deeper. There could be more sites, more clues." She leaned forward, urgency sparking. "We can't stop now."

Eli shifted in his chair, his tone measured but firm. "I was discussing this with Paul earlier. We think the focus should shift, secure these items in a vault in Europe, keep them out of terrorist hands."

Amina crossed her arms, her glare screaming, *Of course you did.*

Joshua hauled himself up, wincing from last night's bruises, his voice raw but resolute. "These items aren't going anywhere. If they leave this temple, they stay in Jerusalem, secured by a religious order here. They belong to the faithful, not some former order chasing fame and relevance."

Noa stepped closer to him, her presence steady. "I'm with him. And I'd bet the rest of us, those without Templar crosses around our necks, agree."

The room stilled, the air thick with defiance. The cloak lay between them, a silent witness, its legacy now a battleground of trust and purpose.

Thomas broke in, voice tight. "We need to do something with them. Word just came, the two ISIS fighters who got away regrouped with a larger force. They're moving this way."

Rabbi Cohen frowned, incredulous. "They wouldn't risk tangling with the IDF. What are they after? What if we get these to the Israel Museum? They'd be safe there, right at home with the Dead Sea Scrolls."

Eli leaned back, exchanging a nod with Thomas and Gideon, who shifted to block the exit. "Well, after all our involvement, we deserve to take these into our custody."

Father Nance raised a hand, searching for calm. "Look, what if we ensure the Templars are part of the official findings? I'll speak to the cardinal, push a recommendation to the pope to recognize your order again. That's no small thing."

Paul turned to Eli, his tone softening, almost pleading. "That's more than we expected, sir. Let the items go with Dr. Khalil, escorted by Gideon and Thomas. We can make it official later, can't we?"

Eli's jaw tightened then relaxed. "I can accept that, for now. But we hold the crate and coins. Insurance for our troubles."

"Fine," Amina snapped, her voice clipped.

The tension eased, but the Templars had tipped their hand. The rest of the team shared a silent glance. ISIS spies, Templar greed, they'd need a new security plan, a way out of this orbit.

They shared a meal, the unspoken rift filling the space between bites. Afterward, Noa, Joshua, and Amina slipped back to the planning room as Dr. Khalil, Gideon, and Thomas moved the scrolls and cloak to the museum. The trio had the translations. No need to risk keeping the originals here.

Alone, they worked like a well-oiled machine, pinning notes to the wall. They theorized: Could this Zechariah, from the scroll, be the priest of Luke 1:8, 23, struck mute after his vision, father to John the Baptist? The letter hinted at "a voice to come" who'd "prepare the way in the wilderness," John's calling (Luke 3:4). Scholars never proved John was an Essene, but his desert life fueled the idea. This text might be the link. With leaps of educated guesswork, they tackled the scroll's cryptic end: "The dove rests where the fisherman mends his net."

Joshua rubbed his bruised jaw, the ache dulling as his mind sharpened. "That's John the Baptist, the dove's the Spirit at Jesus's baptism in the Jordan,

Luke 3:22. The fisherman could be Andrew, John's disciple before he followed Jesus. Nets hint at Peter's banks, but Bethabara's the fit."

Noa nodded, her finger tracing the Jordan's curve on the map. "The shepherd's crook links Elijah's mantle to John, maybe even Jesus's lost sheep parables. It's a thread from Melachim to the Gospels."

Amina pinned the translation higher, her eyes alight. "If this Zechariah is John's father, the scroll's from Qumran to Bethabara, 6 BCE matches his birth. It's near that site again."

Joshua grinned, wincing through the pain. "I'm with you, but it won't be the exact same spot. We need to narrow it down. Last dig showed we've got no time to waste once we're there."

Noa tilted her head, her agreement easy, almost instinctive. "We know the baptism was in the Jordan, but where exactly? Anything in the clues that points to a spot?" Her alignment with Joshua felt natural now, a rhythm growing stronger since they'd both clocked the spark between them.

Amina pulled a worn copy of the Gospels from her bag, flipping to John 1:28. "Here, 'These things were done in Bethany beyond the Jordan, where John was baptizing.' That's Bethabara, east bank, near modern Al-Maghtas. The scroll's 'fisherman mends his net,' Andrew's a solid guess, but nets mean a riverbank spot, not just anywhere."

Joshua leaned over the map, squinting at the Jordan's snaking line, its faded ink curling like the river itself. "Al-Maghtas fits, UNESCO's marked it as a baptism site, with pools and monk cells from later centuries. But the river's shifted since 6 BCE. We found the mantle north of a split stone last time, dove rests could be downstream, where fishing happened."

Noa tapped a spot south of their last dig, near Tell el-Kharrar, Elijah's Hill, her fingertip resting on the ridge's jagged outline. "This overlooks the river. Early Christians built there, believing it's where Elijah ascended in that whirlwind, 2 Kings 2:11. John could've preached nearby, where fishermen worked. Nets get mended on shore, not midstream."

Amina nodded, cross-referencing a photocopied article from her stack, a creased page about Byzantine remains at Al-Maghtas, dog-eared from late-night study. "Right. Excavations turned up pottery, a prayer hall from the third century, but the site's older, Iron Age traces too, predating John. If his ministry overlapped Essene routes from Qumran, dove rests might mean a quiet bend, a fisherman's nook tucked away from the crowds."

Joshua traced a finger downstream from Tell el-Kharrar, stopping at a shallow curve where Wadi al-Kharrar spilled into the Jordan. "Here it makes a natural harbor, calm enough for nets to dry. And it's defensible, caves dot the cliffs above. Last time, ISIS hit us fast; we need cover if they're closing in again."

Noa smirked, catching his eye across the map's worn edges. "You're thinking like a digger and a soldier now, Masa. I like it." Her tone was light, teasing, but her gaze lingered a beat longer, a spark they both felt flickering beneath the urgency.

Amina smirked too, flipping the projector to a satellite image of the area, the screen casting a grainy glow over the room. "Wadi al-Kharrar's a mile south of our last find, close enough to match the scroll's range, far enough to dodge the obvious. 'Fisherman mends his net' could be literal, a spot Andrew knew before he met Jesus, John 1:40. It's our best shot."

Joshua straightened, pain forgotten in the rush, his bruised jaw set with purpose. "Then that's it, Bethabara, Wadi al-Kharrar bend."

Noa glanced at him, her brow furrowing as she took in his slumped shoulders and the shadows under his eyes. "Okay, Masa, look, you're too beat up to move now. We should wait until tomorrow evening at least, give you time to heal and get some energy back. That last dig nearly broke you."

Amina paced around the table, her strides sharp, feeling the weight of their predicament. "I'm worried about the mole issue. They had our notes last time, someone's feeding ISIS or the Templars. We can't risk them beating us there."

"Yes," Joshua replied, wincing as he shifted, but his voice held a stubborn edge. "Which is why we should move now, before it's too late. Every hour we wait, they get closer."

Noa laid a hand on his shoulder, her touch firm but gentle, grounding him. "Please, let's buy some time first. How about a false flag? We know what we need, let's change the info on the wall. If it leaks, they'll chase the wrong lead."

Amina's eyes lit up, a rare grin breaking through. "That could work. I'll copy this to my journal, keep the real plan safe. Then we update the board to send them somewhere else, like Bethlehem."

"Don't make me laugh," Joshua said, chuckling despite the stab of pain it brought, his ribs protesting. He leaned over his tattered leather bag, fishing out a small journal, its cover cracked and faded like an old scroll. "Here, use this one, it's been through worse than me." He handed it to Amina, who took it with a nod, her fingers brushing the worn leather as if it held its own secrets.

Noa grabbed a marker, stepping to the wall where their notes hung pinned and tangled. "Bethlehem's south, plausible enough with the shepherd angle but far from the Jordan. We'll scribble 'crook points west' and some vague coordinates. They'll waste days chasing it."

Amina opened the journal, her pen flying across the page as she transcribed the Wadi al-Kharrar plan, coordinates, cave sketches, the scroll's exact words. "Done. This stays with us. The wall's a decoy now." She snapped the journal shut, tucking it into her vest, her posture easing as the strategy took shape.

Joshua watched them, his grin softening into something quieter, grateful. "Good. We rest tonight, ice my ribs, pack light. Tomorrow, we slip out after dusk, hit the tunnels before Gideon's watch. Tal and Avi can cover us if we time it right."

Noa squeezed his shoulder once more before stepping back, her voice low but firm. "You're still a mess, Masa, but we'll get you there. Wadi al-Kharrar's got answers, I can feel it."

Amina crossed her arms, staring at the doctored wall, now a web of half truths and red herrings. "John's voice, Andrew's nets, the dove's rest, it's all there, waiting. We just have to outrun the bastards first."

The room settled into a charged silence, the map glowing under the projector's hum. The cloak's legacy pulsed in their minds/ Elijah's fire, Elisha's miracles, John's cry, now a beacon pulling them back to the Jordan's edge. Tomorrow night, they'd move, a trio bound by trust and a thread of ancient truth, racing against shadows they couldn't yet name.

17

The Traitor's Shadow

The Templar house hummed with a tense quiet as late afternoon shadows stretched across the planning room. Lockdown had tightened the air. The team gathered around the table, their voices low as they debated the next site. The false map, now pinned to the wall with its Bethlehem decoy, glowed under dim lights, a web of red herrings crafted to mislead. Joshua, Noa, and Amina had finished it hours ago, their real plan for Wadi al-Kharrar bend safely tucked in Amina's journal.

Paul burst in with Gideon and Thomas, his eyes lighting up at the wall. "This is amazing. You all are fantastic." His enthusiasm rang hollow to the trio, who shared a fleeting glance.

Noa flashed a gaslight smile, her expression smooth as glass, betraying nothing. "Yes, we think with this we can rest up till tomorrow and hit it in the evening. It's fresh info. ISIS won't have it yet."

"Right," Paul said, not peeling his gaze from the map, tracing the fake coordinates with a finger. "You all retire to your rooms; we'll shut this down." The Templars lingered, Gideon's shadow looming near the door as Paul scribbled notes, oblivious to the deceit beneath his nose.

The room darkened as the sun's last rays faded through the wall's crack, leaving only the hum of bulbs to bathe the maps and notes in a sickly glow. Joshua lingered, watching Paul, his bruised jaw tightening. The false flag felt like a gamble. One wrong move and they'd lose everything.

Tal and Avi slipped in moments later, faces grim.

"We've got a breach," Tal muttered, voice clipped. "Intercepted chatter. ISIS knows we're here, mentioned the shepherd's notes. Your wall, Joshua." The words hit like a punch, and the room spun.

Suspicion flared fast. Amina's gaze snapped to Paul, still at the wall. "You?" she hissed, pendant glinting as she stepped forward.

He spun, hands up, incredulous. "Me? Check Gideon, his late-night radio calls don't add up."

Gideon bristled, hand twitching toward his belt, but said nothing.

The Templars fractured before their eyes, trust crumbling. Amina rounded on Eli, who'd entered silently behind Thomas. "You planted a mole, didn't you? To control this?" Her pendant flashed with her fury, voice cutting.

Eli's face stayed stone, his reply cryptic: "We guard what the world can't handle."

It fueled her rage, her fists clenching.

Noa, rifling through Paul's bag for a marker, froze as her fingers brushed a crumpled note. She unfolded it. Templar code, scrawled in haste: "Bethabara secured, await signal." Her breath caught, and she thrust it at Joshua.

He snapped awake, guilt slamming him as he read it. His notes, his wall had given ISIS the edge, indirectly. "I wanted to find it, not start a war," he confessed, voice breaking as he met Noa's eyes.

She grabbed his hand, fierce. "We finish this together, Masa. No one dies." Her grip steadied him, a lifeline in the chaos.

Dr. Khalil, who'd been quiet, stepped to the projector, flipping it on. "Let's decode this dove rests clue now, before they close in." He cross-referenced Luke 3:22 and Matthew 3:4, his voice calm but urgent. "Bethabara is John's baptism site, Spirit like a dove. The fisherman could be Andrew, John's disciple before Jesus. A cache from his early ministry, maybe."

Joshua nodded, shaking off the haze. "Near the caves in Bethlehem, the dove's rest hinting at the manger, or so they'll think." He forced a smirk, playing into the decoy for the Templars' ears.

Amina pocketed her journal, glaring at Eli. "We're done here. You've got the info, Bethlehem. Chase it if you want." She turned to Tal and Avi. "You're with us, right? We need Mossad muscle."

Tal smirked. "Always. IDF's too slow for this mess."

The team scattered to their rooms, the false map glowing behind them, a trap set for the traitor. Noa shot Dr. Khalil a quick wink as she passed. He blinked, puzzled, then caught a flicker of understanding, a shallow grin spreading as she nodded slightly. She'd signaled they were hiding something, though he didn't know what. With spies, injuries, and Templar games swirling, who could blame the secrecy?

Noa squeezed Joshua's hand once more then released it, grabbing their gear. "Dusk tomorrow, we hit the tunnels. Wadi al-Kharrar's a mile south of the last dig, caves, cover, the works. We've got one shot."

"Yes, and with the false flag in play, who knows if we even have that long," Joshua said, slinging his old leather bag over his shoulder. He headed for the room he'd crashed in the past few nights, its stone walls a cold comfort.

Sleep wouldn't come easy for anyone, each aching to close this chapter fast. But with moles, bruises, and logistics tangling their path, rushing was a fool's game. Joshua sank onto the cot, staring at the ceiling as if it might spill answers. Exhaustion tugged at him, and at some point, he drifted off.

In the dream, he was eight again, knee-deep in a backyard hole, dirt streaking his hands.

His grandfather knelt beside him, twirling a pocket watch on its chain, the pendulum swinging like a metronome. "Don't give up, Masa," he said, voice warm and rough. "In this business, the one with better effort often wins. It's more than smarts."

"Masa? Grandpa, why're you calling me that?" young Joshua asked, pausing his shovel, curiosity lighting his grubby face.

"Because you've got the tenacity of a man not quitting when the odds stack up. Like those rebels at Masada, holding the line against the world. You'll need that as you go, kid." His grandfather ruffled his hair, the watch glinting in the sun.

The dream jolted Joshua awake, heart pounding in the dark. Masada, fortress, defiance, a name his grandfather had etched into him, now alive in Noa's voice. He rubbed his eyes, the ceiling still blank, but the weight of Masa settled deeper. It wasn't just a nickname, it was a charge, a spark from dirt piles to this war-torn chase. Wadi al-Kharrar waited, and he'd dig through anything to reach it.

Morning broke with a muted gray, the trio slipping into the planning room roughly at the same time. The next steps hung unspoken, waiting for the pieces to align. Meanwhile, Dr. Khalil had unleashed shockwaves through the academic world. Back in Fayetteville, a professor read his email, jaw dropping as he learned Joshua Bennett, once a scrappy undergrad, was behind this. The class buzzed, dubbing him a real-life Indiana Jones, half joking, half awed, their lectures now alive with his name.

At the Israel Museum, Rabbi Cohen and Father Nance pored over the cloak and scrolls with the caretaker, fielding a flood of requests from religious leaders, rabbis, priests, even an imam from Amman, all clamoring to see the find. Historians salivated too; Elijah's mantle and a hint of John the Baptist bridged Melachim to the Gospels like nothing before. The team had leaked the news deliberately, hoping the spotlight would shield them. ISIS wouldn't dare strike now, not with the world watching.

But the gamble cut both ways.

Tal muttered over a breakfast of stale bread and bitter coffee, "They'll want the next site more now, intercept us before we dig it up."

Avi nodded, checking his pistol's clip with a practiced flick, the metal clicking softly. "Publicity's a shield, but it's also a flare."

The Templar house buzzed with controlled chaos that morning. Vehicles, dusty jeeps and unmarked vans, rumbled in and out, their engines growling through the stone courtyard. It was a deliberate ruse, decoy runs to muddy their exit, orchestrated by Tal and Avi to throw off any watchers.

The trio kept low, hunkered in a side room off the main hall, packing light: Joshua's journal, its pages creased with his grandfather's notes; Amina's pendant, tucked under her collar; Noa's map, folded tightly into a waterproof sleeve. Every move was measured, every glance sharp. They couldn't trust the walls here, not anymore.

Joshua sat on a crate, flipping through his journal, pausing at a sketch of Masada his grandfather had drawn decades ago, rugged lines of a fortress perched on a cliff, a scribbled note: *Effort beats odds, Masa.* He traced it with a finger, the dream's echo lingering. "We've got to move smart," he said, voice low. "Wadi al-Kharrar's our shot, but this spotlight's a double-edged sword."

Noa crouched beside him, rechecking her gear: compass, flashlight, a slim knife strapped to her ankle. "It's buying us time," she said, her tone steady but edged. "ISIS won't hit the museum, not with every news crew from here to London camped out. But Tal's right, they'll pivot to the next dig. We've got to beat them to it."

Amina stood by the window, peering through a slit in the shutters at the courtyard below. A jeep screeched out, kicking up dust, its driver a Mossad operative in civilian clothes. "They're good at this," she muttered. "But it's not enough. The mole's still out there, Gideon, Paul, someone. They've got Bethabara's name now, even if they're chasing Bethlehem."

The door creaked open, and a wiry man slipped in, dark eyes, stubbled jaw, a faded keffiyeh loose around his neck. Tal introduced him as Youssef, a local fixer with Mossad ties, his voice a rasp from years of desert air.

"Streets are humming," he said, dropping a satchel on the table. "Word's out, your find's got every imam and priest in a tizzy. But ISIS? They're not scared off. Chatter's up, trucks moving south from Ramallah, armed to the teeth."

Joshua's gut tightened. "South, toward Bethlehem?"

Youssef nodded, pulling a crumpled cigarette from his pocket and lighting it with a flick. "Your decoy's holding, for now. They're sniffing around the caves, hassling shepherds. But they're not stupid. Someone's feeding them scraps, and they know there's more."

Noa stood, crossing her arms. "How close are they to Jerusalem?"

"Too close," Youssef said, exhaling a plume of smoke. "Five miles out, last I heard. IDF's got patrols, but they're stretched thin, Passover's got half the units on leave. You've got a window, but it's shrinking."

Amina turned from the window, her pendant glinting as she moved. "Then we stick to dusk. Tunnels give us cover, Sacred Heart's our best shot out. Wadi al-Kharrar's a mile south of the last dig, caves near the bend. We can't let them cut us off."

Tal stepped forward, his radio clipped to his vest. "Youssef's right, ISIS is hungry now. That cloak, John's hint? It's not just history to them, it's a trophy. We've got decoys running all day, but once you're out, it's on us to keep the tail off." He glanced at Avi, who was testing a drone's controls, its hum faint but steady. "We'll stage you east, throw them off the scent."

Joshua closed his journal, the Masada sketch fading into the leather. "Grandpa said effort wins," he murmured, half to himself. "We've got the spot, Wadi al-Kharrar, where the fisherman mends his net. Andrew's haunt, John's voice. We just need to hold the line."

Noa caught his eye, a flicker of a smile breaking her focus. "You're Masa for a reason, stubborn as that fortress. We'll make it." Her hand brushed his shoulder, a quiet anchor.

The day dragged on, each hour a slow grind. The trio ran drills with Tal and Avi, tunnel routes memorized, signals set: two taps for stop, three for go. Youssef slipped out, promising intel by dusk, his cigarette smoke lingering like a ghost. Outside, the decoy runs kept up their chaos, jeeps peeling off toward the Old City, vans doubling back through alleys.

Amina watched it all, her jaw set. "They're buying it," she said. "But not for long."

As evening crept in, the sky bruising purple, Tal and Avi signaled, *Time*. Mossad whisked them out in a battered sedan, weaving through Jerusalem's backstreets to a nondescript safehouse, a squat concrete box off the grid, its windows shuttered against prying eyes. The air inside was stale, thick with dust and the faint tang of old diesel. The tunnels loomed ahead, Wadi al-Kharrar their prize, but the traitor's shadow stretched longer now, sharpened by the world's gaze.

"Now that we're away from the temple, can we talk about the spy issue?" Noa asked, her voice cutting through the safehouse's stillness. She eyed not just Joshua and Amina but Tal and Avi too, pulling them into the circle.

"Right," Amina said, standing as if facing a tribunal, her pendant catching the dim light. "I still don't know for sure. I'd say it's not Gideon or Thomas, too obvious." She turned to the Mossad agents, voice steady. "Even with that crumpled note, I can't buy Paul either."

"Yeah, he was in as much danger as you two with the gunfire and explosions," Tal said, leaning against a cracked wall, arms crossed. "Caught a bullet graze himself, hardly a mole's move."

Avi chimed in, his tone dry. "And Eli? Head of a Templar order, even a faded one, leaking to a Muslim group like ISIS? Doesn't pass muster. Pride's too thick for that."

"You called out Gideon and Thomas," Joshua said, leaning back in a rickety chair, wincing as his ribs twinged. "Maybe it's from my rescue. Think about it. They took on a small ISIS crew, reveling in the fight, versus tipping off a group to take out rivals. Contrast doesn't prove much." He rubbed his jaw, eyes narrowing. "I'm not sold on anyone, but the Templars as a whole? They're not on our side."

Tal's radio crackled, a burst of static slicing the room. The words were muffled from across the table, but his face tightened. "Roger that," he barked then turned to the trio. "Bethlehem caves are crawling with ISIS fighters, roughing up locals, tearing through the hills."

"As if on cue," Noa said, a wry smile tugging her lips. The false flag had worked, too well maybe.

The sun dipped lower, the sky exploding into wild streaks of orange and purple beyond the safehouse shutters.

"We leave in twenty," Avi announced, slinging a gear bag over his shoulder. "Get your stuff together. Cameras show nothing's tracked us yet."

Joshua hauled his bag closer, checking the journal, his grandfather's legacy pressed between its pages. Amina tucked her pendant under her shirt, a silent vow. Noa folded the map, her fingers lingering on Wadi al-Kharrar's bend. Twenty minutes to dusk, to the tunnels, to the truth, if they could outrun the shadow.

18

Flight into the Night

The dark SUV cruised smoothly down the dusty highway, its tires humming against the cracked asphalt between the Mossad safehouse and the Jordan River, where Wadi al-Kharrar once poured in. The route sliced through the night, a ribbon of shadow flanked by barren hills that loomed like silent sentinels. They passed eerily close to the site of the jeep rollover from their last outing, a mangled memory of twisted metal and Joshua's battered escape, the ditch still scarred with tire tracks under the moonlight. The air inside the vehicle thickened with anxiety, each bump in the road a jolt to already frayed nerves.

Joshua's ribs ached with every lurch, a dull reminder of that night, while Noa's fingers tightened on the map in her lap, her flashlight beam flickering over its creased lines. Tal drove, his eyes flicking between the road and the rearview mirror. Avi sat shotgun, scanning the horizon through a cracked window. Amina hunched in the back, her pendant glinting faintly as she stared out at the passing scrub, silent but taut.

The hum of the engine was their only companion until Tal broke it, voice low. "We're off the grid now, no tails from Jerusalem. But this close to the Jordan, every shadow's a threat."

Joshua shifted, wincing. "How far to the bend?"

"Ten minutes," Noa said, tracing the map with a finger. "Wadi al-Kharrar's shallow curve, where the nets would've dried. Caves are up the cliff, north of the split rock." Her voice steadied him, a thread of calm in the storm brewing inside.

Avi turned, his silhouette sharp against the dashboard glow. "Keep your lights low when we stop. ISIS isn't far. Bethlehem's chaos won't hold them forever." The false flag had worked, drawing fighters south, but the team knew it was a fragile shield.

The moon hung low as they pulled off the highway, its silver sheen bathing the shallow curve ahead, where ancient waters once lapped calmly enough for fishermen to mend their nets. The SUV's engine cut out, and five flashlight beams swung side to side as the team piled out, cutting through the darkness. Joshua, Noa, Amina, Tal, and Avi searched for any hint of the scroll's clues.

Amina's discovery of the split rock last time lingered in her mind, a quiet triumph she couldn't shake, though every few minutes the weight of it pressed harder, her steps deliberate as she swept her beam across the sand.

The radio squawked, a burst of static shattering the silence. Tal snatched the mic, his voice low and cryptic. "We're en route now, arrival in thirty minutes. We'll keep it quiet, no attention drawn." He dropped the mic with a clatter, glancing back at the group. "They're missing us already. We've got thirty minutes tops, less if they're watching the roads."

"Who called?" Joshua asked, his bruised jaw tightening as he scanned Tal's face. "Maybe they're not the spy."

Avi stepped into the middle of the group, his silhouette stark against the moonlight. "I've got this, Tal. While you three have been playing alibi roulette, trying to clear everyone, we knew the traitor would tip their hand. Whoever calls when we miss our check-ins, it's them."

"So?" Amina couldn't resist, her tone sharp, daring them to name her, her flashlight dipping as she turned to face Avi.

Tal's eyes narrowed, unflinching. "Well, to be honest, we knew it'd be you, and whoever you're working with."

"What?" Amina feigned surprise, her pendant catching the flashlight's glare as she stepped back, indignation flaring. "There's no way you think I had anything to do—"

"Paul," Tal cut her off, his voice flat but certain. "Look, we took your cell phone back at the safehouse, slipped it out when you weren't looking. Would've done it sooner, but that was our first clean shot."

Avi picked up the thread, his tone cold, hand hovering near his holster. "We figured that's how they tracked you last time, your phone. Pings matched ISIS movements, right up to the rollover. And why you walked away alive when Joshua took a beating. So, confirm it, Amina, did they use it to pin you?"

Tal swung his flashlight toward her, the beam harsh against her face, pinning her in its glare. "Is that why they called? Not just that we're late but that we haven't moved from the safehouse?"

"It'd be too obvious if they rolled up there," Noa interjected, her voice steady but edged with suspicion, eyes locked on Amina as she stepped closer. "You've been too quick to vouch for Paul, every single time."

Joshua's brow furrowed, piecing it together. "And you couldn't help defending him, every chance you got." He paused, head snapping toward a light on the group's far end. It froze then bobbed wildly, like someone running with it. "Wait, this looks a lot like the last spot. Another split rock."

"Oh, come on," Noa said, exasperated, stepping toward the bouncing beam. "That's too obvious."

The accusation hung heavy as the team fanned out, flashlights carving jagged paths through the scrub and sand. Joshua's light joined the runner's, Avi, now slowing near a hulking shape jutting from the riverbank. It was a split rock, its cleaved face mirroring the last find, though smaller, weathered by centuries of wind and water. The shallow curve of Wadi al-Kharrar stretched before it, the Jordan's ancient bed glinting faintly under the moon.

Amina stayed rooted, her fists clenched as Tal's beam lingered on her. "You think I'd sell us out?" she snapped, voice rising, cutting through the night's stillness. "After everything, ISIS, the Templars, Paul bleeding beside me in that ditch? That note in his bag was a plant, I'd stake my life on it."

"Then why's your phone a beacon?" Avi shot back, his hand resting on his pistol, eyes narrowing. "We traced the signal, pings matching their trucks, right up to the rollover. You're clean, or you're clever, too clever for us to ignore."

Joshua turned from the rock, his light sweeping back to Amina, frustration boiling over. "Enough, both of you. If she's the mole, why's she here, not running? We've got bigger problems." He nodded toward the split rock, his voice steadying. "This fits, 'dove rests where the fisherman mends his net.' Wadi al-Kharrar's bend, caves up the cliff. Let's move."

Noa grabbed Amina's arm, pulling her along, her grip firm but not hostile. "Prove it out there," she muttered, her tone low and urgent. "We'll sort this later, focus."

The team closed ranks, flashlights converging on the rock as Tal's radio crackled again, muffled voices, urgent, but he silenced it with a flick, his jaw tight.

The cliff loomed above, pocked with shallow caves, their mouths dark against the pale stone. Joshua took point, his boots crunching on gravel as he climbed, pain flaring in his ribs but ignored, his flashlight steady despite the tremor in his hands. The others followed, fanning out to scan the crevices.

Noa's beam caught a glint, something wedged in a niche, twelve paces north of the rock, just as the scroll hinted. "Here!" she called, voice tight with adrenaline, her light holding firm.

Avi reached it first, tugging free a clay jar, its wax seal cracked but intact, the faint scent of aged clay rising as he pried it open. Inside, a rotted fisherman's net cradled a scroll fragment, its edges curling with age, brittle as autumn leaves.

Joshua's light trembled as he took it, his voice hoarse with awe: "I, John, son of Zechariah, baptize in water, but He comes with fire..." It was John the Baptist's words, echoing Luke 3:16, a testament from the wilderness.

The cave near Wadi al-Kharrar was a tomb of shadows and secrets, its air thick with the dust of centuries and the faint, earthy tang of ancient soil. Flashlights sliced through the gloom, their jagged beams dancing across rough stone walls to settle on the scroll fragment cradled in Joshua's hands. Beside him, the clay jar that had housed it lay open, its wax seal fractured like a confession finally spoken. Noa, Tal, and Avi pressed close, their breaths shallow with a mix of awe and disbelief. At the cave's mouth, Amina stood apart, her silhouette framed against the moonlight, her posture taut but distant from the unfolding discovery. The four, however, were wholly consumed by the parchment, a brittle, faded relic that seemed to hum with the weight of its maker: John the Baptist.

Joshua unrolled the scroll with trembling care, its edges curling inward as if reluctant to surrender their story. The text was etched in Koiné Greek, faint but legible, and his voice quavered as he translated aloud for the others:

"I, John, son of Zechariah, am but a voice crying in the wilderness, 'Prepare the way of the Lord, make His paths straight.' I baptize in water, but He who comes after me is mightier. I am not worthy to untie His sandals. He will baptize with the Holy Spirit and fire. I saw the Spirit descend like a dove upon Him, and a voice from heaven declared, 'This is My Son, the Beloved, with whom I am well pleased.' I testify that He is the Son of God. He calls me friend, though I am unworthy. His path leads to the cross, and I prepare the way. Repent, for the Kingdom of God is near. He is the Word, and I am but a voice."

The words settled over them like a hush after thunder, a thread stitching the wilderness prophet to the Messiah's dawn.

Joshua lowered the scroll, his flashlight wavering as he swallowed hard. "It's... it's John's own words," he said, voice thick with reverence. "A testament tying the old prophets to the Messiah. From Melachim to the Gospels, right here in his hand."

Noa leaned in, her eyes tracing the faded script as if it might dissolve under her gaze. "It's so personal," she murmured, her voice soft with wonder. "'He calls me friend,' that's not in the gospels, not like this. It's John's heart laid bare. Like he knew his role but felt every ounce of its weight."

Tal's voice came softer, almost reverent, his flashlight steady on the parchment. "It's a missing link. Ties the wilderness preacher to the early church, to Jesus's inner circle. 'He is the Word,' that's straight from John's Gospel, chapter one. But here, it's the Baptist saying it, not the evangelist."

Avi nodded, his pragmatism tempered by the moment's gravity, his beam joining the others. "It's a prelude, setting the stage. John's voice, then the Light comes. Like the overture to the whole story."

A heavy silence fell, each of them adrift in the scroll's echo. Joshua's mind spun through the gospels, Matthew's vivid baptism scene with the heavens torn open, Mark's urgent brevity stripping it to essentials, Luke's lineage rooting John in Zechariah's priesthood, and the Gospel of John's soaring theology, where the Baptist names Jesus the Light of the world. This fragment wove them into a single tapestry, a small book with a reach that spanned centuries, a cry from the wilderness, a whisper of the cross.

Noa broke the quiet, her voice barely above a whisper, her breath visible in the chill. "It's humble, too. 'I am but a voice.' He knew his place, pointing to the Word, not claiming it."

Joshua rolled the scroll back with deliberate care, his fingers brushing the net's decayed strands, nodding slowly. "And that line, 'His path leads to the cross.' It's like he saw it all, even then, before the ax fell."

Tal's flashlight swept the cave, as if more truths might hide in its shadows, his tone hushed but firm. "If this is real, it's seismic. A first-person account from John himself. Theologians will lose their minds. Rabbi Cohen, Father Nance, they'll fight to decipher it."

Avi's smirk flickered, though his eyes stayed sharp, scanning the cave's edges. "Assuming we get it out of here. This isn't a museum yet."

The words jolted them back to the present. Beyond the cave, the night held its breath, but the stillness felt brittle, like glass about to shatter.

Amina shifted at the entrance, her pendant glinting in the moonlight as she peered out, her voice tight with warning. "We've got minutes, not hours. Wrap it and go, now."

Joshua slipped the scroll into his bag, its weight pressing heavier than its size suggested, a tangible link to John's wilderness cry. "This is it, the dove's rest, John's voice. We've got what we came for."

But as they turned to leave, the night erupted. Headlights pierced the darkness, trucks roaring up the highway, their dust clouds swirling like specters in the beams. ISIS had found them, and the cave's fragile peace splintered into chaos.

19

Echoes of Betrayal

The cave's fragile sanctuary shattered as headlights blasted the cliffside, a harsh glare flooding the wall of caves near Wadi al-Kharrar. Trucks growled below, their beams pinning the team like prey caught midflight, the light searing through the night's thin veil. Joshua, Noa, Tal, and Avi dove behind a boulder, its jagged bulk barely shielding them from the onslaught, loose gravel biting into their palms as they hit the ground. Amina lingered a beat longer, her silhouette stark against the glow, her pendant catching a stray beam before she crouched low, half-hidden in the shadow. The air thrummed with diesel fumes and menace, the shallow curve of the Jordan's ancient bed now a battleground under the moon's cold, unblinking watch.

Avi and Tal scanned the hillside, their flashlights extinguished, eyes darting for an escape route through the fractured terrain. The SUV sat over two hundred meters downslope, a distant hope glinting faintly in the dark, its dark hull swallowed by the night's edge.

"Too far," Avi muttered, his voice a rasp, fingers tightening on his pistol as he peered over the boulder's rim.

Tal nodded, his breath shallow, peering through a narrow crack in the stone, tracing the cliff's jagged edge for any path that didn't end in a hail of bullets. The slope was a maze of scrub and loose rock, offering little cover beyond the boulder's meager shield.

Yells erupted below in two tongues, Arabic, sharp and commanding, slicing through the stillness, followed by broken English barking from a megaphone, "Present yourselves with hands up! Lay the articles you found on the ground!" The voice was guttural, amplified, its echo ricocheting off the cliff like a physical blow.

Joshua's pulse hammered, his chest tight as he caught the others' eyes, or lack thereof. No one was looking at him, their gazes fixed on the lights, the threat, the betrayal unfolding below. Seizing the moment, he slipped the scroll fragment deeper into his backpack, tucking it beneath his grandfather's journal, its leather spine a familiar anchor. The clay jar's empty husk lay beside him, a hollow decoy in the dirt.

Amina rose first, her pendant glinting as she stood, hands half raised, a move not lost on the team. Joshua's jaw tightened, a muscle twitching as he watched her silhouette sharpen against the glare. Noa's breath hissed through her teeth, a sharp intake of fury, while Tal's hand froze midcrawl, his fingers digging into the earth. Avi stayed low, his glare boring into her back, a predator sizing up a turncoat, but the others followed suit, rising reluctantly, Joshua with his pack slung tight against his bruised ribs, Noa with a scowl twisting her features, Tal easing up but clinging to the boulder's shadow.

"Now the find," the voice demanded, its echo bouncing off the cliff, relentless. "Is that all of you?"

No one moved, the silence a taut wire stretched to snapping.

Then, impossibly, the megaphone crackled again: "Whoever's hiding, come out." A pause, heavy with unspoken threat, the air thick with the promise of violence. "One of you bring the jar to us."

Amina's gaze flicked to the trio, her expression unreadable, stone-cold or maybe just resigned. "I'll do it," she said, voice clipped, reaching for the jar without a glance inside, her fingers brushing its cracked rim.

"Of course you will," Noa hissed, her words venomous, eyes blazing as Amina gripped the empty vessel. The earlier accusation, her phone, Paul's note, and the pings that led ISIS to their last dig hung between them, a wound torn open anew, raw and bleeding.

Amina moved downslope, her steps deliberate, measured, the jar cradled like a peace offering or a surrender. The trucks loomed closer, their lights blinding as shadowy figures spilled out, black-clad, rifles slung low, boots crunching on the gravel. They made a show of it, grabbing her roughly, one yanking her arm while another shoved her into the bed of a pickup with theatrical force, her body jolting against the metal.

Joshua's fists clenched, nails biting into his palms; it looked staged, too clean, a performance for their benefit or someone else's. The headlights swung off the boulder, plunging the team back into shadow, the sudden dark a jarring reprieve.

"Go now!" Tal barked, seizing the break, his voice cutting through the haze. "This way!" He bolted up the hill, following Avi's earlier path, his boots kicking gravel in a frantic sprint, a trail of dust rising behind him.

Joshua and Noa scrambled after him, the scroll thumping against his spine with every step, a lifeline he wouldn't lose, its weight a tether to John's voice amid the chaos.

They crested the hill, lungs burning, the cold night air clawing at their throats, when a new set of headlights bounced toward them from the east, dust swirling in their wake like a storm front.

"Not again," Joshua rasped, spinning for cover, a ditch, a rock, anything, but the barren slope offered nothing, just exposed earth and thinning scrub under the moon's pale scrutiny.

"No, come on!" Tal countered, veering toward the lights, a wild gamble in his stride, his silhouette a blur against the glow.

The vehicle, a battered jeep, skidded to a stop just ahead, its driver's door flying open, dust billowing around it like a shroud.

Joshua braced, hand on his knife, expecting the worst, his heart thudding a war drum in his chest.

"Get in!" Avi's voice cut through the glare, sharp and urgent, a lifeline thrown from the chaos.

Relief flooded Joshua as he recognized the Mossad agent behind the wheel, his face taut with focus, eyes glinting with the same steel that had pulled them through before. The trio piled in, Joshua in front, Noa and Tal in the back, the jeep spinning in a tight arc, tires spitting dirt in a gritty spray.

Avi killed the lights, plunging them into moonlit gray, and eased toward the highway, slow and deliberate, the engine's growl a low murmur. "Watch for the dip," he muttered, eyes flicking to the side, hands steady on the wheel. "Hit it hard coming up, nearly flipped."

Through the cracked windshield, they saw a line of headlights bouncing parallel, not far to the left, ISIS trucks tearing toward the caves, their beams slashing the night, oblivious to the jeep's detour.

Noa leaned forward, her breath hot on Joshua's neck, her voice a mix of shock and suspicion. "Amina, did she just...?"

"Betray us?" Tal finished, his voice low, bitter, edged with exhaustion as he slumped against the seat. "Looked like it. Took the jar, walked right into their hands."

Joshua's grip tightened on his pack, the scroll's weight a silent rebuttal pressing against his spine. "She didn't check it, didn't know it was empty. If she's with them, why play it blind?"

Avi snorted, steering around a rut with a jolt that rattled the jeep. "Could be cover. Could be she's deeper than we thought. Phone pings, Paul's note, she's been a step ahead too long. Either way, she's theirs now."

"Wait," Noa jumped in, her voice cutting through the hum of the jeep, eyes widening as she turned to Joshua, realization dawning. "You mean you have the scroll on you?"

"Yes. Oh, sorry, I forgot to tell you," Joshua said, sheepish, opening his bag with a rustle that seemed loud in the cramped space. "I was a little distracted, things were happening fast." He pulled the scroll fragment free, its brittle edges catching the faint moonlight seeping through the windshield, the Koiné Greek script a ghostly whisper of the past.

"That's fantastic!" Tal spun in his seat, a grin breaking through the tension as the jeep burst into nervous laughter, a jagged release of fear and adrenaline that echoed off the metal walls. "Okay, so we've got the gospel part, John's testament. Is there more to it?"

Avi glanced over, easing the jeep off the highway into a shallow gully flanked by low scrub, its shadow cloaking them from view as he killed the engine. "I'm pulling in here, gets us out of sight. Let's take a look."

Joshua passed the scroll to the front, Avi and Tal handling it with childlike care, fingers hovering as if it might crumble at a touch, their breaths held in reverence.

Tal unrolled it further, squinting at the faded Greek under the dim glow of a penlight he fished from his vest. "Here, beneath the gospel bit. 'Beneath the dove's shadow, the fisherman's net holds my words.' This feels separate, like a clue after John's message."

Noa's head snapped up, her mind racing back to their planning, her voice quickening with urgency. "Wait, Joshua, didn't we circle a site on the map? Something near here, another spot tied to the Jordan. Considering the mess we're in, maybe we should move now, strike while they're chasing ghosts."

Joshua's thoughts tumbled out in a rush, half-formed but fervent, his hands gesturing as if mapping the air. "Yeah, yeah, the map! We marked a secondary site, downstream from the bend, near Tell el-Kharrar, Elijah's Hill. Could be another cache, John's words, more scrolls, maybe hidden where the dove's shadow falls. We're here, we've got the jeep, ISIS is distracted with the jar and Bethlehem. Let's go before they figure it out and circle back."

Avi nodded, restarting the engine with a low growl that vibrated through the seats. "Smart. They're scattered now. Bethlehem's a mess, and the caves are a dead end with that empty jar. We've got a window, small but real." He eased the jeep back onto the highway, lights still off, the moon their only guide, its pale arc a faint promise overhead.

Joshua clutched the scroll, its new clue burning in his mind: *Beneath the dove's shadow, the fisherman's net holds my words.* John's voice wasn't done echoing, not yet. The jeep rolled on, a battered lifeline threading through the night, carrying them toward Tell el-Kharrar and whatever lay hidden in the shadow of the dove. The cracked asphalt stretched ahead, flanked by low hills that loomed like silent watchers, their silhouettes jagged against the silvered sky. The air inside the jeep was thick with dust and the faint tang of sweat, a testament to the night's relentless grind.

Noa unfolded her map across her knees, her penlight casting a faint circle of light as she traced the Jordan's curve. "Tell el-Kharrar's a mile downstream, east bank, near where early Christians built a shrine for Elijah's ascent. If John hid more, it'd be there, close to his baptism site, under the dove's shadow. Maybe a cave or a crevice."

Tal leaned over, his shoulder brushing hers as he studied the markings. "Makes sense. Fisherman's net could mean Andrew again, or a literal net, like the one in the jar. We need to check the cliffs near the tell, any nook that fits."

Joshua's fingers brushed the scroll, his voice low but firm. "It's John's pattern, Qumran to Bethabara, hiding pieces of his testimony. This clue's got to point to something bigger, maybe what he couldn't say outright." His mind flashed to the gospel fragment: *His path leads to the cross.* A chill ran through him, what else had John foreseen?

Avi's eyes flicked to the rearview mirror, his grip tightening on the wheel. "Hold that thought, company." A faint glow bloomed on the horizon behind them, headlights flickering through the dust, growing closer. "They're backtracking, must've sniffed out the jar trick."

"Wasn't bound to fool them forever," Noa muttered, folding the map with a snap. "How close?"

"Half a mile, maybe less," Avi said, his voice clipped. "We're not outrunning them on this stretch, too straight, too exposed." He scanned the roadside then jerked the wheel hard, veering off into a narrow wadi, the jeep jolting as it plunged into shadow. Branches scraped the sides, a grating screech that set Joshua's teeth on edge, but the gully swallowed them, its banks high enough to mask their silhouette.

The engine idled low, a barely audible hum as they held their breath. The ISIS trucks roared past on the highway, their beams slashing the night, dust swirling in their wake like a phantom army. Joshua's heart thudded, the scroll pressed against his chest, its fragile weight a silent prayer. The lights faded, their growl receding toward Jerusalem, and the team exhaled as one.

"Too close," Tal said, wiping sweat from his brow. "They're not done hunting."

Avi eased the jeep forward, navigating the wadi's twists until it spilled back onto a side track that ran parallel to the highway. "We're clear, for now. Tell el-Kharrar's five minutes if I push it. Gear up."

Down the road, the ISIS trucks barreled toward Jerusalem, their tires chewing the asphalt, Amina in the back of one, sprawled against the tailgate. She wasn't bound, but eyes watched her closely, dark, unblinking stares from the fighters crammed beside her. Arabic chatter volleyed back and forth, rapid and heated, a language she caught only in fragments. The truck slammed on its brakes, a sudden lurch that nearly threw one fighter off, his rifle clattering against the metal as he cursed.

The passenger, a wiry man with a scar slicing his cheek, leaped out, storming to the rear. He snatched the jar from the truck bed and shoved it at Amina, his voice a snarl. "What is this? This is empty! I thought you said there was going to be something!" His English was rough, jagged with fury, his free hand gesturing wildly at the jar's hollow interior.

Amina scrambled to her knees, grabbing the jar with shaking hands, peering inside as if it might conjure the scroll back. "No, there *was* a scroll. It was written by John the Baptist!" Her voice cracked, nerves fraying as she upended it, dust spilling onto her lap. Suddenly, she was very nervous, stammering, trying to explain how it could be empty, her mind racing through excuses: it fell out, it crumbled, it was a fake. But not once did she say the others kept it, her tongue tripping over the truth she couldn't voice.

The scarred man barked something in Arabic, sharp and guttural, to the others in the truck. They jumped out, boots hitting the dirt with a thud, dropping the tailgate with a clang that echoed in the night. Two grabbed Amina, dragging her to the ground, her knees scraping the asphalt as she yelped.

"What have you done with the scroll? Where did you stash it?" the leader demanded, looming over her, his shadow swallowing the moonlight.

Amina's breath hitched, her pendant swinging as she twisted against their grip. "I-I didn't stash it! It was there, I swear!" Her eyes darted, searching for an out, but the highway stretched empty in both directions, ten minutes outside Jerusalem, the city's glow a distant tease. The fighters closed in, rifles glinting, their questions relentless, her fate teetering on the edge of the lie she couldn't escape.

Back in the jeep, Joshua's voice broke the silence, urgent. "She's in deep now, empty jar's a death sentence if they don't buy her story." The scroll's clue pulsed in his mind, a beacon pulling them forward as Avi gunned the engine toward Tell el-Kharrar.

20

The Dove's Shadow

The jeep rumbled through the night, its engine a steady growl beneath the moon's pale arc, threading a dusty path toward Tell el-Kharrar. The cracked windshield framed a landscape of low hills and scrub, the Jordan River's unseen ribbon glinting faintly to their west. Inside, the air was thick with anticipation, the scroll's weight pressing against Joshua's chest as he clutched his backpack, its new clue, *Beneath the dove's shadow, the fisherman's net holds my words*, burning in his mind like a flare. John's voice lingered, a whisper from the wilderness, pulling them deeper into the mystery.

"Masa, we have the location. What are we looking for?" Noa's voice broke the silence, urgent and rapid, her thoughts tumbling over each other as she leaned forward in the backseat. "Where could beneath the dove's shadow even be? Is it a cave, a rock, some kind of marker? How do we—"

"Calm down," Joshua interrupted, his tone firm but gentle, trying to steady her spiraling questions as he turned to meet her gaze.

A collective "Eww!" erupted from the front, Avi and Tal groaning in unison, their faces twisting in mock disgust at the exchange. Avi's hands tightened on the wheel, while Tal shot a sidelong glance at Joshua, one eyebrow arched.

"Calm down?" Noa's eyes flashed, her voice rising as she launched into a tirade, her words a torrent of pent-up energy. "Calm down?! Masa, we're dodging ISIS trucks, Amina's probably getting grilled on the side of the road, and we've got a cryptic clue from a two-thousand-year-old scroll that could lead us anywhere, or nowhere! Don't tell me to calm down when we're this close!" Her hands flailed, nearly knocking the map off her lap, her breath sharp with exasperation.

Avi and Tal exchanged a knowing look, a flicker of amusement beneath their tension. They'd seen this coming. Noa's fire was as predictable as it was fierce, especially after the night's chaos. Tal stifled a smirk while Avi kept his eyes on the road, the jeep's jostle masking his quiet chuckle.

"Okay, sorry," Joshua cut in, raising his hands in surrender, his voice softening as he tried to redirect her. "But if you want to know what I think, maybe we fight later? Right now, I've got a spot that fits the line. Wadi al-Kharrar, near Tell el-Kharrar itself. There's a network of caves there, carved into the marl and limestone cliffs flanking the wadi. Archaeological surveys documented them. Some were used by hermits in the Roman and Byzantine periods. They're scattered along the valley, close to the spring called John the Baptist Spring and the churches near the Jordan's bank."

"How in the world could you know all that off the top of your head?" Tal turned in his seat, peering at Joshua with a mix of incredulity and admiration, as if he'd just sprouted a second head. "You're an encyclopedia back there."

"I don't," Joshua said, stopping him with a grin, reaching into his pack to pull out his weathered notebook. Its leather cover was creased and stained, a relic of countless digs and sleepless nights. "I've got this. As it happens, I studied the location early in this journey, back when we were plotting Bethabara. I circled the caves and jotted notes, thought they might tie to John's ministry. Look." He flipped to a dog-eared page, holding it up so the faint penlight glow caught his cramped handwriting and a rough sketch of the wadi, Tell el-Kharrar marked with a red circle.

Noa snatched the notebook, her eyes darting over the text as she traced the sketch with a finger. "You're serious, caves under the tell? That's got to be it. Beneath the dove's shadow, the Spirit came down like a dove right around here, Luke 3:22. And fisherman's net, Andrew's haunt, or another jar like the last one. It's perfect."

Avi's voice cut through, steady but edged with caution. "If you're right, we're almost there, Tell el-Kharrar's just ahead, half a mile. But we're not strolling in. ISIS might be scattered, but they're not gone. We need a plan, fast."

The jeep slowed as the terrain shifted, the highway giving way to a rutted track veering east toward the wadi. The moon cast long shadows over the low ridge of Tell el-Kharrar, its silhouette a quiet sentinel against the night sky. Joshua squinted through the windshield, the hill's gentle rise sharpening into focus, its eastern slope dropping into the wadi where the caves waited. His pulse quickened. This was it, the next thread of John's legacy.

"Park off the track," Tal said, leaning forward, his tone all business. "We go on foot, lights off, quiet. If those caves are the spot, we'll need cover. The cliffs should shield us from the highway."

Avi nodded, easing the jeep behind a cluster of tamarisk bushes, their gnarled branches scraping the hull as he killed the engine. The silence was immediate, heavy, broken only by the faint rustle of wind through the scrub. The team piled out, boots crunching on the dry earth, their breaths visible in the chill. Joshua slung his pack over his shoulder, the scroll's weight a constant reminder, while Noa tucked the map into her vest, her earlier fire now a focused ember.

"South side of the wadi," Joshua said, pointing toward the cliffs' shadowed bulk, their pale marl faces looming like a weathered fortress. "The caves are carved into the cliffs, some shallow, some deeper. Surveys pegged them as hermit cells, but they're old enough for John's time. Look for anything that fits. Dove's shadow might mean an overhang, a carving, something tied to the baptism."

Noa nodded, her voice low but sharp. "And fisherman's net, we found the last scroll in one. Could be another jar, a bundle, something hidden where Andrew might've walked. Let's split the cliffs, two and two."

"Me and Joshua," Tal said, stepping up, his pistol already in hand, its metal glinting faintly under the moon. "Avi, you take Noa. Stay tight, signal if you spot anything, two taps on the rock for stop, three for found."

Avi checked his clip with a practiced flick, his eyes scanning the horizon where the highway's faint glow lingered. "Agreed. We've got maybe an hour before dawn, or before ISIS doubles back. Move quick, keep low."

The team fanned out, shadows among shadows, descending into the wadi's embrace. The cliffs loomed closer, their pale faces pocked with dark mouths, caves staring back like silent witnesses, their edges softened by centuries of wind and dust. The air grew cooler as they dropped below the tell's ridge, the faint trickle of the John the Baptist Spring audible somewhere to their left, a lifeline in the parched valley.

Joshua's mind raced, the clue's rhythm pulsing with each step: *Beneath the dove's shadow, the fisherman's net holds my words.* John's voice was here, waiting, if they could find it before the night turned against them.

They moved in pairs, Tal's steady stride matching Joshua's as they hugged the cliff's southern base, their boots silent on the loose marl. Noa and Avi veered right, their shapes blurring into the scrub as they scanned the opposite stretch. The moon hung lower now, its light slanting across the cliffs, casting jagged shadows that danced with every gust. Joshua's flashlight stayed off, his eyes adjusting to the dimness, searching for anything, a shape, a hint, that matched the scroll's cryptic call.

When Noa's beam swept across the cliff face, a shadow flickered, its curve resembling a dove's wing against the pale stone. "Hold it, everyone stop!" she called, her voice a sharp whisper as she flashed her light again, trying to recreate the image. "I just saw a dove's wing in the shadow! Let's start with the left. Avi, can you wave your light over the face?"

The group converged, beams slicing the night one by one, a quiet choreography of hope and haste beneath the moon's waning glow. Joshua's light hit an opening ten paces up the cliff face, casting a shadow that could be argued as a wing, faint, its curve more suggestion than certainty, but enough to spark a jolt in his chest. Then Tal's beam struck a higher cave, its angle throwing a shape that might pass for a head, blocky but birdlike if you squinted. Noa and Avi shifted, circling until their combined lights stretched the second wing, an imperfect silhouette, but the dove's form emerged, hovering over the cliff like a ghostly sentinel.

"There, directly below it!" Joshua pointed, his voice tight with adrenaline. Beneath the big shadow, where the dove's imagined breast would rest, a small crack split the wall, a narrow fissure, invisible without the light's interplay, its edges swallowed by the marl's grainy texture. He dashed over, dropping to his knees, his hand reaching for the gap.

"Careful, Masa, there could be a snake in there!" Noa fell in line behind him, her flashlight trembling as she aimed it into the dark slit. "Scorpions, too. This close to the Jordan, anything could be nesting."

Joshua hesitated, his fingers brushing the cool stone, then plunged his hand in, feeling the rough interior widen slightly. His heart thudded, the prize was close, the fisherman's net waiting beneath the dove's shadow. The interior widened just before he hit something solid. "No, this can't be right. We got something wrong."

Noa stood beside him while Tal and Avi kept watch, their beams sweeping the wadi. "What's wrong?" she asked, her hand on his back, trying to ease the tension.

"There's nothing. The hole just stops, a wall, nothing inside." Joshua stepped back, staring at the fissure as if it might confess its secret.

Noa reached in, her arm disappearing into the gap. "Okay, I see." She turned to the others. "Somebody have a knife?"

Tal handed her his combat knife, its blade glinting. "Careful, it's—"

"Don't mansplain a sharp knife," Noa quipped, snatching Tal's blade and driving it into the fissure. With a grunt, she pried loose a chunk of solid wax, handing the knife back with a smirk. "Oh, Masa," she said, pulling out more pieces and piling them at her feet. Minutes later, she extracted a cube of wax, its size barely fitting the hole, its weight sinking her arm as she hefted it into the open.

"What on earth? Haven't seen anything like this before," Joshua said, taking the block. Its heft surprised him. "It's got some weight..."

Avi turned to the group, his voice low and urgent. "We should go now that we have the item. We don't want to risk attracting attention from the authorities."

The team piled into the SUV and began their journey back toward a safehouse in Jerusalem, desperate to secure their find.

But not far from the Israeli border, Amina remained on the side of the road, surrounded by ISIS fighters.

"What did it say?" they demanded, hammering her with questions, but Amina's response stayed steady: "I don't know." Finally, exasperated, they bound her wrists and threw her back into the truck.

"We'll see what you *do* know," one snarled as the engines roared to life, the convoy speeding toward the location Amina had reluctantly surrendered, the team's starting point from earlier that evening.

ISIS trucks soon encircled the compromised safehouse, fighters poised in the shadows, ready to intercept anyone approaching and seize the artifacts.

Inside the team's SUV, Avi's phone buzzed with an alert. He handed it to Tal. "Look this over, I think our site's compromised."

Tal studied the video feed of the area around the safehouse. "Yep, definitely movement near the house. We need to shift to the backup site."

As they drove past the driveway of the original safehouse, nothing seemed amiss from the road.

"They're set in good, then," Tal muttered. "We're heading to another spot, it'll be another twenty minutes. Hang on."

The sun crept up, the eastern sky glowing faintly, casting a cautious sense of safety over the team. Avi radioed the rabbi to report the venue change and confirm the item was secure. Inside the vehicle, conversation was scarce. Two ambushes had already rattled them, and with the safehouse compromised, uncertainty gnawed at their minds. How much had Amina told ISIS? How much did she even know to tell?

But as the dawn warmed the air, Joshua noticed something troubling. The wax cube in his lap was softening, its edges blurring in the rising heat. "Uh, guys," he said, lifting it carefully, "this thing's starting to melt."

Noa leaned over, eyes wide. "We need to cool it down, now. If it melts, we could lose whatever's inside."

Tal swore under his breath. "There's a cooler in the back, grab it. Use the ice from the water bottles."

Joshua fumbled to secure the cube, but as he shifted it, a faint crack split the wax, revealing a glint of metal inside. His breath caught. "Wait, there's something in here. Metal, maybe a tablet or a key."

Avi glanced back, jaw tight. "We can't stop now. The backup site's close. There's shade and tools there. Keep it steady."

But the wax softened faster, beads dripping onto Joshua's hands. "It's not going to hold," he muttered, panic creeping in. "We need to get it out now."

Noa dug into her pack, pulling out a multitool. "Let me try." She chipped at the wax with steady hands, despite the jeep's jostling. Flakes fell away, exposing more of the metal, a small tablet etched with faint Aramaic script. "It's a message," she whispered, squinting at the text. "Something about... 'where the river bends twice, the prophet's mantle rests.'"

Joshua's pulse raced. "Another clue. Maybe Elijah's mantle, linked to the scrolls."

Before they could process it, Avi's phone buzzed again, a text from an unknown number: *Backup site compromised. Do not approach.* The team exchanged tense looks.

"Who sent that?" Tal snapped.

"No clue," Avi said, gripping the wheel harder. "But we can't risk it. If the backup's a trap, we're out of safe spots."

Noa scanned the horizon, where the sun's rays broke over the hills. "We need a new plan, fast. The wax is melting, ISIS is on our tail, and now the backup's off the table."

Joshua clutched the tablet, its weight grounding him. "There's a monastery near Jericho, old Byzantine site. It's off the grid, might have a crypt or vault to stash this. We can regroup there, decode the clue."

Tal nodded, veering onto a side road. "Risky, but better than an ambush. Let's move."

21

Sanctuary Under Siege

The world jolted awake to a seismic shift. News of Elijah's mantle, secured in Israel, blazed across screens and pulpits, a biblical relic reborn. Synagogues swelled with hushed prayers, churches brimmed with seekers, the Israel Museum's claim a thunderclap reshaping faith's fragile edges. Dr. Khalil, Father Nance, and Rabbi Cohen stood as its heralds, their voices lending weight to a find that could rewrite history. But beneath the awe, shadows coiled. ISIS, and perhaps others, were bent on burying the truth to shield the religious order they'd kill to keep.

Joshua, Masa to his crew, trudged on, blind to the storm breaking beyond their reach. The wax cube, its metal tablet etched with Aramaic secrets, weighed heavy in his pack as they slipped into a Byzantine chapel near Jericho. Candlelight danced across ancient stone, the steps of Joshua, Noa, Tal, and Avi, echoing in the stillness, a fragile refuge from the chaos hunting them.

His phone buzzed, a relentless pulse of missed calls and texts from his family.

"Joshua, they're freaking out," Noa said, her voice soft but sharp, nodding at the screen.

Guilt twisted his gut, his jaw tightening. "I'll call when we're safe," he muttered, the word tasting hollow.

Cut off from the world's clamor, they moved to the sanctuary, its air thick with incense and time.

Avi set the cube on the altar, wax softening in the heat. "We crack it now, or we lose it," he said urgently.

Noa chipped away with her multitool, flakes falling to reveal Aramaic script: *Where the river bends twice, the prophet's mantle rests... hidden fire waits.* "Anyone read Aramaic?" Noa laughed, nerves fraying.

Then Avi's phone buzzed, a text: *They're coming. Get out now.* No name, just dread sinking the chapel's peace.

"ISIS?" Noa's voice tightened, adrenaline spiking.

"Or the mole," Tal growled, pistol in hand.

Joshua grabbed the tablet, its chill steadying him as candles flickered low. "Who knew we were here? This was a backup's backup, random as it gets." His mind raced, the thesis-turned-death-game spiraling out of control.

"Even if Amina's the mole, she didn't know this spot," Noa said, pacing the sanctuary's stone floor, her voice sharp as she ticked off possibilities. "Who'd you call, Avi?"

"Father Nance, he suggested it. Rabbi doesn't know squat. Jeep, now." Avi bolted out the side door, the engine roaring to life as the team piled in.

Joshua and Noa traded jittery glances, the tablet's weight pressing against Joshua's bruised ribs, a relentless reminder of their spiraling stakes.

"Israel Museum," Avi barked at Tal, his tone clipped, eyes scanning the shadowed streets beyond the chapel. "Fastest route, the father and rabbi are there, and they don't expect us."

"Got it," Tal replied, peeling out, tires screaming through Jericho's tight, dusty lanes, the jeep lurching as it dodged a cart of overripe figs abandoned in the dawn's chaos.

Joshua gripped the tablet tighter, its Aramaic script burning in his mind. "This started as a thesis," he muttered, voice trembling. "Now it's life or death."

Noa's hand brushed his shoulder, a fleeting anchor, her eyes fixed ahead, wary.

Minutes after the jeep vanished into the haze, a truck screeched to a halt outside the chapel, masked men spilling out, rifles trained on the weathered doors. Dust swirled, the morning sun glinting off barrels as they fanned out, silent and predatory.

In Jerusalem's Templar house, Paul hunched over a screen in the planning room, the grainy feed showing the chapel's empty facade. He dialed a number, voice curt. "Come out, hand it over," he said, hanging up with a scowl. "Voicemail," he muttered to a shadowed figure by the door.

ISIS trucks rumbled up moments later, engines growling against the city's waking hum. They dumped a bound, blindfolded Amina at the Templar door, her body slumping to the cobblestones as tires spat gravel and peeled away. The alert bell clanged, a harsh, metallic cry, and Gideon flung the door open, staring at her crumpled form, her pendant dangling loose, smeared with dust and blood.

"Help, now!" Gideon shouted, voice cracking as he hauled Amina's limp weight into his arms.

Thomas thundered down from a middle floor, stone steps shuddering under his boots, his face a mask of confusion. "What's going on?" he demanded, oblivious to the conflicts tightening around them.

Eli emerged from the planning room, silhouette sharp against flickering oil lamps, expression cold as flint. "Bring her up," he ordered, low and commanding. "We need to discuss something."

Gideon heaved Amina into a wooden chair, her wrists bound, head lolling as he stepped back, uncertain.

Eli waved him off. "Leave us."

Gideon hesitated then retreated, Thomas trailing with a muttered curse. The door thudded shut, leaving Eli and Paul alone with Amina, the air thick with suspicion and sweat.

Paul loomed over a map-strewn table, Qumran, Bethabara, Wadi al-Kharrar pinned in a chaotic tapestry, translations of scrolls, dossiers on the team with question marks beside Tal and Avi's names.

"What's the status, Paul?" Eli asked, pacing from Amina's chair to the screen. "Last I heard, they were at a backup site."

Paul's jaw tightened, fingers drumming the table. "Eli, we need to question her and get rid of her, one way or another." He knelt before Amina, her breath shallow, eyes fluttering beneath the blindfold. "Amina, what do you know?"

"Nothing," she mumbled, words slurring through cracked lips. "The team got away... with the last scroll."

Paul's eyes narrowed, flicking to Eli. "So we don't even know if they found anything at that chapel? We could still be chasing the scroll from Wadi al-Kharrar." He stood, frustration simmering. "We need to find out if the mercs know more than they told us. She's useless like this."

Eli crossed to the screen, its feed showing the chapel truck pulling away, empty-handed. "She's a liability," he said, tone icy. "But she might have a use. If they've got a new find, a tablet, a clue, she could've seen it. Press her harder."

The jeep tore through Jericho's backstreets, Tal weaving past hawkers and stray dogs, the sun climbing higher, heat seeping through the cracked windshield.

Joshua's phone buzzed again, Emily's text: *Masa, you're on CNN! Call us!* He silenced it, guilt gnawing deeper, but the tablet anchored him. "Father Nance," he said, voice tight. "If he's the leak, why send us here just to tip them off?"

"He might not be," Noa countered, multitool in hand, wax flakes dusting her lap. "Could be Paul, Eli's lapdog. Templars have the tech to track us, not ISIS." She squinted at the tablet, tracing its Aramaic. "This says 'hidden fire waits,' a trap or prophecy. Masada fits, Herod knelt there."

"Or Qumran," Avi cut in, eyes on the rearview. "River bends twice near the Dead Sea caves. We're not safe till we decode it." He swerved into an alley as dust rose behind, a truck, too close, horn blaring. "Company, ISIS or Templars. Hold on!"

Tal gunned it, the jeep jolting over ruts, a gunshot cracking the air, grazing the tailgate.

Joshua ducked, clutching the tablet, his grandfather's words flashing: *Effort beats odds, Masa.* "Museum's our shot," he shouted over the roar. "We can't outrun this forever."

Noa braced against the seat, her voice fierce. "Then we make it count." She paused, eyes narrowing. "Masa, maybe call your sister, keep calm. If we're on TV, she might have intel we can trust."

The jeep fell silent, the idea sinking in. A murmur of agreement rippled through. Tal nodded, and Avi grunted assent.

"Okay, I'll need a signal, maybe a free Wi-Fi hotspot," Joshua said, glancing at his phone, its bars flat. "Can't reach anyone with this."

Tal veered toward a bustling market, the air thick with cumin, diesel, and the tang of overripe dates, stalls crowding the street with faded awnings and shouting vendors. "Nice Wi-Fi and the crowd'll keep us hidden," he said, parking just shy of the main thoroughfare, the jeep tucked behind a stack of crates draped with knockoff scarves. "Anyone else thinking breakfast?"

Avi smirked but stayed vigilant, scanning the sky for drones or the glint of trucks they'd lost, for now.

Joshua hopped out, hotspot signal flickering as he dialed Emily.

Her voice burst through, frantic. "Masa! You're all over CNN. Elijah's mantle, John's scroll, crowds at the museum! Churches and synagogues are packed stateside, Muslim clerics are losing it, calling it a hoax."

"What do you mean CNN?" Joshua asked, the team catching his half of the call, enough to piece it together.

They were famous. News swarmed the museum. Global faith teetered, and the Muslim backlash hinted at why Templars might align with ISIS: a shared dread of relics uniting or upending their worlds.

Tal stepped out, returning with falafel wraps, his breakfast hint no joke. "Eat fast," he said, tossing one to Noa. "We're exposed here. Anything from that end?"

"You're famous," Avi replied, unwrapping his meal.

"Finally," Joshua muttered, jumping back in. They ate fast, grease staining their fingers as conversation sparked between bites: fame, religion, the museum overrun.

"It's probably out of the question to approach," Noa said, wiping her mouth. "They'll be watching it."

"CNN said crowds are blocking the streets," Joshua relayed, swallowing a bite. "Protestors, some chanting for the relics, others against. Clerics in Dearborn called it Zionist lies. Dad texted, said the imam down the street's preaching fire and brimstone."

"Fire and brimstone," Avi echoed, eyes narrowing. "Templars and ISIS might both want it buried, one for control, the other for chaos." He scanned the market again, its chaos a shield but fragile, vendors haggling over pomegranates, a motorcycle weaving through, the air humming with life and danger.

Tal crumpled his wrapper, voice low. "Museum's a trap now. Media, guards, whoever's hunting us. We need a new play. Masada's a haul, Qumran closer."

Noa nodded, studying the tablet. "Qumran's caves. We're sitting ducks here—"

Her words cut off as a faint whine pierced the market's din, a drone. Its shadow flitted over the stalls, too small to spot but close.

"Move!" Avi barked, dropping his falafel as the jeep roared back to life.

Tal floored it, crates toppling behind them, a vendor's shout drowned by the engine. The drone buzzed louder, a gunshot cracking from above. Templar tech or ISIS, it didn't matter. A bullet punched the jeep's roof, glass splintering over Joshua's lap.

"Down!" Noa shoved him lower, her arm shielding his head as Tal swerved into a narrower alley, laundry lines snapping overhead. The market was a blur of spices in the air, a donkey braying, faces turning, but the drone clung, its whine a vulture's cry.

"They've got us pinned," Tal growled, tires skidding on loose gravel.

Joshua clutched the tablet, heart hammering. "Qumran, go! We decode it there, lose them in the caves!" His voice cracked, but the call to Emily had lit a spark. Fame was a double-edged sword, and they'd wield it to survive.

Tal yanked the wheel, the jeep bursting out of the market's chaos onto a sun-scorched road snaking south from Jericho. The landscape opened, cracked earth and stunted acacias stretched toward the Dead Sea's shimmering haze, its salt flats glinting like a mirage. Qumran lay twenty miles ahead, a jagged scar of cliffs and caves etched into the wilderness, the ancient Essene stronghold where the Dead Sea Scrolls had once slept. The tablet's Aramaic, *Where the river bends twice, the prophet's mantle rests... hidden fire waits*, remained a locked riddle in Joshua's hands, its script taunting them with secrets they couldn't yet crack.

"Keep it off the main highway," Avi snapped, twisting to scan the sky through the shattered rear window. "They'll have eyes on Route 90, drones, trucks, whatever they've got."

The drone's whine faded then surged again, a black speck darting between wisps of cloud, relentless.

Tal veered onto a rutted dirt track, the jeep bouncing over stones smoothed by centuries of wind and rare flash floods. Dust billowed behind them, a beacon they couldn't shake. "This cuts through Wadi Qelt," he said, voice steady despite the jostling. "Old caravan path, narrow, rough, but it'll spit us out near the caves." The wadi's dry riverbed twisted below, its limestone walls rising sharp and sheer, pocked with hermit caves, echoes of monks who'd once fled the world, now a gauntlet for the team's fight.

Noa gripped the seat, peering at the tablet's etched lines. "We need time to figure this out, river bends twice could mean the wadi's turns, but the hidden fire part? No clue." She glanced at Joshua, his face pale beneath a sheen of sweat. "You okay, Masa?"

"Barely," he muttered, brushing glass off his lap, the tablet's weight grounding him. "Emily said the museum's a circus, crowds, clerics raging. If Templars and ISIS are in bed together, they'll kill to stop this from getting out." His pulse raced, the drone's shadow flickering over the hood.

Outside the Israel Museum, Father Nance and Rabbi Cohen stood shoulder to shoulder on the steps, facing a swarm of press, their voices straining over the clamor of shouted questions and protest chants.

"These finds affirm faith's roots," Nance declared, his cassock fluttering in the breeze, "a bridge between traditions."

Rabbi Cohen nodded, adjusting his kippah. "A testament to our shared history."

Dr. Khalil pushed through the crowd, his face taut, clutching his phone with Noa's text: *Chased. Every stop compromised. Templars with ISIS.* "Father! Rabbi!" he called, voice hoarse. "They're being hunted, shot at. Nance, you told the Templars about the chapel?"

The three froze, eyes locking. "I don't talk to them," Rabbi Cohen said, brow furrowing.

Nance paled, hands clenching. "I... I mentioned it this morning, thought they'd protect the site." His voice faltered as realization sank in. "My God."

Khalil shook his head, typing a reply: *Nance leaked. Don't trust either. Stay clear.* "Hope it reaches them," he muttered, glancing at the chaos, cameras flashing, a cleric's megaphone decrying "infidel lies" from the street below.

Avi's phone buzzed, Dr. Khalil's reply to Noa's earlier SOS. He swore under his breath. "Nance sold us out, explains the tail. Museum's off the table."

The drone's buzz sharpened, a second shot punched the fender, metal screeching.

"Faster!" Joshua yelled, ducking as Tal pushed the jeep to its limit, tires clawing the earth. Ahead, Qumran's cliffs loomed, dark mouths of caves promising shelter... or a trap.

22

Caves of Qumran

The jeep rattled to a halt at the base of Qumran's cliffs, its engine coughing a plume of dust into the predawn stillness. Joshua, Noa, Tal, and Avi spilled out, the wilderness silence wrapping them tightly. No drone whine, no truck growl, just the faint rustle of wind through stunted tamarisks and the Dead Sea's distant lap against its salt-crusted shore. An hour had ticked by since the market escape, and for the first time in days, the absence of pursuit felt like a weight lifted, fragile, untrusted.

"Clear for now," Avi muttered, squinting at the paling sky, hand on his pistol. The cliffs loomed, their jagged faces pocked with caves, dark refuges where Essene scribes had scratched their secrets two millennia ago, now a bolt-hole for a team frayed by flight. "Inside. Open ground's a death sentence."

They hauled gear, packs sagging with tools, the wax tablet's cold weight, and a dented jug sloshing what water remained into a narrow-mouthed cave, its entrance a choke point they could hold if pressed. The air hit cool and dry, thick with ancient dust and the sour tang of bat guano.

Tal flicked his flashlight across limestone walls etched with faint scratches, prayers, tallies, and pleas lost to time. "Home sweet home," he quipped then growled low, swinging the light to cast a bearlike shadow that hulked over the rock.

Joshua jolted, tablet nearly slipping, heart thudding. "Whoa—okay, Tal!"

he hissed, half laughing as adrenaline ebbed.

Noa swatted Tal's arm, glare sharp, lips twitching. "Idiot," she said, tension easing a notch.

Avi grunted, already pacing deeper, flashlight probing the cave's recesses, unfazed by the antics.

"Had to," Tal grinned, voice a welcome crack in the cave's weight.

Laughter flickered brittle, swallowed fast by stone, but it lingered in their eyes, a fleeting shield against the grind of days without rest. The cave stretched around them, its ceiling low and pitted, stalactites dripping shadows that pooled in corners. A faint breeze whistled through unseen cracks, carrying whispers of the past, scrolls hidden, lives spent in solitude, a sect's defiance against Rome's sprawl.

They settled near the mouth, exit framed in dawn's gray glow, the jeep's silhouette a sentinel below. The day dragged, sun climbing beyond the cave's shadow, heat seeping through the rock, a dull pulse against their backs. No drones hummed, no scouts crept, just survival's quiet rhythm, broken only by the scrape of boots and the rustle of gear.

Joshua and Noa hunched over the tablet, its Aramaic script a stubborn knot under their flashlights. "Where the river bends twice..." Joshua traced the etched lines, wax smudging his fingers, the words a lifeline. "We've got this, but 'hidden fire,' 'dove flies' it's gibberish without a key."

Noa scowled, flipping her notebook, pages scrawled with Hebrew from the Copper Scroll's cryptic hoard, Greek from John's fragments at Bethabara, Aramaic guesses from Wadi al-Kharrar's singed wool. "I'm tapped, Masa," she said, frustration biting. "You too. We're blind." She paced the cave's edge, kicking a pebble that skittered into shadow, its clatter echoing like a gunshot in the stillness. "Too much rides on this: ISIS, Templars, the world's eyes now, thanks to Emily's CNN leak."

Joshua nodded, tablet heavy in hand and mind, its edges pressing his palms like a dare. "Dr. Khalil's our shot. The museum, trustworthy, despite Nance's betrayal." He glanced at the cave's roof, imagining satellites overhead, invisible threads tying them to Jerusalem.

Noa hesitated, thumb hovering over her cracked phone, then snapped a photo of the tablet's surface. The signal flickered, faint from their Wadi Qelt relay, a lifeline stitched through desert static. "Hope this doesn't blow up," she muttered, pocketing it, her breath tight with the gamble.

Hours crept by, sunlight slanting to a bruised purple over Qumran's cliffs, the cave's coolness fading as evening pressed in. Tal rigged a barricade, loose rocks stacked with a tarp, a flimsy wall against whatever hunted them, while Avi watched, silhouette taut against the cave mouth, ears straining for the faintest crack of gravel. Joshua's stomach growled, the falafel a ghost on his tongue, but the tablet trumped hunger, its script a tether to his grandfather's spark, *Effort beats odds, Masa.* He ran a finger over the wax, tracing the Aramaic curves, feeling the weight of centuries in its grooves, a relic older than the Essenes who'd once huddled here.

Noa's phone buzzed, sharp in the stillness. They froze, eyes locking. "He's got it," she said, voice rising, scanning Khalil's reply. "Hid it from the museum's press circus. His Aramaic's rusty, not Nance-level, but he tried." She stumbled through the raw text, syllables rough: "B'midbara d'nehara p'nayim t'lata, t'chot tzela d'rama, m'tila d'navi sh'riya. T'reisar q'dam l'tzafona, m'khata d'dayaga sh'mira milay. Yona p'raḥ b'atra d'malka k'ra, v'nura t'mira b'uma d'bira l'dina l'ragiza. Tuvu, d'malkuta q'riva."

Joshua blinked at the guttural tangle, unease prickling. "Sounds cursed," he half joked, the cave's echo amplifying the words into something primal.

Noa read Khalil's translation slowly, "He says, 'Doesn't make sense to me, but might to you; you've been ahead all along.' Here: 'In the wilderness where the river bends twice, beneath the cliff's shadow, the prophet's mantle rests. Twelve paces north, the fisherman's net guards my words. The dove flies where the king knelt, and hidden fire waits in the cistern's depths to judge the greedy. Repent, for the Kingdom dawns.'"

Silence fell, the words sinking like stones into the cave's dust.

Joshua stared at the tablet, script alive, not a map, a warning, a voice across time. "Okay," he said, steadying, breaking it down. "First line, 'river bends twice, prophet's mantle,' that's Elijah's fragment, the singed wool from Wadi al-Kharrar weeks back, when we thought it was just a relic. Second, 'twelve paces north, fisherman's net,' that's here, Qumran, Dead Sea bends nearby.

The rest, 'dove flies, king knelt, hidden fire,' Masada, maybe? Herod's fortress?"

Noa's flashlight swept the cave, its beam slicing shadows over stalactites and worn stone. "Wadi Qelt twisted twice getting us here, cliffs all around. 'Twelve paces north' fits under the right shadow. Let's walk it." Urgency cut her exhaustion; they fanned out, pacing the uneven floor, boots scuffing dust that hadn't stirred since the Essenes fled Rome's wrath.

Tal counted, voice a low chant against the cave's hush. "Ten, eleven, twelve, here." He stopped at the northern wall, a ledge jutting under an overhang, shadow pooling dark even in their beams, a pocket of night carved into the rock.

Joshua crouched, heart pounding, brushing scree, grit under his nails. Then a glint. A rotted weave, coarse and brittle, half buried in centuries of silt. "A net," he breathed, freeing it, dust puffing like a sigh from the past. Inside, a scroll fragment, parchment cracked but legible, ink faded to brown, words sharp as if whispered yesterday.

Noa knelt, light steady, breath held. "Fisherman's net, John's words?"

Joshua unrolled it. The Aramaic was simpler than the tablet's, a voice cutting through the ages. He read, voice shaking, "I, John, son of Zechariah, born of Elizabeth's silence, cry in the wilderness, repent, for the Kingdom nears..." It trailed off. John the Baptist, raw, tying Luke 1:20's miracle to Luke 3:3's mission, a cry that echoed in Joshua's chest louder than the cave's stillness.

"John," Noa whispered, eyes wide, breath catching. "The tablet led us to him, Elijah's mantle, now this. Copper Scroll's shadow everywhere." She snapped photos, fingers trembling, the phone's flash a stark flare against the gloom, sending them to Khalil: *Found it. John's voice. More to come.* The cave seemed to lean in, its walls bearing witness, as if the Essenes themselves nodded from the dust.

Avi's voice sliced from the entrance, sharp as a blade. "Company, truck engine, half a mile. Templars or ISIS, time's up."

Tal hefted a rock, grimacing, flashlight clattering to the floor. "They're tracking us. Gideon, maybe. That drone wasn't blind."

"No, we lost it miles back," Noa snapped, frustration flaring, her voice bouncing off stone. "How'd they find us here? Following our trail?" She grabbed her pack, movements jerky, eyes darting to the barricade, rocks and tarp, a child's fort against a storm. "We need to go, now."

Avi nodded, decisive, shadow shifting as he stepped in. "Come on, I'll get us out. No drone yet, maybe we slip clean."

They bolted for the jeep, parked just below, its dents glinting in dusk's fading light, a battered steed waiting for its riders. Avi gunned it down an ancient Byzantine track, rutted stone snaking beyond the Dead Sea, a merchant's path to northern Israel, worn by sandals and caravans long silenced. The desert sprawled, vast and unyielding, but a vegetation belt clung to the wadi's edge: tamarisks, reeds, acacias masking their dust, a green vein threading the waste. Avi wove through, clearing the wall, tires clawing earth, the track's curves a labyrinth of shadow and scrub.

Joshua clutched the scroll, tablet beside it, mind racing as the jeep jolted over stone. "Masada, 'where the king knelt.' That's where this ends," he muttered, voice low against the engine's roar.

Noa's hand brushed his, fierce, steadying. "Then we make it. John's voice deserves it."

The scroll's parchment crinkled under his grip, its weight more than paper, a call that had outlasted empires.

Half a mile back, a truck bounced down the wadi trail, its headlights slicing dusk. Paul and Eli were grim silhouettes against the cab's glow, dust swirling in their wake.

"We need to catch them there," Paul said, voice taut, gripping the wheel, knuckles white as bone. "If they get away now, they're gone. The market was luck. Gideon's tip barely held."

Eli twirled a cross on his finger, eyes cold, calculating, the metal glinting in the dashboard's dim light. "You sure no one knows we're hitting them? If the government catches us shooting their guys, this religious war blows wide, Jews, Christians, Muslims, all at once." He leaned forward, breath fogging the windshield, voice dropping. "ISIS needs to stay blind too, keep their eyes off us. We're not their pawns."

Paul's jaw tightened, truck lurching over a rut, suspension groaning. "Gideon swore they're in that cave. He tracked their dust from the market turnoff. If he's right, we end it now." His voice dipped, edged with doubt, eyes flicking to the rearview. "If he's wrong, we're chasing ghosts and losing time."

The caves loomed ahead. They approached at speed but didn't see the other truck leaving the trail. They would arrive a few minutes late, finding nothing but tracks and a wrapper from a street vendor. Paul howled as if shot, frustration permeating the pair as they drove to the end of the wall and found nothing that would give them the information needed to chase them.

Back at the temple, Gideon received a call from Eli's sat phone. "We don't see anything. Amina is still here. But what could she offer?"

Thomas sat behind the computer, panning the satellite images looking for anything that might be a way out of the area for the other team.

The jeep's dust trail thinned as Avi pushed north, Byzantine stone crunching beneath, Qumran's cliffs shrinking to a jagged memory against the twilight. Joshua's pulse hammered, scroll and tablet in his lap. Noa leaned against the door, eyes falling in the subtle rumbling of the stone. The team hadn't slept in almost two days, and the physical effects were impacting everyone.

"Let's pull over and get some z's, I'm passing out, and I don't want you falling asleep behind the wheel." Tal pointed out the cover between them and the road. They hadn't seen anyone else.

Avi didn't argue. He simply slowed to a stop under a palm tree with high brush on both sides.

John's cry, Elijah's legacy, a map to Masada's fire. "Repent, for the Kingdom dawns," Joshua murmured, the words a tether through the dark, a whisper louder than the desert's roar. He fell asleep, the script running over and over in his mind, the feeling of missing something in connection from the Copper Scroll to John's words.

Tal stayed awake while Avi slept.

After a couple of hours, Avi leaned up. "Okay I'll get us moving again. Why don't you switch places with one of them in the back?"

23

The Net's Shadow

Avi eased the jeep back onto the Byzantine track, the engine's low growl a stark contrast to the stillness that had cloaked them for hours. Nothing had stirred since they'd stopped, no drones whining overhead, no trucks roaring through the dawn. He could have slept for a week, his bones aching with a fatigue mirrored in the slumped forms around him. The team felt it too, Tal's head lolling against the window, Noa's eyes half shut in the backseat, Joshua clutching the scroll and fisherman's net like lifelines.

Dr. Khalil's last message lingered in their minds. He'd taken refuge with Rabbi Cohen, Father Nance still under suspicion after his Templar leak. They were on their own now, pushing south toward Masada.

The ancient trail intersected a rough road about two miles from where they'd rested under that palm tree, its high brush a fleeting shield against the world hunting them. Masada loomed some thirty kilometers ahead, a jagged silhouette on the eastern edge of the Judaean Desert, overlooking the Dead Sea's salt-crusted shimmer.

Avi rubbed his eyes, fighting the pull of sleep. "Tal's going to snooze a bit," he said, voice rough. "Joshua, can you jump up here to give him room and make sure I don't nod off?"

Joshua climbed into the front, his leather backpack thudding beside him. "Got it," he muttered, peering out as the sun breached the horizon, its first rays casting long shadows across the cracked earth.

Avi started slow, scanning for anything, dust trails, glints of metal silhouetted against the light. The drive stretched quietly, the desert unrolling in a monotony of stunted acacias and wind-smoothed stone. Only as they neared Masada did the air shift, a faint hum of anticipation rising with the hill itself, an ancient site of defiance, its name echoing Joshua's own nickname, Masa, like a tree standing stubbornly in a storm.

The jeep's steady hum lulled Joshua's mind as the desert rolled past, the horizon sharpening with Masada's faint outline. Exhaustion dulled his edges, but the name, Masa, echoed in his head, tugging him back to a sunlit day years ago when the fortress had first planted its roots in him.

He was seven, sprawled on the worn rug of his grandparents' living room in suburban Illinois, the air thick with the scent of his grandmother's cinnamon bread cooling on the counter. Summer light streamed through the bay window, glinting off the brass compass his grandfather held like a talisman. Joshua's small hands clutched an old library book, *Masada: Herod's Fortress and the Zealots' Last Stand*, its pages yellowed, spine cracked from his relentless flipping. The black and white photos of the clifftop ruins had captivated him: ramparts baking under a relentless sun, the Dead Sea a shimmering mirage below.

"See this, Joshua?" His grandfather's gravelly voice cut through the quiet, his finger tracing the book's map of Masada's plateau. "Last stand of the Zealots, 967 of 'em, holed up against Rome's legions. Held out three years, built walls, stored grain, fought till the end." He leaned closer, his khaki shirt rumpled from a morning in the garden, eyes glinting with a storyteller's fire. "Herod knelt there first, built it strong, but those rebels, they made it a symbol. Defiance in the dirt."

Joshua's brow furrowed, the name lodging in his mind like a burr. "Masada," he tried, the word clumsy on his tongue. "M'sada?"

His grandfather chuckled, a deep rumble that shook his wiry frame. "Close enough, kiddo. Masa, short and sharp, like you." He ruffled Joshua's dark hair, the nickname slipping out as naturally as breath. "You've got that stubborn streak, digging for answers. My little Masada."

The memory shifted to later that day, out back under the gnarled oak tree. Joshua knelt in the loamy dirt, his chipped red shovel scraping at the earth, a garage sale prize he'd begged for.

His grandfather crouched beside him, khaki pants stained at the knees, guiding his hands to unearth a rusted bottle cap and a shard of blue glass. "Treasures, Masa," he'd said, grinning as Joshua clutched them like relics. "Just like Masada's secrets, waiting for someone to find 'em."

He'd handed Joshua an old map of the Middle East, its edges curling, and traced a line to Masada.

"Prophets and rebels hid their lives there, scrolls, hopes, everything Rome wanted to crush. Someday, you'll chase those stories yourself."

The jeep jolted over a rut, yanking Joshua back to the present. Masada loomed closer now, its cliffs stark against the morning sky, no longer a photo in a book but a real, breathing challenge. The nickname had stuck that day, Masa, a badge of his endless curiosity, his refusal to quit. His grandfather's voice lingered, a whisper against the engine's growl: *Effort beats odds, Masa.* This was his fortress now, its shadow calling him to finish what that backyard dig had started.

"Okay, here we go," Joshua said, his excitement betraying the weariness in his tone. "Remember, the temple's a tourist spot now, no need to draw attention."

Avi pulled the jeep off the track, parking it behind a low ridge near the base of Masada's cliffs. He and Tal dismounted, submachine guns slung under their arms, their movements deliberate despite the fatigue dragging at them. Noa followed, her multitool dangling from her belt, eyes sharp as she scanned the cable car station in the distance, its modern lines a jarring contrast to the fortress above.

The team climbed to the fortress, the walls crumbling with age, making the hints in the scroll's lines harder to decipher. They walked the inner perimeter, staying low to avoid the scattered tourists snapping photos of the ruins. Joshua's pulse quickened as they found an opening covered by rusted bars, a cistern, its dark maw leading down to where Masada's water supply once sustained its defenders. The air hung thick with ancient stone, moss creeping through the cracks, a damp breath from centuries past.

Staying out of sight, they recovered rope from the jeep, its frayed coils a lifeline as they rigged it to the bars. Avi went first, descending into the shadows, followed by Tal, then Noa. Joshua brought up the rear, the scroll and net tucked in his pack, their weight pressing against his spine. The rope burned his palms as he lowered himself, the cistern's walls closing in, slick with moisture and history. A few minutes later, they hit the bottom, boots splashing into shallow water. Tunnels snaked around the wet cellar, their echoes carrying the faint drip of unseen leaks.

Noa's flashlight swept the space, its beam catching on rough-hewn stone and patches of green slime. "This has to be it," she whispered, her voice tight with anticipation. "'The dove flies where the king knelt,' Herod's cistern."

Tal moved ahead, his light probing a tunnel that curved left, its walls narrowing. Joshua followed, the tablet's words looping in his mind: *The dove flies where the king knelt, and hidden fire waits in the cistern's depths to judge the greedy.* His grandfather's voice layered over it, *Herod knelt there first, built it strong*, a fortress now whispering secrets through the stone. Then, Noa's beam snagged on something, a shallow niche carved into the wall, arched like a small altar, its edges smoothed by time. Above it, etched faintly, a dove with outstretched wings stared back, crude but unmistakable.

"Here!" Noa hissed, her light steadying.

Below the niche, the floor dipped into a circular basin, its edges scorched black, ash dusting the stone like a memory of fire. Joshua knelt, his breath catching as he traced the dove's lines. "The dove's perch, where the king knelt. This is it."

Avi crouched beside him, peering into the niche. A glint flickered within, metal or clay, too shadowed to tell. "Hidden fire waited here once," he murmured, brushing the ash. "Whatever's left, it's ours now."

Another porcelain encasement, no opening so it would have to be broken. The impact of ruining a genuine treasure to reveal another was a real feeling of sacrifice. Joshua took a deep breath then threw the case on the ground. A small piece of a fisherman's net and another scroll displaying Hebrew writing this time. Joshua passed it to Avi, he looked at the letter. *The disciple who saw the dove follows the shepherd, hands grasping nets for men. Fire awaits the greedy where the waters call. Repent, for the Kingdom dawns.*

Meanwhile, Paul and Eli had seized the chaos of the ISIS ambush, sliding into the passenger side door of their truck. Paul got it started, tires spinning as he floored it forward. The middle ISIS truck split its fire between the two others, caught in the crossfire. Headlights flared ahead, IDF forces, responding to shots in the temple district, their sirens cutting through the din. Paul veered off, the truck lurching toward Masada, leaving the firefight behind.

As Paul drove toward the fortress, he grabbed his arm, seeing blood on his hand from a stray bullet that had grazed him. Eli wasn't hit but sat rigid, in shock over the unexpected betrayal. The Templar leader had only read about such combat in holy wars, glorifying it in texts. Now, the reality left him pale. The truck came to a stop at the bottom of Masada, and Paul stumbled out, climbing the steep path alone. He searched the ruins, spotting signs of the team's passage, fresh scuffs on the stone, a snapped twig near the cistern. Reaching the opening, he collapsed against the bars, blood streaking his side.

Down in the cistern, the team heard a shout from above, followed by the grind of Paul's truck engine. Dust sifted down as he stumbled into view, collapsing against the bars. "ISIS turned, Gideon's with them," he gasped, his voice raw.

Noa scrambled up the rope, reaching through the bars to press a wad of cloth from her pack against his wound. "You're one of them, give me a reason to trust you," she snapped, her glare fierce.

Paul coughed, wincing. "Gideon's the mole. Stole Joshua's notes in Amman, sold them to ISIS for gold. I knew, didn't act. ISIS double-crossed us, shot up the temple, ambushed us on the road."

Avi climbed beside Noa, his gun trained on Paul. "You sat on it? You're as bad as he is."

Tal joined them, his jaw clenched. "He's bleeding out. Let him talk, then we decide."

Joshua stood in the cellar, the fisherman's net heavy in his hands. Gideon's betrayal stung. Those Amman notes, his wild theories, now a weapon against them. But the net's weave spoke of unity, a thread through the chaos. He climbed up, meeting Paul's pained gaze. "You messed up, Paul. We all have. But this, it's bigger than us. We share it, or it dies here."

Noa's eyes flicked to Joshua, a flicker of respect cutting through her doubt. "Fine," she said, her voice clipped but resolute. "He's in but watched."

Paul nodded, relief shadowing his shame as Tal hauled him down the rope, his blood-slick hands slipping on the frayed coils. Above, the rumble of more trucks grew sharper, ISIS or IDF, the pursuit closing in, their engines snarling like beasts circling prey.

Joshua's breath hitched, the words igniting a spark through his fatigue. "John would be speaking of a disciple that witnessed both the dove and the shepherd, with the net a dead ringer for one of the fishermen out of Capernaum—"

The thought was cut short as gunfire erupted above. Bullets pinged off the cistern's edge, spitting stone chips into the dark. The team dropped back farther into the cellar, dragging Paul with them as chaos swarmed the fortress.

"Tunnels, now!" Avi barked, his flashlight slicing through the gloom as he led them into the narrowing passage.

The scroll's promise echoed in their steps, a rhythm against the damp stone, but the fight above roared louder, reminiscent of the rebel stand in 73 A.D. when Masada's walls held against Rome's legions. Joshua stumbled, Paul's weight heavy against his shoulder, the net in his pack a lifeline tethering him to John's ancient cry. The tunnel twisted, its walls pressing tighter, slick with moss and the sweat of centuries.

Tal's boots splashed ahead, his light bouncing off jagged corners as he scouted the path. "Keep moving!" he shouted, voice hoarse over the distant crack of gunfire.

The air thickened, the drip of water a counterpoint to the chaos above, ISIS fighters shouting in Arabic, IDF sirens wailing, a war breaking over the fortress like a storm.

Joshua's mind churned as they pressed deeper. The dove's perch lingered in his vision, the carved bird, the ash basin, the glint of something waiting.

John's prophecy wasn't just history; it was a map, a thread pulling them through Masada's depths. A shepherd? The Copper Scroll's riddles flashed back, its talk of shepherds' paths near Qumran, and his grandfather's voice: *Prophets and rebels hid their lives here.* Was John sending them beyond Masada, to a final piece that Rome, and now ISIS, couldn't touch?

Paul groaned, sagging against the wall, his breath ragged. "They'll burn it all," he muttered, eyes glassy. "Gideon, ISIS, doesn't matter who. They want it gone."

"Not if we get there first," Noa snapped, shoving him forward. Her flashlight caught a fork ahead, two tunnels, one sloping down, the other climbing toward a faint glow.

Avi paused, sweat beading on his brow. "Down's safer, up might lead out."

"Out's a fight," Tal said, glancing back. The gunfire spiked, a scream cutting through the stone, someone had breached the cistern's mouth.

Joshua clutched the net, its coarse weave grounding him. "The shepherd, John, is pointing us somewhere. We have to get off this hill, I don't think there is anything else here." His voice trembled with certainty, Masa's stubborn streak flaring. The rebels of 73 A.D. hadn't surrendered; they'd defied the odds until the end. This was their stand now.

Avi nodded, sharp and decisive. "Up it is. Move!"

They surged toward the glow, Paul staggering between them, the tunnel widening as light bled through cracks above. Bullets ricocheted somewhere close, the war spilling into Masada's bones, but the net's shadow stretched behind them, a fragile thread binding John's cry to the fortress's depths.

The glow brightened, revealing a rusted grate half buried in rubble, daylight seeping through. Tal kicked at it, metal groaning as it gave way. Beyond lay a ledge overlooking the Dead Sea, its salt flats glinting like a promise, or a trap. Joshua peered out, heart pounding. The shepherd's clue dangled just out of reach, on the other side of this war, and the fight above mirrored the Zealots' last defiance, years after John's scrolls foretold a kingdom greater than Rome's.

A truck screeched below, dust billowing as figures spilled out, ISIS, IDF, or both, it didn't matter. They were cornered but not done.

"We're not dying here," Noa said, her voice steel. "John's map ends somewhere. Let's find it."

The team slipped through the grate, the net's shadow trailing them into the light, a lifeline to the fight still to come.

24

The Shepherd's Echo

The team clawed their way out of Masada's cistern, muscles screaming as they swung around the fortress wall to a ledge overlooking the Dead Sea. The shelf jutted from the eastern flank like a broken tooth, barely wide enough for them to stand shoulder to shoulder. Below, the Dead Sea's salt flats glared under the rising sun, a cracked mirror stretching to the horizon. Joshua gripped the fisherman's net, its coarse weave biting his palm, dust whipping across the stone in the wind. Noa crouched at the grate's edge, peering down. Trucks screeched to a halt, ISIS fighters spilling out, black scarves snapping, rifles glinting. IDF jeeps roared in, soldiers barking orders, a snarl of chaos converging at the base.

"We're pinned," Tal said, voice low, submachine gun slung tightly against his chest. His eyes flicked to the drop, hundreds of feet, sheer and unforgiving.

"Not yet," Avi snapped, scanning the ledge. It stretched east, hugging the cliff, narrowing into a threadbare path snaking toward the desert floor. "That's our shot. Move!"

Paul staggered as they shoved him forward, blood-soaked shirt clinging to his side, breath shallow. "They'll see us," he rasped, but Noa hauled him along, her grip iron.

"Then we're faster," she said, flashlight dangling, useless in daylight. She had swapped it for the multitool, clutched like a weapon.

Joshua's mind raced, the scroll's weight heavy in his pack from the interrupted find. The dove's perch had been John's cry; this shepherd was his next whisper, pulling them beyond Masada. His grandfather's map flickered in his memory, prophets scattering secrets across these hills. They bolted down the path, boots skidding on loose shale, the cliff's shadow their only shield.

Gunfire cracked above, bullets chewing the ledge's lip where they'd stood. ISIS had breached the tunnels, and shouts echoed through the stone. IDF fire answered, a firefight blooming across Masada's peak, but it wouldn't hold. The team was a speck against the cliff, exposed to any sharp eye.

The path steepened, gravel sliding as they descended. Tal took point, his wiry frame cutting the drop with grim precision, while Avi covered the rear, gun trained upward.

Joshua stumbled, catching himself on the rock face, Paul's weight dragging at his side. "Hang on," he muttered, Masa's stubborn streak flaring. The wind howled, tugging at their clothes, the Dead Sea a silent witness below.

Halfway down, the ledge widened into a shallow shelf, a natural overhang cloaking them in shadow. Noa dropped to a knee, peering over. Two ISIS trucks peeled off, dust billowing as they circled the eastern slope, hunting for their descent. "They've got our scent," she said, voice taut, her breath visible in the cool shade.

Avi cursed, wiping sweat from his brow. "We hit the desert, we're done. Open ground, no cover."

Joshua's gaze snagged on a crevice, a narrow gash in the cliff, barely shoulder-wide, cutting into the rock. "There," he pointed, voice urgent. "Tunnels or caves, could give us a way out."

Tal squinted, skeptical, his shadow sharp against the stone. "Or a dead end."

"Better than a bullet," Noa shot back, already moving. She squeezed through, flashlight flickering to life, its beam swallowed by dark.

Tal followed, then Joshua, pushing Paul ahead, the wounded man's groans echoing in the tight space. Avi slipped in last, the crevice scraping his shoulders as gunfire faded behind stone.

The passage twisted, damp and cool, its walls slick with moisture that glistened in Noa's light. The air thickened, heavy with the scent of earth and ancient stillness, a stark contrast to the chaos above. It widened into a low chamber, stalactites hanging like jagged teeth, water pooling in shallow dips across the uneven floor. Noa's flashlight swept the space, catching a crude etching, three lines curving into a crook, a shepherd's staff scratched into the wall. Below it, a flat stone lay flush, edges too neat to be chance.

Joshua knelt, pulse hammering, the net's weight grounding him. "The shepherd's echo, John's mark."

Paul coughed, blood flecking his lips, his back sliding down the wall as he slumped. "Gideon knows, tracked your notes, Joshua. They'll follow wherever we go."

"Shut it," Avi growled, propping him up. "We're not dead yet." He nodded at the stone. "Check it, now."

Noa wedged her multitool under the slab, prying with a grunt. It shifted, scraping against rock, revealing a hollow beneath. A cracked clay jar was nestled in dirt, its surface pitted with age. Joshua lifted it, hands trembling as he brushed off dust, the chamber's silence pressing in. A scroll fragment peeked out, brittle but intact, its edges curling like a secret unfurling.

"Got it," Noa breathed, awe cutting her edge. She pulled her phone, snapping photos, the flash stark against the gloom, illuminating the shepherd's staff in sharp relief.

Joshua unrolled it gingerly, Aramaic staring back, John's hand, jagged and urgent: *The disciple who saw the dove follows the shepherd, hands grasping nets for men. Fire awaits the greedy where the waters call. Repent, for the Kingdom dawns.* His breath caught, the words igniting through fatigue. "Andrew, Capernaum?"

Noa leaned in, eyes narrowing as she traced the script. "The baptism witness, then Jesus's fisherman. Waters call, the Sea of Galilee."

Tal crouched, frowning. "That's north, far north. We're talking one hundred fifty kilometers."

"John's endgame," Joshua said, certainty flaring. "Where Andrew cast nets for men."

The chamber shuddered, boots echoing louder through the crevice, voices barking in Arabic. ISIS had found the trail. "Keep moving!" Avi barked, hauling Paul up, his blood smearing the stone.

They pushed deeper, the cave sloping down, walls tightening until a sliver of light cracked through at the end. Noa wove through, her frame slipping out onto the desert floor, the team scrambling behind her, dust stinging their eyes as they emerged.

ISIS trucks growled closer, circling the slope, their engines a low rumble shaking the air.

Tal pointed west, a wadi snaked through the desert, its dry bed offering scant cover between jagged banks. "That's our road," he said, breaking into a run, his boots kicking up sand.

They hit the desert floor sprinting, the wadi's banks swallowing them as gunfire erupted behind them. Bullets churned sand, ISIS fighters leaping from trucks, black shapes stark against the sun. IDF jeeps swerved in, a three-way clash igniting at Masada's base, chaos buying seconds. The wadi twisted, its walls rising as they pushed west, the sun climbing higher, baking the earth beneath their feet.

Joshua's legs burned, Paul's weight a relentless drag, but the net's shadow spurred him, John's voice threading through dust.

"The jeep's around that corner," Noa panted, glancing back, eyes sharp against the glare. "Points the way around the cliff, if we make it, we'll find the next step."

A drone whined overhead, its buzz slicing through gunfire, a Templar scout, Eli shaking off shock.

Paul's head lolled, voice slurring through pain. "Eli's alive, won't stop..."

Avi fired upward, the drone veering off in a sharp arc, but it had marked them. "They've got eyes," he growled, sweat streaking his face. The wadi forked, left to open desert, right climbing back toward the cliff's corner where the jeep waited. "Right!"

They veered, scrambling up the incline, rocks tumbling underfoot, the air thick with dust and heat. The hill crested into a plateau, scrub and boulders dotting the expanse between them and the jeep, parked where they'd left it, behind the ridge.

"In!" Noa shouted, diving for the passenger side, her boots sliding on loose gravel.

They piled inside, Paul collapsing against the door, blood dripping to the floor, staining the cracked leather.

Avi peeked through a gap. ISIS trucks roared into the wadi, IDF trailing in a haze of dust, the drone circling back with a relentless hum. "Boxed," he said, voice grim, his knuckles white on his gun.

Joshua clutched the pack, the scroll's lines searing: *Hands grasping nets for men, fire awaits the greedy where the waters call.* "We need a direction," he said, urgency cracking his voice, the jeep's stale air pressing in.

Tal checked his ammo, jaw tight, slamming a fresh clip into his submachine gun. "Then hold 'em off, buy time. Where are we going?"

Noa's head whipped to Joshua, her eyes fierce. "Say the last two lines again."

"Hands grasping nets for men. Fire awaits the greedy where the waters call," he recited, the Aramaic echoing in his mind like a drumbeat.

Paul's eyes fluttered, a whisper escaping through bloodied lips. "Gideon's close, saw him at the trucks..."

A shadow flickered against the cliff wall, boots crunching gravel nearby. Joshua's pulse spiked as Gideon loomed beyond the jeep's window, rifle aimed, gold glinting at his neck from ISIS's payout, a smug glint in his eye. "You're done," he sneered, voice cold as steel. "Hand it over, Masa."

Avi slipped out the front, circling low through the scrub, his movements silent against the wind. Gideon fired, a warning shot splintering stone near the jeep's hood. Tal seized the distraction, tackling him low, the two crashing into the dirt, fists flying in a flurry of dust and grunts. Noa yanked Joshua back, Paul groaning as the drone buzzed louder. IDF sirens closed in, time bleeding out like sand through their fingers.

Joshua gripped the net, Masa's defiance roaring. "Not yet," he hissed, diving for Gideon's legs.

They hit the ground hard, Tal pinning his arms as Noa ripped the rifle free, its barrel clattering against rock. Gideon thrashed, gold chain snapping, betrayal bared in the dust as his curses filled the air.

Avi dragged him up, binding his wrists with rope from the pack, the knots tight and unforgiving. "You're finished," he spat, kicking the chain aside into a tangle of thorns.

They exhaled, regaining composure, the jeep's engine rumbling as Tal fired it up.

"Capernaum!" Noa shouted, slamming the door. "Let's go."

"Good a place as any," Tal replied, swinging into the driver's seat, hands steady on the wheel. "We leaving him?" He jerked a thumb at Gideon, sprawled in the dirt.

"Yep," Avi said, climbing in, his tone flat with disgust. "Never liked Templar scum anyway."

"Okay," Joshua said, turning to Noa as the jeep lurched forward, weaving around the cliff wall, tires spinning as they fought to outrun the ISIS trucks. "Why Capernaum?"

"Hands grasping nets for men. Fire awaits the greedy where the waters call," she repeated, Joshua nodding as it clicked, the words aligning like stars. "What disciple witnessed the baptism as John's disciple then followed the shepherd, Jesus?"

"Andrew comes to mind," Joshua said, gears turning, the net's significance flaring bright.

"Yes, his occupation?" She didn't wait. "Fisherman." She leaned back, the reveal landing hard, her voice cutting through the jeep's roar. "Capernaum's his home, where Jesus called him and the others to be fishers of men."

The jeep roared on, Tal pushing it north through scrub and sand, the wadi fading behind as the desert stretched wide. Joshua's breath steadied, the net's weight anchoring him against the jostling ride. Andrew, the dove's witness at the Jordan, John's disciple, Jesus's fisherman, tied it together. Capernaum, by the Sea of Galilee, where waters called and fire waited, a beacon to the north. "That's John's endgame," he said, voice firm, the scroll's promise pulsing in his chest.

Avi glanced back, ISIS dust clouds shrinking but relentless on the horizon. "Long haul, they'll chase us the whole way."

"Then we don't stop," Noa said, checking Paul's pulse, weak but stubborn, his chest rising shallowly. "John's shepherd leads to Capernaum, let's follow."

The jeep thundered across the desert, the net's shadow stretching long, a fragile thread binding John's echo to the fight ahead, Capernaum burning on the horizon.

Behind them, chaos reigned at the plateau's edge. ISIS trucks idled, engines growling, as fighters circled Gideon where he knelt, wrists bound, dust caking his face. They'd halted their pursuit, rifles trained on him as a scarred leader barked questions in Arabic, his voice sharp with suspicion.

Gideon glared back, spitting defiance. "Set me free, now! You've got no play without me."

Eli emerged from the haze not far off, his drone feed flickering on a handheld screen clipped to his belt. He'd watched it unfold, the jeep's escape, Gideon's fall, his mind racing to salvage the mess. Hands raised in a defensive arc, he approached slowly, boots crunching over gravel, voice steady despite the guns. "I think there's room for a deal here. Neither of us profit from anything more being released."

The ISIS leader turned, eyes narrowing under his scarf, rifle steady as he sized Eli up. "You're Templar. Why should we trust you?" His tone was cold, but curiosity lingered, a crack in his resolve.

Eli kept his hands high, his cross glinting faintly at his neck. "Because we both lose if those scrolls hit the light. Joshua's team, they're stirring a fire we can't control. Gideon knows their path; I know their goal. We stop them together, we bury this."

Gideon's jaw twitched, his silence a snarl as he strained against the ropes. "You're fools," he spat, dust grinding between his teeth. "They're already gone. Capernaum's next, and you'll never catch them."

The leader's gaze flicked between them, weighing the gold chain in the dirt against Eli's calm plea. "Capernaum?" he echoed, suspicion hardening. "What's there?"

"John's last secret," Eli said, voice low, almost reverent. "A fire to burn us all if it gets out. We split it, your gold, my silence. Deal?"

The ISIS fighter hesitated, rifle dipping slightly, the drone's hum a steady pulse overhead. Gideon's eyes burned, but he stayed mute, the gold at his feet glinting like a broken promise. A fragile truce hung in the desert heat, dust swirling as the jeep's trail faded north, Capernaum a distant flame drawing nearer with every mile.

25

The Road North

The jeep roared north through the Judaean Desert, its engine a steady growl against the fading echoes of Masada's chaos. Dust swirled in their wake, the Dead Sea's salt flats shrinking behind as the landscape flattened into a blur of scrub and stone. Joshua gripped the net, its coarse weave a lifeline in his lap, the scroll fragment's weight pressing against his spine. *The disciple who saw the dove follows the shepherd, hands grasping nets for men. Fire awaits the greedy where the waters call. Repent, for the Kingdom dawns.* Capernaum burned on the horizon, 150 kilometers away, a beacon pulling them through the haze.

The tide of action had subsided, the gunfire and drones of Masada swallowed by distance, but tension clung like damp heat. Paul slumped against the passenger door, blood-soaked shirt crusting dark, his breath a shallow rasp. The wound had stopped bleeding, stanched by Noa's makeshift bandage back on the plateau, but he'd lost too much, his face pale, eyes fluttering beneath bruised lids. He was a ghost of the man who'd stumbled into the cistern, his Templar secrets bleeding out with him.

"Jericho's close," Avi said, voice rough from the driver's seat, eyes flicking to the rearview mirror. "Ten kilometers. We drop him there, hospital's our best shot."

Tal nodded from the back, submachine gun cradled across his knees, his jaw tight. "He's fading. We can't drag him to Capernaum like this."

Joshua glanced at Paul, guilt gnawing at him. The man had betrayed them, sat on Gideon's treachery in Amman, but he'd also crawled to Masada, bleeding, to warn them. Redemption or desperation, it didn't matter now; he was dying. "He's fought this far," Joshua said, voice low. "We owe him a chance."

Noa, beside Joshua in the front, adjusted the map on her lap, tapping her multitool absently against her thigh. "Jericho's got an ER, small, but it'll do. We're off the grid enough to slip in and out." Her eyes met Joshua's, steady despite the weariness etching her face. "Then we keep moving."

The jeep jolted over a rut, Paul groaning as his head lolled against the window. Darkness rolled in, the third day since they'd unearthed the mantle in Qumran, a relic that sparked this relentless spiral. Every hour since had been harrowing, drones whining overhead, bullets spitting sand, Gideon's gold-glinting sneer. Joshua's fingers tightened on the net, his grandfather's voice whispering through the engine's hum: *Effort beats odds, Masa.* Three days felt like three years, each moment a thread unraveling time back to the Essenes who'd buried John's secrets.

They rolled into Jericho as dusk bled purple across the sky, the city's lights flickering awake. The jeep wove through narrow streets, past date palms swaying in the cooling breeze and squat buildings casting long shadows, until they reached a low-slung hospital on the outskirts. Avi pulled into an alley, tires crunching gravel, the engine idling as they scanned for threats. The last drone, Eli's Templar scout, had buzzed them thirty kilometers back, its silhouette lost in the desert haze. Freedom hung fragile, a breath before the next chase.

"Quick," Noa said, hopping out, her boots hitting the ground with purpose. She yanked open Paul's door, his limp form sagging against her. "Tal, help me."

Tal slid out, slinging his gun over his shoulder, and together they hauled Paul from the jeep, his legs dragging as they half carried him toward the hospital's glass doors. Joshua followed, heart pounding, the net tucked under his arm like a shield. Avi stayed at the wheel, eyes darting to the mirrors, ready to bolt. Inside, the ER hummed with quiet urgency, beeping monitors, a nurse's sharp voice calling orders over the shuffle of feet.

Noa flagged a doctor, her words clipped: "Gunshot wound, lost blood, stable but critical."

The staff swarmed, wheeling Paul into a curtained bay, his blood-streaked hand slipping from Tal's grip. Joshua lingered at the edge, watching as they cut away his shirt, tubes snaking into his arm, the sterile light glinting off the metal. Paul's eyes flickered open, finding Joshua's, a ghost of a plea in them, *Stay alive*, before he faded under the doctor's hands, the beep of the monitor a fragile lifeline.

"He'll make it or he won't," Tal said, voice flat, wiping blood from his palms onto his pants as he turned away. "We can't wait."

Noa nodded, her jaw set, brushing a strand of hair from her face with a blood-smudged hand. "Back to the jeep. Capernaum's still north."

They slipped out, the hospital's lights fading behind as they piled back into the jeep. Avi gunned it, tires spitting gravel as they peeled onto the highway, Jericho's skyline swallowed by night. The drone was gone, the desert silent, but the weight of pursuit lingered. ISIS, Templars, IDF, all trailed their dust like hounds on a scent.

Noa laid her hand on Joshua's, her touch warm against his calloused skin, grounding him as the jeep rumbled north. Three days of life-altering encounters had forged something concrete between them: trust, maybe more, carved in the crucible of survival. "Masa," she said, her voice soft but piercing the engine's drone, "is this the end of the road?"

Joshua stared at the dark ribbon of highway stretching ahead, the Sea of Galilee a distant promise shimmering in his mind. "I guess there could always be another message," he said, his thumb brushing hers, tracing the lifeline there, feeling the pulse beneath. "Another find to chase. But it feels like our travel through time's catching up to the Essenes burying the scrolls, to John's last whisper. Capernaum might be it."

She squeezed his hand, a flicker of a smile breaking her fatigue, her eyes reflecting the dashboard's faint glow. "Then we finish it together."

Farther south, in Jerusalem, the museum buzzed with a different kind of tension. The day had been filled with inquiries, reporters, scholars, pilgrims, all clamoring to see the mantle and scrolls unearthed from Qumran and Bethabara. The staff held firm, citing preservation concerns, the items too fragile for air exposure after centuries in clay jars. But the excuse was thinning, and the voices decrying it a hoax grew louder across the Middle East, online forums, street protests, and clerics shouting from minarets. Soon, they'd have to relent to keep the find alive, to prove John's words weren't dust and fable. Father Nance paced the museum's back room, his cassock swishing, while Rabbi Cohen pored over a tablet translation, glasses slipping down his nose.

Dr. Khalil stood by the window, phone in hand, tracking the team's last message from Masada. "They're north," he said, voice tight. "Capernaum, if the scroll holds. But this..." He gestured at the locked case holding the mantle. "This'll draw more than we can handle."

Cohen looked up, eyes weary. "ISIS cells, those Templar fanatics, governments burying history, they've got the team on the run already. If we show this, it's a beacon. Every treasure hunter from here to Cairo'll join the chase."

Nance stopped pacing, his hands clasped behind him. "Or it's a shield, proof John's voice matters. We publish, we protect them by spreading the truth."

Khalil shook his head, his gaze on the city's glow. "Truth's a weapon now. They're racing to Capernaum. Let's pray they get there first."

Back on the road, Avi slowed as they neared a bend, the Sea of Galilee's shimmer peeking through hills, its surface a faint silver under dawn's creeping light. "Checkpoint ahead, IDF," he muttered, nodding at faint lights flashing red and blue through the trees. "They'll be looking for us."

Noa tucked the map away, her hand lingering on Joshua's, her touch a quiet anchor. "Side road, now."

Avi veered left, tires crunching onto a dirt track, the jeep bouncing through ruts as they skirted the checkpoint, branches scraping the roof. Joshua's pulse spiked, the net a steady weight against his chest, its weave a silent promise. The drone was thirty kilometers back, but Eli's Templars, or worse, weren't far behind. Paul's fight hung in Jericho, a thread they couldn't pull, and Capernaum loomed closer, its promise shadowed by fire.

Meanwhile, Eli and Gideon rolled into Jericho under the same dawn, their truck rattling over the city's edge, dust still clinging to their boots from Masada's plateau. They'd watched the jeep peel north, Gideon's wrists raw from cut ropes. ISIS had freed him after Eli's deal, a tenuous pact fraying at the edges.

"They're headed somewhere big," Eli said, voice low, eyes on the drone feed replaying the team's escape. "Only a few places fit. Capernaum's top of the list."

Gideon smirked, rubbing his wrists, the gold chain gone but his arrogance intact. "You're guessing. I *know*. Joshua's notes screamed fisherman, nets, water. Capernaum's it."

Eli shot him a look, his cross glinting faintly. "Then we find leverage."

Word of a wounded man dropped at the ER the night before had reached them, too perfect to ignore. They pulled up to the hospital, the hum of the ER broken by two sets of heavy footsteps cutting through the antiseptic air. Eli flashed a badge, forged but convincing, while Gideon loomed behind, his presence a threat wrapped in silence. A nurse, harried and oblivious, glanced up from her clipboard.

"Looking for a gunshot victim, dropped last night, critical," Eli said, voice smooth.

She nodded, pointing down the hall. "Bay three, surgery overnight. He's stable now."

The curtain slid open with a sharp rasp, revealing Paul in a hospital bed, monitors beeping a steady rhythm, relaying the news of life clinging on. His chest rose faintly under a white sheet, tubes snaking from his arm, his face a mask of exhaustion even in sleep. Eli and Gideon towered over him, their shadows eclipsing the light on his pale skin, the room shrinking under their weight.

A doctor stepped in, clipboard in hand, his tone clipped. "You family?"

"Close enough," Eli lied, his hands folding calmly. "Status?"

"Through surgery, bullet missed the lung, but he lost blood. Been recovering for hours, asleep for at least three more. Might talk then, if he's lucky."

Gideon's eyes narrowed, a predator sizing prey. "We'll wait," he said, voice a low growl, his fingers flexing as if itching for the gold he'd lost.

Eli nodded, stepping back, his mind already spinning, Paul alive was a card to play, a thread to pull the team back.

The jeep roared north of Jericho, its headlights slicing through the Jordan Valley's creeping dark, the hospital's antiseptic hum a fading memory. Paul's fate hung in the empty passenger seat, stable, maybe alive, a Templar thread they'd severed to keep moving. Joshua gripped the fisherman's net, its coarse weave biting his palms, the scroll fragment's weight a steady ache against his spine. Noa sat beside him, map folded, her hand brushing his, a quiet anchor in the jeep's stale air. Avi drove, eyes locked on the road, submachine gun across his lap, while Tal cleaned his weapon in the back, the metallic clicks a restless pulse against the engine's growl.

Hours bled into silence, the desert's edge softening into greener hills as Beit Yerah passed, the Sea of Galilee's tang seeping through cracked windows. Dawn streaked gray across the horizon, painting the landscape in muted silver, Capernaum's promise shimmering closer, seventy kilometers down, eighty to go.

Joshua pulled the scroll from his pack, its Aramaic jagged under the dashboard glow. "The disciple who saw the dove follows the shepherd, hands grasping nets for men. Fire awaits the greedy where the waters call. Repent, for the Kingdom dawns." Andrew's path, from John's Jordan to Jesus's Galilee, mirrored their own, a lifeline through dust and blood.

Noa traced the script, her voice low. "Synagogue or shore, Andrew's ground. Paul's map marked a cave by the water. That's our shot."

"Paul's map?" Avi grunted, glancing over.

"Stole it in Amman," she said, unfolding the crumpled sheet to show Templar ink, cryptic lines. "Masada was too late to use it, Capernaum's where it fits."

Joshua studied it, the net heavy in his lap, its weave catching the light. Three days since Qumran's mantle, a relic tying Elijah to John, now this scroll linking John to Jesus through Andrew. The thrill he'd chased, backyard bottle caps, Copper Scroll dreams, had curdled into survival, not just his but the team's, and the voices in these artifacts pleading to be heard. His gaze drifted to Tal and Avi, Mossad legends forged in Jewish defiance, now bleeding for words pointing to Jesus. Was it a crack in their faith, fighting for a Christian dawn, or a bridge to stories bigger than dogma?

"Masa," he muttered, the nickname a tether to his grandfather's gravelly whisper: *Effort beats odds. Prophets hid their lives here.* Those prophets hadn't just buried treasure, they'd left a legacy, a dominion he carried, not claimed. Tal and Avi weren't breaking; they were honoring truth, no matter whose God it served.

"Joshua?" Noa's voice cut in, firm, her elbow nudging him. "You're muttering. Stay here. This isn't over."

He blinked, Capernaum sharpening ahead, the Sea of Galilee a faint gleam. "Yeah," he said, forcing a grin, net steady. "John's running us ragged."

"Better than dirt-digging," Tal quipped, eyes flicking to the rearview. "Though I'd kill for falafel."

Avi snorted. "Dream on. Fire's waiting, hope it's not ours."

Joshua's laugh was brittle, steadying him. Stress clawed, with Eli scheming, ISIS trailing, and Paul's fate dangling, but the net's shadow stretched long, binding them to Capernaum. John's endgame loomed, and whatever fire awaited, he'd face it, not as a treasure hunter but as Masa, stubborn to the end.

The jeep rolled on, dust swirling, Capernaum a flame flickering closer.

26

The Fire at the Waters

The jeep crested a ridge as dusk bled across the Sea of Galilee, its waters a dark mirror rippling under a bruise-purple sky. Capernaum's ruins sprawled ahead, synagogue stones stark against the shore, Peter's house a squat shadow among basalt walls, the air thick with fish and wet earth. Avi eased to a stop behind tamarisk trees, their gnarled branches cloaking the vehicle, the engine ticking quietly.

Joshua stepped out, boots crunching gravel, the fisherman's net heavy in his hands, scroll fragment a steady weight in his pack. Noa flanked him, multitool ready, her breath misting in the cooling air. Tal and Avi followed, guns low, shadows stretching as the last light faded.

"Masa, move," Noa snapped, her hand on his arm, pulling him toward the ruins. "We're exposed. Synagogue or shore, pick fast."

He nodded, the scroll's lines flaring: *Hands grasping nets for men. Fire awaits the greedy where the waters call.* "Shore," he said, decisive. "Andrew's nets, Paul's map marked a cave."

They moved low, shadows among shadows, the synagogue's limestone glowing faintly under the moon. The lake's breath wove through broken arches, waves lapping softly, a deceptive calm before the fire. Joshua led, staying below the shadow line, the team hugging the shoreline's edge to avoid the moon's pale spotlight. The quiet was jarring, a stark antithesis to the chaos of every other find: Qumran's caves, Masada's cistern, the wadi's dust-choked sprint. Each step crunched softly on pebbles, the silence amplifying anticipation, a held breath waiting for the shoe to drop.

Small dark openings pocked the shore, shallow cuts in the basalt, some natural, some carved by hands long gone. Joshua's pulse quickened, the net heavy in his grip. Where would a fisherman place a shepherd? John's clues twisted through his mind. Andrew, witness to the dove at the Jordan, follower of the shepherd Jesus, casting nets for men by these waters. The cave had to be here, hidden where the lake's call met the scroll's fire. He scanned the shadows, eyes tracing each crevice, the stillness a taut wire ready to snap.

Noa crouched beside him, her flashlight off, relying on moonlight as she brushed reeds aside. "Paul's map showed a dip near the synagogue, low, close to the water. Could be overgrown." Her voice was a whisper, tight with the same unease that prickled Joshua's spine.

Tal lingered back, gun low, his silhouette sharp against the ruins. "Too quiet," he muttered, eyes flicking to the horizon. "They're out there, ISIS, Templars, someone's watching."

Avi nodded, scanning the ridge where the jeep hid. "We've got minutes, not hours. Find it fast."

Joshua's fingers tightened on the net, its weave a silent guide. He stepped closer to the water, waves licking his boots, and spotted a shadow deeper than the rest, a narrow gash in the rock, half swallowed by silt and tangled reeds, its mouth barely wide enough for a man. "There," he hissed, pointing, his breath catching. "That's it." Joshua dropped to his knees, brushing silt from the cave's mouth, the net dangling at his side.

Noa joined him, her multitool prying at roots, the lake's lapping a soft counterpoint to their quick breaths. The opening widened, dark, damp, a faint whiff of earth and rot seeping out. "John's pattern," she whispered, awe cutting her edge. "Jars in caves, Qumran, Wadi al-Kharrar, now here."

Tal crouched behind, gun ready, his voice a hiss. "Hurry, moon's climbing. We're lit up soon."

Avi flanked the shore, eyes on the ridge. "No drones yet, but they're coming. Move."

Joshua squeezed through first, the cave's walls scraping his shoulders, the net catching on jagged stone. Darkness swallowed him, the air cool and thick with mildew, the drip of water off stalactites ringing through the chamber like a distant bell. Noa followed, her flashlight flicking on, its beam skittering across basalt, smooth in places, pitted in others, centuries of water carving its mark. Tal and Avi slipped in behind, the passage twisting, narrowing, then widening into a low auditorium, stalactites dripping shadows onto a silt-dusted floor.

The cave wasn't nondescript. Its contours suggested use, but nothing screamed preservation. Had others walked here over centuries, pocketing what they found? Joshua's mind swirled with doubt, *Are the items still here, or are they in some nearby hoard?*, but Noa's steady presence cut through, her hand brushing his arm as if sensing his spiral.

"Focus, Masa," she murmured, keeping the crew calm. "It's here, look."

Flashlights swept the walls, hunting for a hint. In the back right, a stalagmite jutted up, its base hollowed into a negative space that formed a shepherd's hook. Joshua's instinct flared, his legs carrying him slowly toward it, eyes tracing its angles. From one vantage, the light cast a shepherd's crook onto the far wall, a faint, deliberate shadow. He pointed, voice tight. "There, it's got to be it."

Noa reached it first, Joshua holding still to preserve the angle. She pressed a rock just small enough to shift. It slid and fell away with a dull thud, revealing a hidden nook. *No one would've tried that without reason,* Joshua thought, the answer to his earlier fears settling in.

Noa reached in, her fingers brushing moss and mud, then the familiar curve of porcelain, jars, tucked deep. "Pots," she called, voice sharp with triumph. "Help me with these." She climbed atop the outcropping where the stone had rested, lifting the jars straight out through the narrow gap. "Someone really wanted these hidden," she grunted, pulling the first, a pristine vessel, mud dripping in splats as she handed it to Tal. The second bore a small crack above its muddy base, fragile but intact. The third gleamed immaculately but was missing its bottom. She passed it to Joshua with a nod. "There's more, grab my legs."

Tal and Avi anchored her as she went on her stomach, top half vanishing into the nook. Her flashlight beam danced inside, muffled grunts echoing back.

"Pull me up," she said after a moment, emerging with a leather pouch, its edges rotten but sealed, and a wooden shard caked in mud, its surface splintered. She brushed it off, revealing faint lettering, *NVS*, the *I* lost to grime, and two rusted nails protruding from its grain.

Joshua's breath caught, the net trembling in his hands. "Andrew's stash," he whispered, taking the first jar from Tal. He cracked its wax seal, porcelain chipping as a scroll unfurled. Greek, Andrew's hand: "I, Andrew, son of Jonah, followed the Baptist's cry and the shepherd's call. Here, where nets caught men, the fire of truth burns the greedy. The Kingdom dawns." Inside, coins glinted, silver, thirty pieces, unspent, a note tucked beneath: "The betrayer's price, untouched by his hands."

Noa opened the cracked jar, her fingers gentle. A small net fragment, its weave like Joshua's, and more coins, tarnished but whole. The third jar held the pouch and wood. Joshua lifted the leather, its rot crumbling, spilling more silver onto the silt, Judas's payment, hoarded not spent. The wood's *NVS* glowed under Noa's light, nails stark against its decay. "INRI?" she murmured, parsing it. "The thief's cross, the one Jesus blessed."

Tal's eyes widened, gun lowering. "Judas's silver, the thief's plank, John led us to this?"

Meanwhile, eighty kilometers south in Jericho, night fell heavily on the hospital. Paul stirred in his bed, the beep of monitors a faint lifeline.

Gideon, patience snapping, grabbed his arm, voice a growl. "Where are they? They dropped you here after fleeing. You must've heard something."

Eli touched Gideon's arm, steadying him, his tone smooth but urgent. "Paul, we're in this together. Think of your brothers and sisters. They've struggled to get us here. If this crew displays these items, all the sacrifice is for nothing."

Paul's eyes fluttered, morphine haze clouding his mind, the weight of what he'd protected slipping through. "Capernaum," he rasped, voice breaking. "Last place I heard... fisherman, something else. I was in and out."

"Perfect," Eli said, a glint in his eye. "Get better. We'll come for you after."

The pair bolted, Paul nodding faintly before his eyes closed again, sinking back into the fog.

Outside, an ISIS truck idled nearby, its scarred leader's dark face covering defiant in the waning light. He tapped his driver as the Templars stepped out, engines growling to life. They trailed Eli and Gideon north out of Jericho, patience honed by numbers, following to Capernaum's city walls. The moon rose, casting dim light on the shoreline, highlighting every disturbance in the sand.

Eli and Gideon entered the city, weaving toward the synagogue, but the ISIS leader grunted, pointing to the sea. His men crept onto a ledge overlooking the shore, spotting four sets of fresh footprints. They split, some flanking the rise, others tracing the tracks to a small cave opening.

Barking orders, two men crawled in, following the team's path within hours of their arrival. Flashlights swept the cave, its walls worn but unremarkable, a teenage hangout, not a vault. They emerged, shaking heads, the leader's tantrum erupting, shouts in Arabic, a fist slamming the rock.

Eli and Gideon rounded the synagogue, freezing as the shouting echoed from the shore. They watched the ISIS men crawl out, the leader's rage a beacon.

"Maybe we're not too late," Gideon said, voice low, a smirk flickering. "He wouldn't act like that if they'd found the prize."

Filled with a new sense of hope, the two stepped out to parley with their tenuous ally.

The ISIS leader turned, his scar casting a shadow in the moonlight, a gold tooth glinting in place of his front left incisor as he grinned, a predator's smile, cold and calculating. "We tracked them here, supposedly," he said, voice rough with an edge of doubt, "but all we've got is four sets of footprints in sand. Could be teenagers partying in a cave for all we know."

Eli's cross spun faintly as he shifted, eyes narrowing. "Or it's them, and they're still close. Paul wouldn't send us on a wild chase."

The argument flared, shouts bouncing off the ancient walls as lights flickered on in Capernaum's windows, the town stirring awake. The synagogue loomed silently, its doors shut tight.

"Fan out," Gideon snapped, frustration boiling over. "Paul wouldn't have named this place if it wasn't the endgame."

They split, scouring the town, Eli and Gideon glaring at inhabitants darkening doorways, demanding answers, their forged badges flashing in the moonlight. ISIS fanned across the shore and ruins, rifles low, their numbers a creeping threat. Shockwaves rippled through the community, curtains twitched, whispers spread, but no treasure hunters emerged. The rabbis' quarters stayed dark, the bell unanswered, the town a maze of dead ends.

The ISIS leader paced the ledge, boots grinding sand into the rock, his gold tooth catching the moon's gleam as he barked into a radio. Static crackled back, voices reporting from the northern ridge, nothing but wind and tamarisk shadows. He slammed the device down, spitting into the dirt, his scar twitching with each curse. "They're ghosts," he growled, turning to his men. "Comb the shore again, every hole, every ripple."

A faint whine pierced the night, a drone lifting off from their truck, its red eye blinking as it climbed, sweeping the coastline with a mechanical hum. The leader's grin returned, tighter now, as he watched its feed on a handheld screen, waves glinting, ruins stark, but no jeep, no figures darting through the dark.

"They can't hide forever," he muttered, fingers drumming the rifle's stock.

Eli and Gideon pushed deeper into Capernaum, their steps echoing off stone alleys, the air growing thick with the scent of olive oil lamps and fear. A dog barked somewhere near Peter's house, sharp and insistent, its chain rattling as a woman hushed it from a window.

Gideon kicked a loose stone, sending it skittering into the dark, his patience fraying to threads. "They're here," he hissed, eyes darting to every shadow. "Paul's word, those prints, too fresh to be nothing."

Eli paused, hand on his cross, listening as the drone's buzz layered over the lake's soft lapping. "Or they were," he said, voice low, a chill settling in his gut. "If they've got it, they're running. We need more than footprints."

The ISIS contingent spread wider, some wading ankle-deep into the Galilee's edge, flashlights slicing through reeds, others climbing the rise toward the tamarisk grove. A man stumbled, cursing as his boot sank into silt, the beam catching a glint, metal, half buried, but just a rusted fishhook, not a relic. The leader's radio crackled again, another truck circling north, headlights probing the hills, finding only goats and dust. His tantrum simmered into a cold fury, eyes narrowing as he scanned the horizon, the drone's hum a relentless pulse overhead.

In the town, a child's cry broke the silence, quickly muffled by a parent's hand, windows slamming shut as Eli's forged badge met blank stares and shaken heads.

Gideon pounded a door near the synagogue, wood groaning under his fist, but no answer came, just the echo of his own frustration bouncing back. "They're shielding them," he snarled, turning to Eli. "Or they're gone."

Eli's gaze drifted to the shore, where ISIS lights danced like fireflies, the drone's red eye sweeping closer to the ridge. A faint rumble teased the air, tires on gravel, distant but sharp, swallowed quickly by the night. His cross stilled, breath catching. "They're moving," he whispered, a predator's certainty flaring. "We're out of time."

27

The Narrow Way

The team had just unearthed the items hidden in the cave along the Sea of Galilee's shore, their flashlights casting jagged shadows across the damp basalt. The excitement was palpable as they inventoried the haul: Andrew's scroll, Judas's unspent silver, the thief's splintered cross with its rusted nails, a small net fragment tying it all to the fisherman's call. Joshua's hands shook as he tucked the relics into his pack, the weight of history pressing against his spine, adrenaline spiking so high they nearly missed the noises echoing into the chamber, boots crunching gravel outside, Arabic voices barking, sharp and close.

Tal scrambled to the cave mouth, peering through the narrow gap just in time to see a group of figures spill onto the shoreline, black scarves snapping in the breeze, rifles glinting under the moon. "ISIS," he hissed, sliding back, his face tight. "Too many, too close."

Frantic, the team huddled, minds racing through escape scenarios. Joshua's breath hitched, chest tightening as visions of bullets and blood spiraled. He'd dodged death too many times already.

Noa grabbed his arm, her grip firm, voice steady despite the chaos. "Masa, breathe. We've got this."

He gasped, the cavern's cool air suddenly suffocating, though it wasn't small, just felt that way in the moment. "Okay, I can't be the only one freaking out here," he wheezed, hands on his knees.

"The only one acting like a baby, Masa," Noa shot back, giving him a side-eyed glare, her tone dry but grounding.

"Not exactly the move I'd make to impress a girl, Masa," Tal chimed in, a smirk tugging his lips as he checked his gun.

"Ha, if we go, at least we go picking on Masa first," Avi added, his gravelly voice cutting through with a dark chuckle.

"Great, a bunch of comedians," Joshua muttered, steadying himself, nerves settling into a familiar jitter. "Now let's figure out what we're doing."

"I say we stay and fight it out right here," Tal said, nodding toward the entrance. "That wedge gives us cover. They don't have a clear shot."

Avi glanced back, frowning. "I agree, but we're screwed if they've got a grenade."

"Good point," Tal conceded, rubbing his jaw.

Joshua's limit for gallows humor was fraying. He needed a plan, not quips about dying. "Okay, let's be serious," he said, eyes flicking to the opening. "Any way to block it, make it look like there's no cave?"

"Hey, that's not bad," Tal replied, holstering his gun. "Here, help me with this rock." He pointed to a boulder near the nook, just small enough to roll.

Joshua and Avi joined him, shoulders straining as they heaved it toward the entrance, grunts and muffled curses filling the space. The rock budged a foot then two of the ten they needed, dust clouding the air with each shove.

"Guys," Noa called, her voice cutting through their racket. "Guys!" Louder now, sharp enough to snap their heads around. "When you're done with that, let's go this way. I found a way out."

The three froze, exchanging looks, then abandoned the rock midpush, its progress a futile tease. They followed Noa to the cave's back, beyond where they'd shifted the stalagmite's stone earlier. A narrow walkway snaked through the shadows, barely shoulder-wide, its walls slick with moss. It twisted upward, the air growing fresher, until it spat them out through a jagged hole between two weathered cottages on Capernaum's edge.

They crouched low, packs heavy with relics, peering through the gap. Moonlight bathed the town, casting long shadows from the synagogue at the street's end. Below, the shore crawled with movement, ISIS fighters fanning out, flashlights slicing the dark, their shouts a dull roar. Farther up, Eli and Gideon prowled the alleys, their silhouettes sharp against flickering lamplight.

"There," Avi whispered, pointing to the synagogue. "If we hurry, we can beat Eli and Gideon to it."

Staying behind the cottages, they moved methodically, timing each dash across gaps when the Templars' backs were turned, their steps muffled by the soft earth. ISIS lights danced closer to the tamarisk grove, oblivious. They reached the synagogue's weathered door, breath ragged, and Tal knocked, three quick raps.

A weary rabbi cracked it open, his eyes sunken, voice gruff. "No more for the day, come back tomorrow."

Tal didn't wait for the sentence to land, shoving through with a hand over the rabbi's mouth, silencing his protest. "Inside, now," he hissed, ushering the team in. "Listen, Rabbi, there's Philistines after us. We need to hide." He eased the door shut, the lock clicking softly as they slipped to the back, a cramped room just outside the living quarters.

The back room was a cramped sanctuary, its walls lined with sagging shelves of scrolls and dusty tomes, the air heavy with parchment and wax. A single oil lamp flickered on a wooden table, casting long shadows as Joshua slumped against a chair, his pack thudding to the floor. Noa stood near the door, multitool in hand, ear pressed to the wood, while Avi paced, gun low but ready. Tal loomed over the rabbi, who'd retreated to a corner, his gray beard trembling as he clutched a worn prayer shawl.

"Who are you people?" the rabbi demanded, voice a hoarse whisper, eyes darting between them. "Philistines, you said, barging in like this, armed, at night? This is a house of peace!"

Tal eased back, hands up, his tone firm but placating. "We're not here to hurt you, Rabbi. Name's Tal. We're running from trouble, not bringing it. Those Philistines out there? They're after what we've got, and they won't care who's in their way."

The rabbi's gaze narrowed, flicking to Joshua's pack. "What you've got? Thieves, then, looting ruins, stirring up chaos in my town? I heard shouting, saw lights on the shore."

"Not thieves," Joshua cut in, steadying his breath, the net's weight grounding him. "I'm Joshua, Masa. We're archaeologists, sort of. Found something by the lake, old, sacred. Scrolls, coins, a piece of wood tied to the Baptist and the Nazarene. They're hunting us for it."

The rabbi's brow furrowed, skepticism warring with curiosity. "The Baptist? John? And... Jesus?" He stepped closer, peering at the pack. "You expect me to believe you've dug up relics here, under our noses, while men with guns chase you?"

"It's true," Noa said, turning from the door, her voice sharp but earnest. "I'm Noa. We've been at it for days. Qumran, Masada, now here. It's Andrew's stash, Judas's silver, the thief's cross. They want it buried or burned, not shared."

"Judas?" The rabbi's eyes widened, hand tightening on his shawl. "The betrayer's silver, here? And you brought this storm to my doorstep?"

"We didn't have a choice," Avi growled, pausing his pacing, his silhouette stark against the lamp. "I'm Avi. ISIS is out there, fanatics with rifles. Templars too, some cult with badges. They'll tear this place apart if they think we're still on the shore."

The rabbi sank into a chair, rubbing his temples. "ISIS... Templars... and you, what? Heroes? Fools? This town's quiet. We don't need blood on our stones."

"We're not heroes," Joshua said, meeting his gaze. "Just trying to keep these stories alive. John's, Andrew's, even the thief's. They're out there because greed blinds them. Help us, Rabbi, and we're gone by dawn."

The rabbi exhaled, long and weary. "Dawn, then. Stay quiet. Those lights are too close." Outside, a drone buzzed, its hum a knife in the silence. He rose, shuffling toward a curtained alcove, his movements slow, deliberate.

The team settled, exhaustion creeping in, but his eyes flickered with something unspoken, doubt or resolve.

Unseen, the rabbi slipped behind the curtain, a small phone trembling in his hand. His voice was a murmur, barely audible over the lamp's faint hiss. "Yes, authorities, armed strangers in the synagogue. Relics, they say. Hurry."

He hung up, guilt shadowing his face but his jaw set firm. This was his town, his peace to protect.

Outside, Capernaum churned under the moon's cold glare, the Sea of Galilee's waves a mocking whisper against the shore. Eli and Gideon prowled the alleys, boots scuffing stone, the air thick with olive oil fumes and frustration. The drone hummed overhead, its feed empty, ruins, tamarisks, a goat blinking into the lens.

Gideon slammed a fist against a wall near Peter's house, the crack echoing as a dog's bark flared and died, hushed from a window. "They're here," Gideon snarled, eyes wild. "Those prints, Paul's word, too fresh. They're laughing at us, Eli."

Eli's hand tightened on his cross, calm fraying. "If they are, they're quiet about it," he muttered, peering down a street where lamplight flickered. "Every door's a wall, blank stares or slammed wood. They're gone, or this town's a vault."

On the shore, the ISIS leader's patience snapped, gold tooth glinting as he barked orders. His men waded knee-deep into the Galilee, flashlights stabbing reeds and silt. One slipped, rifle clattering, pulling up a sodden sandal. No relic, just trash. The leader's radio crackled, and another truck circling north found faded dust trails, nothing more.

He kicked a rock into the waves, the drone's whine swallowing the splash, his scar twitching as he glared at the ridge. "Ghosts," he spat. "Spread out, every cave again. They don't vanish."

His men fanned wider, climbing the rise, boots slipping, probing shoreline holes. A flashlight caught a rusted hook in seaweed, useless. The leader's fury hardened, fingers drumming his rifle, the drone's feed taunting with empty shadows.

Back in town, Eli pounded a synagogue side door, wood shuddering, but silence answered, just his fist's echo and a child's stifled whimper.

"They're shielding them," Gideon hissed, kicking dirt, badge glinting. "Or they've slipped us, again."

Eli eyed the shore, ISIS lights darting, drone buzzing closer. "We're chasing echoes," he said, a chill settling. "If they've got it, they're gone or too close."

Eli's voice carried down the street, frustration raw. "We're headed back to Jerusalem. If this isn't over, they'll go there anyway."

"There'll be a small contingent to make sure we didn't miss them," the ISIS leader added, voice clipped, giving away a nugget. "But we have to leave, our presence'll be reported to Israeli enforcement by now."

Inside the synagogue's back room, the team rested fitfully, the oil lamp's flicker casting jagged shadows on the walls. The search hadn't died. Boots thudded past, fists rapped doors, voices barked in Arabic and English, each near miss spiking their pulses. Hours dragged, the night a slow bleed.

"At this rate, they won't be gone by dawn," Avi muttered, gun across his lap, eyes on the door as another knock echoed down the street.

An hour had passed since the last disturbance, the drone's hum fading, shouts dying to whispers. With dawn a couple hours off, exhaustion won, three days of relentless chase crashing down. They slumped against chairs and walls, packs guarded, adrenaline fading to a dull ache, eyes closing despite the risk.

A sharp rap jolted them awake, dawn's gray light seeping through cracks, boots stomping, Hebrew commands barking outside. The door burst open, IDF soldiers flooding in, rifles raised.

"Hands up, now!" a captain snapped, eyes hard.

Joshua blinked, groggy, relics heavy at his side as cuffs clicked on wrists, Tal cursing under his breath, Noa glaring, Avi silent and still.

The local rabbi stepped forward, his shawl clutched tightly, guilt and resolve warring in his eyes. He raised a hand to the captain, voice steady but low. "Thank you, gentlemen. These aren't the threat. They've already left the town. These are the ones escaping them. Any chance you could help with an escort?"

The captain's gaze flicked between the rabbi and the team then softened a fraction. He barked an order, and the soldiers lowered their rifles, stepping back. "We'll sort it," he said gruffly then turned, leaving the front door hanging open.

Sunlight spilled in, the dawn fully greeting the team as they stirred, rolling over to rise, cuffs still biting but tension easing.

Not far off, in the synagogue's main chamber, Rabbi Cohen sat at a table, glasses low on his nose, sifting through the scrolls and silver coins from the jars, his fingers tracing Andrew's Greek script. Beside him, Father Nance hunched over the splintered wood, studying the *NVS* and rusted nails under a magnifying glass, muttering about crucifixion relics. Dr. Khalil rolled the jars in his hands, peering at etchings. *Deliberate shepherd hooks scratched into the clay or mere wear?* His brow furrowed in thought. Joshua stumbled in, rubbing his wrists, pack slung over one shoulder, the others trailing behind.

Cohen looked up, a wry smile breaking his stern face. "You're awake, Masa. Quite a mess you've dragged us into."

"Us?" Noa snapped, brushing dust off her jacket, multitool still clutched. "You're sitting pretty while we're dodging bullets."

"Fair," Nance said, setting the wood down, his cassock rustling. "But we've been tracking you since Masada. Khalil's calls, my prayers, Cohen's nagging. You've got half the Middle East in a tizzy."

Khalil snorted, placing a jar gently on the table. "Tizzy's mild. ISIS, Templars, now IDF? These pots..." He tapped one. "They're first, century, deliberate marks. Andrew's, maybe. You've stirred a hornet's nest."

Joshua sank into a chair, the net's weight a comfort. "We didn't plan this. Found John's trail. Qumran, Masada, here. Andrew's stash and Judas's silver, the thief's cross. It's not a treasure, it's the truth. They want it gone."

Cohen nodded, pushing his glasses up. "Truth's a weapon now. The mantle's already got Jerusalem buzzing with reporters, clerics, doubters. This?" He gestured to the relics. "It'll light a fire. Eli and Gideon'll be waiting there."

"Great," Tal muttered, leaning against a pillar, rubbing his arm where a graze had scabbed. "More fanatics. What's the play?"

"Escort," Avi said, voice flat, eyeing the open door where soldiers milled. "Rabbi called in the cavalry. IDF's our ticket out. Back to Jerusalem?"

"Exactly," the local rabbi interjected, hovering near the soldiers. "I couldn't risk you here. Too many guns, too close. They'll take you south, safe."

Nance clasped his hands. "Well, not exactly. He called IDF on the whole lot.

We just happened to get here to talk the good rabbi into leniency." His eyes on the wood, he continued, "And safe's relative. Templars want this buried, literally. ISIS'll sell it or burn it. Jerusalem's a gauntlet, but the museum's secure. We can publish, protect it."

"Publish?" Noa raised an eyebrow, skeptical. "After all this, you think ink'll stop bullets?"

"It'll spread the story," Cohen countered, tapping the scroll. "Andrew's words, Judas's shame, the thief's grace, too big to silence. IDF'll get you there; we'll handle the rest."

Joshua rubbed his face, exhaustion warring with resolve. "Three long days for this. Masada's tunnels, Capernaum's shore. If we're going back, what's the catch?"

Khalil smirked, rolling a coin between his fingers. "Catch is you're still wanted. IDF's not thrilled about armed foreigners. We've got pull, but you'll ride in cuffs till Jerusalem. Relics stay with us."

"Fine," Avi said, holstering his gun, voice resigned. "Cuffs beat coffins. Let's move before that contingent doubles back."

Cohen stood, gathering the jars. "Dawn's here. Truck's outside. You've done the hard part, Masa. Now we carry it home."

Joshua hefted his pack, the net a lifeline, meeting Cohen's gaze. "Home's where the fight is, right?"

"Always," Nance said, a faint smile breaking through. "Let's not keep the soldiers waiting."

Word of the team's safe retrieval and the IDF escort back to Jerusalem rippled fast, a whisper on the wind that sent ISIS melting into the shadows. The small contingent left in Capernaum pulled back, their trucks vanishing into the hills, the drone's hum silenced as Israeli enforcement loomed too close.

In a dim Jericho safehouse, Eli, Gideon, Paul—pale but upright from his hospital stint—and Thomas hunched over a grainy news feed, the TV flickering with images of an IDF convoy rolling into Jerusalem's museum district. The anchor droned about "archaeological personnel secured," but the relics stayed a glaring blank. No mention of scrolls, silver, or crosses.

"They've got it," Gideon growled, slamming a fist on the table, his raw wrists twitching. "And we're stuck watching."

Paul rubbed his bandaged side, voice weak but sharp. "No details. That means they're hiding it. Museum's a fortress now."

Eli's cross glinted as he leaned forward, eyes narrow. "Or stalling. Cohen's there, Nance too. They'll publish eventually, and we're out of moves."

Thomas, silent until now, smirked, a scar tugging his lip. "Not out, just late. Jerusalem's their endgame. We wait."

Meanwhile, the museum buzzed, a hive of historians and security, the team's truck grinding to a halt in its shadowed courtyard. Amina stood at the edge, arms crossed, her welcome smile faltering as soldiers waved her back. The inner sanctum, Cohen, Nance, Khalil, and a swarm of bigwigs, closed ranks around the relics, leaving her on the outside, peering through a glass door at the flurry of white gloves and hushed awe.

Inside, Joshua stretched, wrists raw but the cuffs finally off. The trip's quiet was a jarring shift from car chases and gunfights, scenes he'd pictured in a movie not his life. "Feels wrong," he said, voice low, slumping against a wall as Noa joined him, her multitool pocketed. "No bullets, no running. What's next, tea and medals?"

Tal snorted, flexing his arm where the graze had scabbed. "I'd settle for that nap. But this?" He nodded at the historians swarming the table, scrolls unrolled, silver glinting, wood under lights. "This is why we bled."

Avi stayed near the door, eyes scanning the courtyard. "Quiet's temporary. Eli's not done, nor is ISIS, shadows or not."

Cohen approached, glasses fogged from hours bent over the finds, a tablet glowing in his hand. "You're right, Avi. But for now, you're safe. IDF's got this locked down, relics too." He paused, eyeing their haggard faces, then added, "If you want, we can find you a place to sleep, or go get some food. This'll be a big process. You're not missing anything."

"Food?" Joshua perked up, a tired grin breaking through. "What I wouldn't give for a falafel from my guy in Amman. It's only been days, but feels like a lifetime."

Noa chuckled, nudging him. "Masa's got priorities, scrolls then shawarma."

"Falafel, not shawarma," he corrected, mock offended. "There's a difference."

Tal leaned in, smirking. "I'd kill for one, greasy, hot, with that tahini drip. Jerusalem's got spots. Let's move."

Avi shrugged, holstering his gun. "Beats museum coffee. Lead on."

Cohen waved them out, Nance and Khalil trailing, jars and scrolls left with the historians. "Café's two blocks. IDF's got eyes, you're fine," Cohen said, his tone dry but warm. "You've earned it."

They shuffled into the sun, badges clipped to hips, unneeded, their faces now infamous in this corner of the world. The café was a hole-in-the-wall, its air thick with cumin and frying oil. Falafels hit the table, crisp and steaming, and they ate quietly, the TV above the counter scrolling their names: *Joshua "Masa" Bennett, Noa Lev, Tal Ben, Avi Katz, Archaeological Team Secured After Galilee Clash*. No relics mentioned, just vague heroics.

Joshua chewed slowly, the taste grounding him. "Feels like someone else's life up there," he said, nodding at the screen.

"Better than a body count," Noa replied, wiping tahini from her chin. "Though I'd rather they spelled my name right, Lev not Levi."

Tal laughed, a rare crack in his edge. "Fame's a bitch. At least they got my scar in the photo."

Avi stayed silent, eyes on the door, falafel untouched. "Quiet's nice," he said finally, "but it's a lull. They're regrouping, Eli, Gideon, those bastards."

Nance sipped his tea, his cassock out of place amid the grease. "They are. But the museum's a wall. IDF's not letting anyone near. These finds..." He gestured vaguely. "They're already shifting things. Clerics are calling, skeptics too."

Khalil nodded, breaking a falafel in half. "Scroll's Andrew, carbon dating'll confirm it. Silver's Roman, first century. The wood? Nails match crucifixion specs. It's real, and they know it."

"Real enough to keep us running," Joshua said, leaning back, exhaustion creeping in. "Don't get me wrong, I'm thrilled we got it. Just feel like I could sleep a week."

Cohen adjusted his glasses, tablet dimming. "You could. But you won't. Back to the museum after this. We're cataloging, and you're the story. Badges or not, they'll want you there."

Noa groaned, dropping her napkin. "Fame's overrated. Can't we just send a memo?"

"Not how it works," Nance said, smiling faintly. "You're the faces. John's trail ends with you."

They finished, the café's hum a brief reprieve, then trudged back, sunlight glinting off the museum's glass doors. Joshua led, badges at their hips, but no one asked. Guards nodded, and historians stared. Their names were a quiet buzz. Inside, the relics waited on a steel table, jars gleaming, scrolls unfurled, the wood's *NVS* stark under halogen lights. Cohen waved them to a corner where chairs ringed a smaller desk, Nance and Khalil already there, papers and laptops scattered.

"Sit," Cohen said, voice brisk. "Debrief, tell us everything. Qumran to Capernaum, every step."

Joshua sank down, pack at his feet. "Started with the Copper Scroll, thought it was treasure, turned into survival. Qumran's mantle, Masada's cistern, Capernaum's cave, John's trail, Andrew's end. ISIS wanted it torched, Templars buried. We just ran."

Noa picked up, voice sharp. "Paul's map got us there, stole it in Amman. Cave had jars, scrolls, silver, that cross piece. Judas didn't spend it; the thief got grace. Fire's truth, not gold."

Tal rubbed his scar, smirking faintly. "Fought our way out. Masada was a soup sandwich, Capernaum a trap. IDF saved our butts, but it's not over."

Avi's eyes stayed on the door. "They're out there, Eli's crew, ISIS remnants. Museum's safe till they regroup."

Khalil tapped a jar, frowning. "This etch, shepherd's hook, is deliberate. Ties to Andrew's net. We're dating it now and should have results in days. This'll rewrite books."

Nance traced the wood's nails, reverent. "Thief's cross, Luke's account, real. Clerics'll fight it, but evidence doesn't lie."

Cohen leaned forward, tablet alive again. "Publishing's the goal. Spread it wide, kill their leverage. IDF's here, but we need time. You're staying as faces for the press, witnesses to the find."

Outside, Amina paced the courtyard, her shadow long against the glass. She rapped on the door, voice muffled but insistent. "Cohen, let me in! I've been with this from Amman. I deserve a piece!"

Cohen sighed, waving a guard off. "Amina, later. We're locked down. Process first."

Her glare burned through the glass, fists clenched. "You owe me! Khalil's calls, my intel! Don't shut me out!"

"Later," Khalil barked, not looking up. "This isn't personal. Security's tight."

She stormed off, muttering, her exclusion a raw wound.

Inside, Joshua watched her go, unease prickling. "She's pissed, but we can't trust her. She has switched sides back and forth."

Nance shrugged. "Right, ambition's her fuel. She'll push again. Maybe even go back to the Templars."

Noa jumped in, voice firm. "I don't care how she feels, I'm not trusting her at all. I'm worried she'll find her way back in with the Templar crew. She may do that then come back and be a spy, again."

Tal nodded, his smirk fading. "She's a wildcard. If she flips, we're blindsided. Keep her out."

Avi's gaze hardened, still on the door. "She's a leak waiting to happen. Museum's secure but not if she talks."

Cohen rubbed his temples, tablet dim. "Noted. We'll watch her, restrict access. She's got no leverage here, yet."

Hours bled into dusk, the debrief stretching as historians swarmed, cataloging jars, photographing scrolls, testing the wood's grain.

Cohen finally stood, stretching. "Enough for today. IDF's got rooms upstairs, crash there. Tomorrow's press and tests. Rest while you can."

Tal yawned, scar twitching. "Finally, that nap." He shuffled off with Avi, their boots heavy on the stairs, Tal muttering, "If I dream of caves, shoot me."

Joshua lingered, pack slung over his shoulder, Noa beside him. The museum hall was quieter now, historians thinning out, the relics glowing under soft lights. "Upstairs?" he asked, voice soft.

She nodded, multitool twirling in her fingers. "Yeah, but I need air first. Let's hit the roof, watch the city for a bit."

They climbed a back stairwell, emerging onto the museum's flat roof, Jerusalem's skyline a jagged glow against the twilight. The air was cool, tinged with dust and distant cumin, a relief after the day's sterile hum. They settled on a crate, perched to watch the sun's last hint vanish over the hill.

A desert chill swept in, catching Noa off, guard; she leaned into Joshua. "Survived," she said, half, smiling. "No bullets today."

"Barely," he replied. "You kept me sane down there, you know. Not just today, but the last few days, feels like a week." He draped an arm around her shoulder, awkward but warm, feeling her shiver against the sudden cold. Only days ago, they'd cracked the cave's vases, unlocking the scroll that led to the mantle.

She shrugged, eyes on the city. "Someone had to. You're a mess under pressure, Masa." Was it a jab or endearment? Tonight, it felt like the latter, but with Noa, he could never be sure.

"Fair. But you're not." He edged closer, voice dropping. "Been meaning to say, this whole thing, us, it's more than just the team now. Isn't it?"

Noa pulled back, eyes meeting his, sharp yet warm, a grin tugging her lips. "Maybe. You're not wrong. Three days of chaos, and I'm still here, not running solo. That's something." She leaned in again, the city's hum fading with the light. "Still not over you being a jerk in class, though," she added, grinning wider.

He laughed, soft and nervous, her quip hitting a spot he'd buried. "I don't even remember that. You weren't exactly rolling out the welcome mat. I was smitten from day one, and you turned my honest nickname into a stinger."

They both laughed, her edge softening. "Don't get cocky. But yeah, it's something." She started to lean closer, a confirmation brewing, but a buzz broke the quiet, Joshua's phone vibrating in his pocket.

He pulled it out, squinting. "Family FaceTime. Forgot I promised." He hesitated then tapped accept, propping it on the railing.

His mom's face filled the screen, Illinois behind her; his dad waved over her shoulder. "Josh! You're alive!" she half shouted, relief thick. "Saw you on the news. What's going on?"

"Long story," he said, grinning. "Found old stuff, ran from bad guys, IDF hauled us back. I'm fine, Mom."

"Fine?" His dad leaned in, skeptical. "You look like you haven't slept in a week, and your sister's mad you're ignoring her."

"Feels like a week," Joshua said, shoulders easing. "But it's over, mostly. Wrapping up here."

Noa shifted closer, peering over his shoulder, hair brushing his cheek.

His mom's eyes widened. "Who's that, Josh?"

A squeal erupted offscreen, his sister. "Is that Noa?"

"Oh, uh," he stammered, heat rising. "Yeah, this is Noa, my, uh, girl-friend?" It slipped out, half questioning; he froze, glancing at her.

Noa's eyebrows shot up, but she smirked, leaning in. "Hi, guess I'm the girlfriend now. Kept him from dying, so there's that."

His sister's face shoved into view, laughing. "Oh, I like her! Josh said you were ugly. He's such a liar!" As Noa's hand swung to swat Joshua's head, she added, "Kidding. He's had a crush since day one."

"Oh, Masa," they chimed in unison, giggling.

"Great," he muttered, red-faced. "Well, that happened."

His dad chuckled. "Better lock that down, son. She's tougher than you."

"Clearly," Noa said, nudging him. "Nice to meet you, even if he kept me a secret."

They chatted, his family grilling Noa, her quips keeping them laughing until the call ended.

Joshua pocketed the phone, sheepish. "Sorry, didn't mean to spring that on you."

She shrugged, grin lingering. "Not mad. Girlfriend's fine, Masa. Just don't screw it up."

"Deal," he said, relieved.

Their hands brushed as the city hummed below. They sat a moment longer, the quiet wrapping them like a blanket, Jerusalem's lights a constellation of what they'd fought for.

Back downstairs, the museum had stilled, the halls dim save for a few historians murmuring over laptops. Tal and Avi were gone, likely snoring upstairs, while Cohen, Nance, and Khalil lingered by the relics, debating in hushed tones. Carbon dates, shepherd hooks, the thief's nails.

Joshua and Noa slipped into the IDF-provided rooms, a spartan setup: cots, a sink, a window cracked to let in the night air.

Joshua dropped his pack, the net's weight a silent anchor, and sank onto a cot, Noa taking the one beside him. "Think they'll publish tomorrow?" he asked, voice low, staring at the ceiling.

"Hope so," she murmured, multitool resting on her chest. "If Amina doesn't screw it first. Or Eli."

He nodded, the day's weight settling. "Feels like we won, but not yet."

"Close enough," she said, a yawn breaking through. "Sleep, Masa. Tomorrow's another fight."

He smiled faintly, eyes closing, the city's hum lulling him under.

In Jericho, Gideon paced a cramped safehouse, the TV off, dust motes swirling in lamplight. Maps sprawled across a table, Jerusalem circled in red, pins marking the contacts of Thomas's network, shadowy figures from Amman to the Old City. "The museum'll give them a false sense of hope," he said, voice taut. "They'll hold out any real explanation till they've studied the artifacts to death. That's our window: find out what the experts say then grab and stash."

Eli leaned back, cross still, voice calm. "Yes, and the world won't believe it anyway. People need to see it, hear it from celebrity priests, rabbis, rock star documentary hacks. Patience and truth's their weapon, but it's ours to twist."

Thomas cracked his knuckles, smirking wider. "They'll lock it down, study slowly, days maybe weeks. Gives us time. My guy in Jerusalem's watching the museum, says it's a fortress but not airtight. We wait, hit when it's ripe."

Paul coughed, wincing, but nodded, his pallor stark against the dim light. "Let them dig their hole. We'll bury them in it. Amina's our edge. She's pissed, sidelined. She'll flip if we nudge her."

Gideon stopped pacing, eyes narrowing. "She's a gamble. Burned us once, could again."

"Worth it," Eli said, fingers tracing his cross. "She knows their moves, their weak spots. We get her in, she's our eyes. Then we take it, scrolls, silver, wood, bury it where no one digs."

Thomas agreed, "Museum's got cracks, guards change at dawn, historians sleep. We've got time to plan."

Paul smirked, pain etching his face. "They think they've won. Victory's a blindfold."

The room fell quiet, the Templars' resolve hardening, Jericho's night pressing in as their scheme took root.

28

April 10, 2025

Four days had passed since the team pried open the cave along the Sea of Galilee, unearthing Andrew's scroll, Judas's unspent silver, and the thief's splintered cross. The world teetered on a razor's edge, rumors of the finds igniting a firestorm that dwarfed even the mantle's leak days earlier. News outlets blared from religious capitals: Jerusalem, Rome, Mecca. Religious scholars and pundits screamed over each other, parsing every whisper from the museum district. Major holy sites swelled with the faithful, hands clasped in prayer or raised in protest, from the Western Wall to St. Peter's Square. Teams of scientists, archaeologists, and clerics toiled in Jerusalem's museum, hunched over artifacts, their debates spilling into the streets. Whose world would these relics reshape most? Jews, Christians, historians, or skeptics?

Inside the museum's courtyard, Joshua, Noa, Avi, and Tal strolled under a late morning sun, the chaos a dull roar beyond the IDF cordon. The air buzzed with a strange calm, their steps light despite the weight of the past week.

Joshua flipped a Roman silver coin between his fingers, its edges worn but gleaming, one of Judas's thirty pulled from the Capernaum jars. "Remember this?" he said, grinning at Noa. "You were shaking like a leaf when we found it."

She snorted, nudging him with her elbow, multitool twirling in her other hand. "Me? You were the one hyperventilating, Masa. Thought you'd faint before we got it out."

Avi chuckled, his gravelly voice cutting through. "She's right. You looked like a kid who'd lost his lunch money."

Tal smirked, flexing his scabbed arm. "I was too busy dodging bullets to notice. But yeah, Masa, you're not winning any poker-face awards."

Joshua laughed, pocketing the coin, the memory grounding him. "Fair. Guess I'm still here, though. Thanks to you lot." He glanced at Noa, her sharp eyes softening for a split second, and felt a warmth from their nighttime roof confession. Girlfriend now, officially.

Avi clapped Tal on the shoulder, grinning. "Told you they'd figure it out. Day one, I saw it. Him tripping over himself, her pretending not to care."

"Obviously," Tal agreed, his scar twitching with amusement. "Took a relic chase to get 'em honest."

Noa rolled her eyes, but her grin betrayed her. "Keep it up, super agents. I'll bury you both in the next cave."

Their laughter echoed off the courtyard stones, a rare bubble of levity amid the storm. Beyond the gates, Jerusalem pulsed with madness. Reporters jostled for soundbites, clerics waved texts at cameras, social media feeds flooded with the hashtags #GalileeFinds, #AndrewsTruth, #ThiefsGrace. Inside, the museum was a hive, historians swarming the relics, carbon-dating machines humming, while Cohen, Nance, and Khalil orchestrated the chaos.

A familiar figure strode toward them, gray hair wilder than ever, a broad smile splitting his face. Professor Thaddeus Luke, Joshua's mentor from Arkansas, fresh off a plane from the states. He'd arrived that morning, swept into a motorcade that made him feel like a head of state, his excitement a mix of scholarly glee and boyish awe. "Joshua!" he boomed, clapping his student's shoulder. "You've outdone every wild theory I ever fed you. This..." He gestured at the museum, the relics within. "This is history breathing!"

"Couldn't have done it without you, Professor," Joshua said, grinning back. "Your Copper Scroll rants stuck with me."

Luke laughed, a storm cloud of energy. "And now look. Kings and presidents begging for a peek! I rode in with sirens, Masa, sirens! Felt like a actual dignitary."

Noa smirked. "Better get used to it. They're turning us into statues next."

The courtyard hummed with their chatter, but beyond, the world was a circus. Heads of state vied for VIP tours, their aides flooding a hastily assembled call center with requests. Photo ops with the "heroic treasure hunters," images to hang in palaces and parliaments for posterity. The Israeli government, overwhelmed, slapped a travel ban on the airspace, issuing warnings. "Closed until further notice." Joshua caught snippets on a guard's radio. The president's people negotiating, the pope's envoy en route, even a Saudi prince offering a private jet's worth of gold for a glimpse.

"Madness," Avi muttered, eyeing the gates where IDF soldiers rebuffed a swarm of press. "All this for some old jars?"

"It's not the jars," Joshua said, voice low. "It's what they mean. Andrew's words, the thief's nails. People want to believe or debunk it."

Tal nodded, scar glinting in the sun. "And Eli's out there, betting on the chaos."

The thought sobered them, but Luke's grin held. "Let 'em come. We've got the truth on our side. Well, most of it. Tomorrow's the big reveal, right?"

"Carbon dates, full scroll," Noa confirmed. "Cohen's itching to publish. Says it'll shut the doubters up."

"Good," Luke said, rubbing his hands. "I'll be front row, watching history crack open."

They wandered toward the museum's heart, past guards who nodded at their now-famous faces. Inside, the relics glowed under halogen lights. Jars etched with shepherd hooks, scrolls unfurled, silver coins stacked, the wood's *NVS* stark and haunting. Historians buzzed, a few glancing up to whisper, "Masa" or "Lev," fame a double-edged blade. Joshua felt it, the weight of eyes, but the coin in his pocket anchored him. Proof they'd survived to tell this story.

Meanwhile, in a Jericho safehouse, the Templars seethed. The TV flickered with a Jerusalem feed. Clerics shouting, crowds chanting, #AndrewsTruth trending.

Gideon paced a dusty room, boots scuffing a cracked tile floor. "Four days," he snarled, slamming a fist on a table littered with maps and burner phones.

"Four long days since Capernaum, and they're parading it like a circus!"

Eli sat still, cross glinting in lamplight, voice calm but edged. "This is our shot, Gideon. Chaos is cover. They're too busy arguing to see us move."

Thomas smirked, scar tugging his lip, scrolling his feed on a cracked phone. "Carbon dates leak tomorrow, they say. Museum's a fortress, but the world's distracted. Prayers, protests, VIPs clogging the streets. Perfect."

Paul coughed, his hospital pallor a bit less stark as he leaned against a wall. "They're cocky. Think they've won. Let 'em. We've got Amina."

Gideon spun, eyes wild. "Amina? She's a snake. Burned us in Amman, flirted with ISIS, now what? She'll sell us out again!"

Eli said, "She's ripe to flip. She knows their cracks. One call, she's ours."

Thomas dialed a number scratched on a scrap of paper, the line buzzing before Amina's voice crackled through, sharp and bitter.

"What do you want, Templar? I'm done with your games."

"Meet us," Thomas said, voice smooth. "Jerusalem, Old City alley. Near the Lion's Fountain, dusk. You're out, we're in. Let's fix that."

A beat of silence then a hiss. "They shut me out. Cohen, Khalil, that bitch Noa. I gave them everything, and I'm nothing now. What's in it for me?"

"Relics," Eli cut in, taking the phone. "Or cash. Your pick. You get us in, you get a piece. Deal?"

Her laugh was cold. "Fine. Dusk. Don't screw me, or I'll bury you."

The call ended, and Gideon glared. "She's a gamble. Always has been."

"She's a key," Paul rasped, coughing blood into a rag. "Museum's guarded, but she's been inside. Knows the shifts, the weak spots. We strike tomorrow, dawn."

They huddled over the maps, Jericho's dust swirling as Eli traced a route. Museum to a cave north of the Dead Sea, a burial site no one'd find.

"Power cuts at dawn," Thomas said. "She distracts. Flirts, cries, whatever. My guy cuts the grid. Ten minutes, tops. We're in, out, gone."

Gideon scowled, fists clenched. "Burn it. Scrolls, silver, wood. No trace, no truth for them to twist."

"No," Eli snapped, eyes hard. "We bury it. Control it. Truth's ours, not theirs to parade. Andrew's gospel, Judas's shame. It's sacred, not a headline."

Paul nodded, sketching a path through Jerusalem's backstreets. "IDF's stretched. VIPs, press, protests. Dawn's quiet. Guards change, historians sleep. Amina gets us past the gate, and we take it all."

Thomas smirked, cracking his knuckles. "She's our eyes. Resentment's a strong motivator."

Dusk fell, and they met Amina in the Old City, shadows long against ancient stone. She stood by the Lion's Fountain, arms crossed, eyes blazing. Hurt turned to venom.

"Museum's a zoo," she said, voice low. "IDF's thick, but the historians are sloppy. Relics moved at night, basement vault. Dawn shift's lazy. Two guards, half-asleep. Power box is outside, east wall."

Eli stepped closer, cross glinting. "You're sure?"

"I was there," she spat. "They locked me out, but I saw. Vault's keycard, guards swap at 5 a.m. Ten-minute window."

"What do you want?" Gideon growled, mistrust thick.

Amina's gaze hardened. "A cut. Silver or cash to disappear. I'm done being their dog."

Eli pulled a cross pendant from his pocket, gold and worn, dangling it before her. "This and a share. Our word. Get us in, you're free."

She snatched it, testing its weight, then nodded. "Tomorrow, dawn. I'll signal. Don't choke." She vanished into the alleys, her footsteps a fading echo.

Gideon spat into the dust. "She'll turn. I feel it."

"She won't," Paul said, wiping blood from his lip. "She's got no one else. Hates them more than us."

Eli's eyes narrowed, cross still in hand. "She's our wedge. Dawn, we take it. Bury it deep. No museum, no headlines."

They returned to Jericho under a moonless sky, tension coiling. Thomas prepped his contact. Power cut confirmed. Paul mapped the cave, breath shallow but mind sharp. Gideon paced, muttering about fire, while Eli prayed over his cross, doubt flickering in the silence. Tomorrow, they'd strike. Or fall.

Back in Jerusalem, dusk painted the museum in shadow, the day's frenzy simmering into an uneasy hum. Joshua and Noa slipped away from the basement, where Cohen, Nance, and Khalil still pored over relics, and climbed the back stairwell to the roof. The city sprawled below, a tidal wave of chaos crashing against the calm of the previous night. Where yesterday's twilight had cradled them in quiet, Jerusalem's skyline a jagged glow, their hands brushing as the girlfriend label settled, tonight was a beast unleashed. The sun's last rays bled out, swallowed by a chilling wave that prickled their skin, sharper than the desert's usual bite. Voices clamored below. Reporters shouting, clerics preaching, horns blaring. They stood at the railing, the crate abandoned, too restless to sit.

Joshua gripped the coin still in his pocket, the metal a cold weight. "This is different," he said, voice tight, eyes scanning the streets where lights flared. Protests near the Old City, prayer vigils by the museum gates. "Last night, it was us. Now it's everything."

Noa nodded, multitool still in her fingers, her gaze hard on the horizon. "Yeah. Felt safe up here. Stupid, maybe. Now it's like the world's clawing at us." Her voice shook, not with fear but with the weight of it. The known and unknown staring them down, a shadow deeper than the Templars' threat.

He turned to her, the wind tugging at his hair. "You okay? I mean, really?"

She laughed, sharp and brittle, leaning into the railing beside him. "No, Masa. You? This..." She waved at the chaos below. "It's bigger than caves and bullets. They're praying and fighting over what we found. Feels like it's not ours anymore."

"It's not," he said, throat tight. "Never was. We just held it till now. But us... " He hesitated, reaching for her hand, the gesture clumsy but firm. "That's still ours, right? Even with this?"

Her fingers curled around his, warm despite the chill, but her eyes stayed on the city. "Maybe. I thought so. Your family, that silly call, made it real. Now? I don't know. This could break everything."

The words hit him like a punch, shaking the foundation they'd built. Tentative, raw, born in Qumran's dust and Capernaum's dark. He'd seen her steady under fire, but this was different. Fear not of death but of losing what they'd clawed out of the chaos. "It won't," he said, voice low, insistent. "Not if we don't let it. We've survived worse. ISIS, Templars, Masada's tunnels. This is just noise."

She pulled back, meeting his gaze, her sharpness returning. "Noise that'll drown us. You saw Amina today. Pissed, lurking. Eli's out there, Gideon too. They're not done, and this"—she nodded at the streets—"gives 'em cover."

He swallowed, the coin digging into his thigh. "I know. But we've got Cohen, Nance, the IDF. Luke, even. We're not alone in this."

"Doesn't feel like it," she muttered, turning back to the city.

Below, a cleric's megaphone blared. Greek, Latin, and Hebrew clashed. A news chopper buzzed overhead, its spotlight slicing the dusk. The museum glowed, a beacon in the storm, but beyond, shadows moved. Protesters, pilgrims, or something darker?

Joshua stepped closer, shoulder brushing hers, the contact a lifeline. "You said, 'don't screw it up.' I won't. Not this, not us. Whatever's coming, we face it. Together?"

She exhaled a shaky breath then squeezed his hand, her grin faint but real. "Yeah, Masa. Together. Just don't faint on me tomorrow."

He laughed, tension easing a fraction. "Deal. No fainting, no screwing up."

They lingered, the city's roar a relentless tide, their hands locked as the night deepened. The calm of yesterday was gone, replaced by a storm they couldn't outrun. But up here, for a moment, they held their ground.

29

Trap of Truth

The museum courtyard blazed with floodlights, pushing back the night's threat to the relics within—Andrew's scroll, Judas's silver, thief's cross—truths now guarded by steel and soldiers. Darkness clung to alleys across the street, tamarisk trees swaying in Jerusalem's restless hum, pilgrims' chants and reporters' murmurs pulsing beyond the IDF cordon. Among the shadows, Amina watched, scarf low, eyes glinting, as a gray-haired figure approached the front doors, his pass clipped to a rumpled shirt. Professor Thaddeus Luke, fresh from a falafel run at the team's café, passed the guards with a nod, unaware of the gaze tracking him from the dark.

Inside, Luke's boots echoed down the stairwell to the basement lab, bathed in halogen glow, relics gleaming on a steel table. Tal and Avi, submachine guns slung low, offered quick hellos and smiles as they headed up. "Roof, Professor," Tal said, scar twitching. "Gonna crash Masa and Noa's rooftop time."

Luke's smile faltered, unease creasing his face, puzzling the operatives who'd seen him jovial hours ago. "Not now," he said, brushing past, his urgency a stark shift from the falafel-bound scholar. He crossed into the clean room, where Father Nance, Rabbi Cohen, and Dr. Khalil hunched over a jar, its shepherd hook etching sharp under light. Luke's expression—tight jaw, wide eyes—drew their attention before his words. "I was at the café, falafel in hand, when someone approached." He paused, breathless, hand trembling on his pass.

Cohen, glasses low, broke the silence, voice light but probing. "By that look, not the woman you were hoping for, Professor." His quip, tied to Luke's bachelor reveal earlier, drew chuckles, which was part of easing the priest's mock-condemnation and their earlier debate on life choices and career vows.

"Right," Luke said, catching his breath, the laughter fading. "He asked if I was with the museum team, saw my pass. I confirmed, and said I'd just arrived to evaluate. Then he slid this across." He placed a note, Hebrew scrawled in black ink, on the table, its weight heavier than paper.

Cohen's eyes scanned it, his face tightening, concern sharper than Luke's. "We need the team," he said, voice clipped, rising fast. "Does anyone know where they are?"

Luke nodded upward. "I just saw Avi and Tal, they were headed up in the stairwell, headed to interrupt Noa and Masa, and that they were probably having a moment."

Cohen exhaled, relief fleeting. "Good. Let's get to the roof, now." He turned to the custodians, their white gloves frozen mid-task. "Keep the relics here, we'll return." He led the charge, boots pounding, Nance, Khalil, and Luke trailing, questions swirling as the rabbi outpaced them, the note's warning burning in his grip.

On the roof, Jerusalem's skyline sprawled, a patchwork of lights under a moonless sky, the city's clamor of megaphones, horns, prayers that were a restless undercurrent. Joshua and Noa stood at the railing, shoulders brushing, the Judas coin warm in his pocket, their bond being sealed by "girlfriend" on family FaceTime, it was now holding against the world's chaos. His Masa faith stirred, cross pendant pressing his chest, Andrew's humility (Matthew 4:19) a guide. "Feels bigger every night," he said, voice low, eyes on the Old City's glow. "Relics, us, all of it."

Noa nodded, multi-tool twirling, her gaze hard. "We can't let it be too big. Fame will be a cage, Masa. The Templars, Amina, you know they're out there, waiting." Her voice wavered, doubt from their rooftop vow creeping in, their future a shadow beyond the relics.

Before he could reply, boots scuffed behind them, Tal's smirk breaking the quiet. "Caught you, well just gazing I guess, lovebirds," he teased, scar glinting, leaning on the railing. "The city's prettier without Masa's puppy eyes."

Avi chuckled, flanking him, gun holstered but eyes scanning the horizon. "Sorry to crash, but rooftop quiet will beat the basement hum. What's the word, Noa? You picking Amman or America yet?" His quip, dry but warm, masked unease from Luke's odd demeanor on the stairs.

Noa rolled her eyes, multi-tool twirl pausing. "It's not me picking, super agents. I've picked Masa, so where he goes, I'm there. But this—" she waved at the city— "feels like a trap closing." Her hand brushed Joshua's, a lifeline, but tension lingered, fame's weight and Eli's threat heavy.

Joshua rubbed the coin, Masa legacy, Effort beats odds rolling through his head. "Trap's right. Amina's lurking, Templars are too. The press reveal's tomorrow, but tonight's too quiet." His voice trembled, Capernaum's cave gunfire echoing, his faith clashing with fear.

Tal's smirk faded, hand on his gun. "Quiet's always bad. ISIS has melted, but Eli's crew—Gideon, Paul—they're desperate. We need eyes on the ground." His soldier's instinct, honed in Masada's dust, sharpened, his gaze flicking to the courtyard's floodlights.

Avi nodded, pacing, silhouette stark. "East wall's weak, the power box is unprotected, the guards swap at dawn. I've seen it before, guardes can get sloppy and distracted, especially when they think their shift is over. We should do a scouting mission." His Mossad edge cut through, Qumran's chase a ghost in his stance.

The stairwell door banged open, Cohen bursting through, the note in hand, Nance, Khalil, and Luke trailing, breathless. Cohen's glasses glinted, his voice sounding urgent. "Team, now, we need to talk, there's trouble." He waved the note, the Hebrew stark against the white. "Luke got this at the café. The Templars, Amina, they are striking at dawn, there will be a power cut, then the plan a vault grab."

Joshua's pulse spiked, the coin suddenly seeming cold. "Amina? Is any of this Confirmed?" His eyes met Noa's, her multi-tool still, fear mirroring his, it was Amman's betrayal reborn.

Cohen nodded, his tablet coming alive, X feeds dimmed. "A contact in Jericho caught chatter, they were going over guard schedules, the east wall box, 5 a.m. shift change. Amina's feeding them the information, obviously she's bitter from being sidelined." His voice was steel, a rabbi's trust in order, but worry shadowed his eyes.

Nance stepped forward, cassock rustling, cross glinting, holding a second note "This is the only thing that goes in the safe tonight," he said, voice calm. "Your plot's exposed, drop to knees, no harm. They'll walk into IDF's net." His priest's faith, held firm, Luke 23:43—thief's grace—guiding his gambit.

Khalil, the jar he was studying in his memory, snorted. "Amina's not just leaking, she's scheming. Chatter mentioned 'Templar house,' some base she wants. She'll slip the ambush, watch her." His historian's mind mapped her path, relics vulnerable despite steel.

Tal cracked his knuckles, and smirked faintly. "So, we wait, let the IDF clean up, and let them smile for the cameras? Too easy." His bravado masked unease, hand on gun, ready for chaos.

"Easy's just a trap," Avi growled, stopping, eyes on city lights. "Eli's sharp, Gideon's unhinged, Paul's cunning, even if he is dying. Hard hit, Amina or not." His hand brushed his gun, "we need to be fully prepared."

Noa's voice cut through, restarting her multi-tool spinning. "We cannot afford to be sitting ducks. If the IDF slips, we need to be ready. The vault, relics, us." Her eyes locked with Joshua's, fierce, their bond a shield, doubt buried under resolve.

Cohen waved them down, voice brisk. "Tal, Avi, please scout the east wall, check the power box, and the exits. Joshua, Noa, come and go over vault protocols with me. No heroics, stay sharp." He led them downstairs, the lab's hum heavy, IDF radios crackling, the patrols clear, and the east wall secure.

Tal and Avi hit the courtyard, the floodlights were harsh, tamarisks swaying, the power box a rusted square under a tree, and as guessed unguarded, Amina's intel chillingly true. "We are sitting ducks," Tal muttered, radioing Cohen. "Guards need some eyes here." Avi nodded, scanning shadows, IDF patrols a rhythm too thin for comfort.

In the vault room, Cohen swiped his keycard, the door began hissing. Locking in the note that would signal the trap that had been set.

The relics gleaming, the jars, scrolls, silver, NVS stark moved to a different room and escorted by custodians. Joshua's breath caught, as his fingers brushed the scroll's case, Andrew's Greek whispering mercy. "This is why they can't have it."

Noa inspected the lock. "Keycard's single-use, it resets at shift change. Amina knows the procedures, how?" Her suspicion sharpened, fame's weight real with reporters' stares and unknown questions gnawing.

"Jericho chatter," Cohen said, "Amina's in deep with them, we know she has been leaking since Amman.The IDF's staging, soldiers ready when lights drop." An IDF captain joined, rifle slung, confirming patrols doubled, and the halls were lined.

In the Old City, Amina stood by the Lion's Fountain, the spice air thick, her scarf low, eyes full of venom. Eli, Gideon, Thomas, Paul approached, dust from Jericho clinging to their clothes, Eli's cross glinting, Paul's pallor was stark. "Schedules written out, the power box, it should lead us to the gold," Eli said. "What's your price?"

Amina's resentment flared, all of the slights coming out, Cohen's Amman dismissal, Noa's Masada glare, Khalil's gate coldness. "Silver, cash, and the Templar house, your base will be my base," she hissed, her plan sharp: use the Templars, slip the ambush, seize the network, and the relics would be hers. "The vault's keycard, it needs to be swiped at 5 a.m., the two guards on duty are lazy. From the time the east wall box is hit, you have a ten-minute window. Scarf's the signal, don't choke."

Eli offered a gold cross pendant, the meaning heavier than the necklace. "You can take this, we will welcome you back and forget any transgressions." His eyes narrowed, knife at the ready, no doubt flickering in his eyes. "But if you take it, we share responsibility, the treasure stays hidden and we stay engaged on any future Joshua might have."

She snatched it without saying a word, then vanished into the alleys, her mind churning using the Templars as tools, the IDF her challenge for now, the

Templar house destined to be her throne. But doubt gnawed, as she thought about Joshua and his coin, and Noa's resolve, but venom won, her path to betrayal locked.

Back in the lab, as midnight passed, the radios were quieter. Cohen had dismissed the team, urging them to get some rest, insisting that the plan in place would work. The team had more to worry about the next day then what the Templar's had planned.

Upstairs Joshua paced the hall, his shoes clicking, interrupted the vents hissing, the coin cold in his pocket. Noa sat at the end of the hallway watching Joshua turn and repeat his line of steps. Tal and Avi stood in a door discussing their future after this whole thing was over. Professor Luke sat on his cot scrolling through emails from the school back in Arkansas. Nothing passed between the team members, just an air that felt charged and ready for an explosion.

Radio chatter suddenly pierced the quiet as the Templar van approached one of the two suspected alleyways. For the plan to work, the team could not engage at any point leading up to the ambush. Only after the Templars were in custody were they allowed to leave their floor. Two IDF Soldiers stood at the door to make sure.

Rabbi Cohen, in the office, confirmed their presence, his tablet coming alive. "The Lion's Fountain, Amina's there. The IDF's ready, the note is set, and soldiers are waiting. Stay back everyone, we don't want to alert them."

Noa gripped Joshua's arm, voice steel. "I'm not planning to sit in hiding. They will know we're here."

Tal grinned, "I know I can take those two, but I would rather not. However, I am itching for a fight with those Templar wannabes."

Nance smiled, as he watched his cross as his hand rolled through his rosary, repeating his prayer for safety of the team and a swift end to the operation. "Faith holds, if those articles say nothing else, the two thousand years of sitting in caves a proof to the faith of the Essenes. We all owe it to them to have faith the truth will win out" Joshua's coin hummed, as dawn's fire looming.

Outside, Amina watched the museum, her scarf sitting low, the signal at the ready. Her venomous stare missing what really awaited them inside the walls.

30

April 11, 2025

The museum's quiet held through the night, a fragile shell against the chanting and shouting that rang out in Jerusalem's streets. The upstairs rooms stood closed and dark where Joshua, Noa, Avi, and Tal took their well-needed slumber. Not just from the relentless days past, but for what dawn would unleash. Cots creaked under their weight, the city's hum a restless lullaby threading through cracked windows and laced with the clamor of pilgrims and press beyond the IDF cordon.

Downstairs, a lone security guard paced a hallway, the click and clack of his shoes echoing off bare walls in the unoccupied space. Keys jingled at his hip, the hiss of air through ceiling ducts sounding like rushing water in the stillness. This was his last walk of the night. He'd missed the action of the past week, car chases, cave digs, gunfire, but this morning felt different. He couldn't name it, just a prickling at his neck, like a bomb ticking down. The museum's treasures, glowing under lock and key, seemed to hum with their own unease.

Outside, two guards approached from the street, rounding the corner as they always did. Amina had watched them for days, clocking their ritual, pausing just beyond the museum's shadow for a last drag of nicotine before crossing the threshold. This dawn, two figures waited in the dark, breath held. As lighters flared and flames caught the tips of cigarettes, the guards didn't see the hands until they clamped down. A swift grab from behind then muffled grunts swallowed by the night. The pairs swapped clothing in seconds, the uniforms stripped from limp bodies donned by the intruders. A car idled nearby, taillights glowing red, backing up to the spot. Two more men dragged the unconscious guards into the backseat, doors slamming shut. The car peeled away, tires whispering on asphalt.

When the figures stepped into the light, anyone who knew them would've seen Gideon and Thomas, faces grim under stolen caps. They marched toward the museum like modern knights storming a wall in the Crusades, keycards clipped to belts, rifles hidden beneath coats.

The crowd out front milled, mostly calm in the early dark hours, though larger than any night before. Pilgrims praying, reporters dozing against vans, all awaiting the press reveal. Gideon swiped his card at the door, the lock clicking open.

The security officer behind the counter barely glanced up. "All right, have a good day," he mumbled, shuffling papers before disappearing into the street, shift done.

The night guard, the one with the bad feeling, rounded the corner, as he always did at shift's end. "It's very eerie in here," he said, voice low, nodding at the two behind the counter. "Must be all those new treasures everyone's talking about."

Gideon and Thomas nodded, grunting in vague agreement, faces shadowed by caps.

With a "Well, see you later" wave, the guard slipped out, leaving only the sleepy IDF soldiers, two by the safe, a contingent at the lab doors. Everything that moved between would be escorted by one of these groups.

"So far, so good," Gideon keyed his radio, voice a low growl. "Phase one complete." The museum was infiltrated. Now they'd neutralize the rest.

Upstairs, Joshua stirred, the cot's springs digging into his back. Dawn's gray light seeped through the window, the city's noise sharper now, megaphones, chants, a chopper's distant buzz. He rubbed his eyes, the coin from Judas's stash a cold lump in his pocket. Noa lay on the cot beside him, multitool resting on her chest, her breathing steady but shallow. Avi and Tal snored across the room, exhaustion claiming them.

He nudged her gently. "Hey. It's time."

She groaned, cracking an eye. "Already? Feels like I just closed 'em."

"Cohen's circus," he said, managing a tired grin. "Press, clerics, chaos. You ready?"

She sat up, stretching, multitool spinning in her fingers. "No. But let's go."

They roused Avi and Tal, the four shuffling downstairs, badges clipped to hips, faces infamous enough to need no check. The museum's heart buzzed, historians prepping, IDF milling, Cohen's voice barking orders. The relics waited on a steel table, jars gleaming, scrolls unfurled, silver stacked, the wood's NVS stark under lights. Nance hovered over the piece of the cross, muttering prayers, while Khalil adjusted a camera, capturing every angle.

Cohen spotted them, glasses low, a smirk breaking his stern face. "Morning, heroes. Carbon dates are in, first century, spot-on. Andrew's scroll's ready. Press is outside, clerics too. We're live in ten."

Joshua nodded, the coin grounding him. "Let's light that fire."

Outside, Gideon and Thomas moved fast. Gideon slipped to the basement stairs, Thomas toward the power box on the east wall, Amina's intel guiding them. She waited near the vault, hair tucked under a scarf, feigning a delivery and flirting with an IDF soldier, her laugh loud, distracting. Thomas pried the box open, cutters snipping wires. Lights flickered then died. A ten-minute window opened.

Gideon keyed his radio. "Eli, power's down. Move."

In the shadows beyond the gates, Eli and Paul emerged from a van, cross glinting on Eli's chest, Paul's pallor stark as he limped. They slipped past the crowd on Amina's signal, a dropped scarf clearing their path.

Inside, Gideon reached the safe, the two IDF soldiers stirring, hands on rifles.

"Shift change," he barked, voice gruff, stolen uniform selling it.

They hesitated then stepped aside.

The lights went out, and two cracks echoed through the hallway, the IDF soldiers crumpling, silenced by Gideon's quick shots. Paul and Eli reached the bottom of the stairs, moving fast to claim the divine objects. Thomas joined them, lockpicks flashing. The safe clicked open, revealing jars, scrolls, silver, wood, and a note from Father Nance tucked atop the relics.

Gideon snatched it, eyes narrowing as he read:

Dear Templars,

It is with the utmost respect that I inform you of your plot being exposed. As you have no doubt killed the power by now, I expect you have not seen the contingent of IDF soldiers standing by in preparation for this action. If you stop, drop to your knees, and await your fate, no physical harm will come to you. We greatly respect the contributions of your team that brought us here, but at this time we graciously accept your resignation from the team.

God Bless,

Fr. Nance

A beat later, boots thundered down the halls from every direction, converging on the group. Amina, who'd walked back down the hallway, ducked into the shadow under the stairs, holding her breath as soldiers stormed past. She slipped out the front door, unnoticed, blending into the crowd.

Gideon spun, firing, a wild shot cracking stone. Thomas bolted, pack slung, but a soldier tackled him, and the scar on his lip split anew as he hit the floor. Eli and Paul dropped to their knees, hands raised, restraint gone, narrowly missed by return fire that caught Gideon square in the chest. He fell, blood pooling, a final snarl fading.

Amina lingered outside, watching from the crowd's edge, unknown to those beyond the doors. She was the lone survivor of the five Templars who'd set out. As Gideon's body was wheeled out on a gurney accompanied by Thomas and Eli in cuffs, Paul limping beside them, she knew it was safe to reclaim Templar house, her betrayal complete.

In the lab, the crew sighed, waiting for the lights to return.

Rabbi Cohen urged calm, voice steady, "Patience, everyone. We're secure."

When the lights flickered back on, Joshua, Noa, Tal, and Avi saw the artifacts safe on display, untouched by the chaos below.

Cohen adjusted his glasses. "Okay, we're ready to present the findings. Just facts, what the items are, that they're first century, safe here for study under strict guidelines."

"No translations?" Joshua replied, disappointment clear in his pitch. He walked to the last scroll they'd unearthed, fingers brushing the case. "I was really ready to learn what everything said."

"We didn't say we hadn't translated some," Father Nance said, placing a hand on Joshua's shoulder. "But we're not releasing the words yet. That time will come shortly." He slipped a paper from behind the case. "Here's the translation for the scroll you're looking at."

Joshua took it, reading silently, Greek rendered into English: *I, Andrew, cast my net for men, not gold. The betrayer's coin stayed cold, the thief's wood bore grace. Seek not wealth but mercy.*

His breath caught, the words sinking in, until Noa cleared her throat. "Ahem, out loud, please."

He grinned, reading it aloud, voice steady. The room stilled, Tal and Avi nodding, Noa's eyes sharp but warm. Soon, the press and badge-holders flooded the lab, ushered through in waves, each getting time to see, touch, take notes. Experts stood by, Khalil on the jars, Nance on the wood, Cohen on the scrolls, answering questions, explaining dates, provenance, significance.

The world waited, the promise of revelation unfulfilled yet tantalizing. The day dragged, the West waking, the East still on edge. At the appointed times, news outlets went live, anchors describing the items. The porcelain jars: some in better shape than others, some bearing intricate designs, some even with Hebrew that could possibly describe the original contents. The shepherd's crook the pundits discussed at length: which shepherd, popular or not, is it the actual staff that matters or the meaning? Then the silver: unspent coins that cost so many lives and were a cornerstone to the start of a fire that consumed the world. A cross splinter with rusted nails: vivid and awe-inspiring, Jesus's or a thief's, was it even a cross splinter from that moment in time? "No translations as of yet, but we'll keep you updated," rang through every screen in every language, a refrain of suspense.

The lack of translations did not stop each religious or government entity from speculating and, ultimately, claiming it meant their moral superiority. Some obviously speculated the end of the world now, with all that had been found. Networks booked scholars and clerics to debate whether this was a call to humility or a relic of doom. Governments issued statements, aligning the finds with national pride, while social media erupted with theories, #EndTimes trending fiercely.

Evening fell, the museum quiet again, relics locked in a reinforced vault. Joshua and Noa climbed to the roof, Jerusalem's skyline softer now the chaos was ebbing. The day's weight lingered: Templars broken, Gideon dead, Eli and Thomas cuffed, Paul surrendered, Amina vanished, the scroll's grace echoing. They sat on the crate, hands brushing, the coin warm in his pocket. Noa leaned into Joshua's shoulder, now watching the quiet city, having been up here every day as more information leaked, the skyline shifting with each wave of reaction.

The remainder of the crew, having watched as much coverage as they could stand, tracked them down, boots scuffing the stairwell. On the roof now, each member spread out, facing different directions, the city a patchwork of lights and shadows below.

"I understand why you all didn't want the translations getting out," Joshua began, voice low, eyes on the Old City's glow. "If the world reacts like this with just artifacts being found, they're not ready for anything else."

Nance, Cohen, Khalil, and Luke nodded in unison, murmurs overlapping.

"Exactly," Nance said, cassock rustling as he crossed his arms. "It's rocked everything. Balance or topple, that scroll's words won't settle it either way."

Cohen adjusted his glasses, gazing west. "They'll fight over it. Humility or apocalypse, doesn't matter what Andrew meant."

Khalil, facing east, snorted. "Speculation's enough. Translations would be fuel on a fire already blazing."

Luke, peering north, grinned faintly. "World's not ready, Masa, but it's awake now. That's something."

Noa shifted, multitool twirling, her voice cutting through. "Awake and screaming. What's it mean for us, though? This doesn't just end here."

Cohen turned, eyes sharp. "It doesn't. Amman's calling, digs lined up, research grants. They want you two, Tal, Avi too, to keep this going. Real work, real stakes."

Luke chuckled, clapping Joshua's back. "And America's got offers, kid.

Arkansas's drooling, tenure track for me if I bring you back, Masa. Big labs, big funding, your name on it."

Joshua blinked, the coin heavy in his hand now. "Amman or America? That's quite opposing options."

Tal smirked, scar glinting as he faced south. "Amman's dirt and sweat, more caves, more fights. Suits us."

Avi grunted, eyes on the horizon. "America's soft, safe. Labs over bullets. I could breathe there."

"But you two weren't even archaeologists a week ago," Joshua said, and the group laughed, tension breaking. "It's okay, agent men, your secret's safe with us."

Noa looked at Joshua, eyes steady. "Wherever, whenever, I'm with you, Masa, but I'm not picking."

"Right," was all he could muster, the word hanging heavily.

The crew retired for the night, boots fading down the stairwell, but sleep wouldn't come for Joshua. He was plenty tired, bone-deep from Qumran to Capernaum, but the thought of choosing one way, maybe closing a door he wanted open, kept him restless. He slipped from the cot, pacing the hall, echoes of his shoes clicking off the walls, the hiss of vents a faint roar in his ears.

Amman meant caves, Noa, the life they'd forged, dust and danger he knew. America was family, a reset, labs where the coin's weight might lighten. He leaned against a window, city lights blurring, the fork unyielding, Andrew's grace a quiet hum in his pocket.

31

August 2025

Months had passed since Masa and Noa stood in the museum, the air thick with dust and anticipation, listening to the scroll's translated words unfurl like a secret too heavy to hold. Masa was picking Noa up at her apartment just down the street from his, the humid Arkansas summer pressing against their skin.

They'd decided to spend the summer here in Northwest Arkansas, the rolling green hills a stark contrast to Jerusalem's sun and scorched stone. Weekdays found them with Professor Luke, hunched over scrolls in his cluttered office, the faint hum of cicadas seeping through the windows as they pored over meanings they couldn't share. Keeping those powerful words secret was not hard in public. There, they could dodge with a smile. But in church, Bible study, any gathering where fellow believers hung on their every syllable, it gnawed at them like a splinter under a nail.

They'd visited churches all over, Fayetteville's steeples, Springdale's clapboard sanctuaries. Anyone who asked, they tried to oblige, shedding light on the hunt's sweat and adrenaline. What did it mean to them, and was there anything else they could share? The questions buzzed like flies, relentless, and the sting of withholding pierced deeper each time. They were believers too, and the necessity of silence felt like a betrayal, even if the world wasn't ready for the truth simmering in their chests.

Noa slid into the car, the leather seat creaking under her and the Villines

Trio's familiar refrain spilling from the speakers: "Echoing across Calvary's hill, I could almost hear Him say..." The twang of gospel strings filled the air, thick with summer heat. "Oh, Masa, every day," she laughed, her voice bright but brittle, masking the weight of the decision they faced. Not the one about getting married, a month of living near each other—no bullets flying, just the quiet rustle of oak leaves and shared glances over coffee—had sealed that with a certainty as solid as the Ozark soil. No, it was the schoolyear looming a week away, the thought of facing crowds daily, each eager face a mirror to their own guilt, demanding answers they couldn't give.

The song looped back, its refrain marking the end of their short morning drive through Fayetteville's tree-lined streets. Joshua parked, the gravel crunching under the tires, and they stepped out, the air heavy with the scent of cut grass and distant barbecue smoke. They walked into Professor Luke's lab at the university, the cool blast of air conditioning a relief.

"Morning, you two," Luke greeted, his voice upbeat, his gray hair wilder than ever as he bent over samples from the jars they'd recovered. Shards of porcelain etched with faint Hebrew glinted under his desk lamp. He was hiding his own secret: the joy that two people he'd come to cherish like family would wed tomorrow and leave Monday to rejoin Rabbi Cohen in the fields. "Coffee?"

"Absolutely," Noa replied, her multitool spinning absently in her fingers, a habit from the caves that never left her.

The trio ambled to the Brew Hut down the block, a squat brick shop where the barista knew their orders: black for Luke, a splash of cream for Masa, Noa's with a hint of cinnamon. They settled at a wobbly table by the window, the murmur of students and the clink of mugs wrapping around them as they sipped, reminiscing about the museum's sterile glow, the weight of that scroll in their hands.

"You sure you don't want to come with us?" Noa asked, her tone teasing but edged with something deeper. "You have to pretend too."

"Oh yeah, maybe someday," Luke said, his grin crinkling his eyes. "They just gave me my tenure. Maybe they didn't know you were leaving and rewarded me for bringing the conquering heroes to the door." He glanced past her, spotting a figure weaving through the tables. "Incoming..."

"It is you, three of the finders," the young woman said, her voice trembling with awe as she clutched a notebook, her ponytail bouncing with each step. They'd long given up correcting folks—two finders and a tagalong, they'd said, but it never stuck. "I heard something and wrote it down, been dying to get a confirmation." She looked like Joshua had two years ago, starstruck in Luke's presence, back when the professor was a legend for his Copper Scroll theories, before this find eclipsed them all. "I'm taking your classes this semester, Dr. Luke. Are you going to make me as good as Joshua?"

The trio laughed, not at her, they clarified when her cheeks flushed, but at the mirror she held up to their own beginnings. The wide-eyed wonder, the hunger for discovery, it was etched in her like it had been in them.

"I'll do my best," Luke said, his tone warm, steadying her nerves.

"Will you two be around?" she asked, pencil poised, hope lighting her face.

The three froze, the words on the scroll flashing in their minds, Andrew's truth, the Essenes' legacy, a flame they guarded in silence. The air thickened, the hum of the coffee shop fading as those words pulsed, a secret too vast to let loose.

A Restless Heart

I, Andrew, son of Jonah, was a fisherman of Bethsaida, my days spent hauling nets with my brother Simon by the Sea of Galilee. The sun scorched our backs, the wind whipping salt and fish, scent through our hair, but my soul ached for more. The prophets whispered of a Messiah, and I sought Him in the wilderness, where John the Baptist's voice cut through the reeds. I stood by the Jordan, the cool water lapping my ankles, as John roared, "Prepare the way of the Lord!" I became his disciple, my heart restless for the one he promised.

The Dove Descends

One day, as John baptized the throng, Jesus of Nazareth came to the river, His steps steady on the muddy bank. I watched as John plunged Him beneath the current, the water rippling silver, and when He rose, the sky split open. A dove descended, white as dawn, hovering over Him, its wings a soft hum in the stillness, and a voice rolled from the heavens: "This is My beloved Son, in whom I am well pleased" (Matthew 3:17). My knees trembled beneath me. John turned, his eyes fierce with fire, and cried, "Behold, the Lamb of God, who takes away the sin of the world!" (John 1:29). The air shivered, and I knew the wait had ended.

Finding the Messiah

The next day, I trailed Jesus with another disciple, the dust of His sandals clinging to our feet. He turned, His gaze piercing, and asked, "What do you seek?" (John 1:38). My tongue stumbled. "Rabbi, where are you staying?" He smiled, gentle as the dawn. "Come and see" (John 1:39). We lingered with Him, His words washing over us like the Galilee's tide. I ran to Simon, my voice breaking with wonder. "We have found the Messiah!" (John 1:41). He followed, and when Jesus saw him, He said, "You are Simon, son of Jonah. You shall be called Peter" (John 1:42). I stood in awe, my simple call weaving my brother into His net.

The Call to Fish for Men

Later, as Simon and I mended our nets, the hemp rough against my palms, Jesus walked by, the sea glinting behind Him. His eyes met ours, steady as stone, and He called, "Follow me, and I will make you fishers of men" (Matthew 4:19). Our nets dropped, tangling in the sand, and we stepped away, the brine fading for the dust of roads and a greater haul.

Bread for Thousands

His power stunned me daily. Once, near the Passover, a crowd of thousands pressed close, their murmurs hungry for His teaching. Jesus asked Philip, "Where shall we buy bread for these people to eat?" (John 6:5). Philip faltered, "Two hundred denarii would not buy enough!" (John 6:7). But I'd glimpsed a boy, his basket clutched tight. "There is a lad here with five barley loaves and two fish," I said, my voice small, "but what are they among so many?" (John 6:9). Jesus took them, gave thanks, the scent of bread rising, and broke them apart. I handed out pieces, my hands trembling as they multiplied, feeding five thousand, twelve baskets spilling over. My meager find turned vast in His grasp.

The Greeks Come

In Jerusalem, during the feast, some Greeks approached Philip, their accents sharp with curiosity, saying, "Sir, we wish to see Jesus" (John 12:21). Philip brought them to me, and together we sought Him, the city's clamor ringing in our ears. He looked at us, His voice grave. "The hour has come for the Son of Man to be glorified. Unless a grain of wheat falls into the earth and dies, it bears no fruit" (John 12:23, 24). His words hung heavy, a shadow I couldn't yet grasp.

The Cross and the Empty Tomb

When the hour struck, I faltered. They seized Him in the night, the torchlight flickering on Gethsemane's leaves, and I hid, my courage a wisp in the wind. From a distance, I saw the cross rise, the sky darkening, His cry, "It is finished" (John 19:30), piercing the air like a spear. My hope bled out, or so I thought. On the third day, Mary Magdalene burst in, her voice wild, "I have seen the Lord!" (John 20:18). Then He stood among us, His scarred hands outstretched, saying, "Peace be with you" (John 20:19). The dove at the river, the Lamb on the cross, He lived, and my faith flared anew.

Find us when you are ready

The End

About the Author

Nicholas Teeguarden is a husband, father and veteran. A devoted Christian and award-winning author from small-town Oklahoma. His global military service fuels the vivid, action-packed world of *The Masa Chronicles: The Copper Scroll*, a Christian thriller honored with the Christlit Award, a Readers' Favorite 5-star review.

You can connect with me on:
- 🌐 https://nickteeguarden.com
- 🐦 https://x.com/nickteeguarden
- 🔗 https://www.instagram.com/nickteeguarden

www.ingramcontent.com/pod-product-compliance
Lightning Source LLC
Chambersburg PA
CBHW020139120726
47903CB00007B/2326